SECONDARY STAGES

SECONDARY STAGES
revitalizing high school theatre

JEFF BENNETT
Foreword by D. B. Sweeney

HEINEMANN
Portsmouth, NH

Heinemann

361 Hanover Street
Portsmouth, NH 03801–3912
www.heinemanndrama.com

Offices and agents throughout the world

The author and publisher wish to thank those who have generously given permission to reprint borrowed material:

Excerpt from "Bachelor Pad" by Brian Baumeister is used by permission of the author.

Library of Congress Cataloging-in-Publication Data
Bennett, Jeff.
     Secondary stages : revitalizing high school theatre / Jeff Bennett.
        p.   cm.
     Includes bibliographical references.
     ISBN 0-325-00313-0 (pbk.)
     1. College and school drama. I. Title.

PN3175 .B46 2001

2001024126

Editor: Lisa Barnett
Production: Lynne Reed
Cover design: Jenny Jensen Greenleaf
Manufacturing: Steve Bernier

Printed in the United States of America on acid-free paper
Docutech T&C 2009

For
Sherri

Contents

Foreword

Jeff Bennett's first year at Shoreham-Wading River High School was my last. Like many seniors, I was prepared to go through on bluff and bluster. Instead, I discovered something that changed my life. I was challenged to rethink my assumptions about a concept—*theatre*—that I abhorred, and in the process reexamine myself. And that's what this remarkable book does. High school theatre need not be marginalized—or worse, eliminated—as a staid, dying anachronism. Bennett shows how to awaken it and put it at the very center of a school's life. In bold, concise strokes he shows how to make theatre cool. And that's no mean feat.

Secondary Stages is the work of a wily master. In typically understated fashion, Bennett calls it a cookbook, but it's much more than that. It's part memoir, part acting manual, part philosophical tract, and part rallying cry. He's been through the funding wars, the scheduling dilemmas, the dearth of material, and the parents flipping out over coarse dialogue. He's got his finger on the teen pulse without sacrificing his sensitivity to the school and community. His heart may be with the kids but his head is with the parents. And in *Secondary Stages* he's laid it all out: a realistic program that's both entertaining and readable.

The real bonus here is the insight into the craft of acting. So few books come close to being practically useful and this is a shining exception. Bennett has clearly digested most of what's in print on the subject and distilled it down to a startlingly clear system. Geared toward the sensitivities of teens, this book will nonetheless stimulate any actor.

High school is a harrowing crucible for many kids. A vibrant theatre experience offers salvation. This book is a great start for anyone interested in the challenge of creating a program that moves out of the wings and into the mainstream.

—D. B. Sweeney

Acknowledgments

My theatre days have been spent in the rowdy company of adolescents. It's an exciting period in the development of the human organism—a time when kids are just old enough to achieve astonishing levels of excellence on- and backstage, just young enough to remain open to the limits of possibility. Whatever I know about the craft, I've learned from them. Many contributed directly to the pages of this book, and I'd like to thank them first: Henry Bittner, for identifying "the acting voice"; Allysa Adams, Kevin Baier, Jay Janoski, Jackie Geary, Shawn Reed, Chris Baier, Craig Donnelly, Chris Gibbons, and Steve Lankau, for their concrete suggestions; Brian Baumeister, for permission to quote from "Bachelor Pad"; and Matt Lembo and Lauren Thogersen, for help in taming "the machine."

I'm infinitely grateful, too, to my colleagues and friends at Shoreham-Wading River High School, so many of whom donated their time, advice, and expertise to every stage of this project: Tim Dolan, Mark Goldberg, Lucio Costanzo, Roberta Wenger, Ed Weiss, David Jackson, Robin Dorsty, Ron Broussard, Liz Weiss, Stephanie Costanzo, George Dorsty, and—on an almost weekly basis—Mike Stegman and Bernard Scherer.

For ready assistance and generous counsel, I'd like to thank Bill Bruehl, Suzie Peck, Hal Ackerman, Michael Weisbarth, George Axelrod, David Friedman, Ghislaine Grillo, Kate Kelly, Mike Apostoli, Jim Hoare, John Shorter, James Malone, and Charlotte Koons.

For T.L.C. "above and beyond the call": Laurey Bennett and Aron Lewis.

For hand-holding during endless outpourings of self-pity: Marian Thurm.

For making the production phase such smooth sailing: Lynne Reed.

Thanks, D. B. Sweeney, for honoring me with your Foreword.

And thanks, last and most of all, to my editor, Lisa Barnett, who practices tough love with compassion and sensitivity.

Introduction

High school theatre is an anomaly in the education curriculum, neither exactly a mainstay nor a nonentity—a kind of eager stepchild no one knows quite what to do with. If you've ever taught the subject or directed the school play, you already know most of the story. When kids in an acting course conquer their shyness and emerge poised and alert, their parents swell with pride. When students present their best work for an audience of their friends, the cheers, laughter, and applause can rock the house. And when budget cuts are approved, absolutely *nothing* lands faster on the chopping block. Even teachers who would fight to protect a drama program might hesitate to challenge the old assumption that high school theatre is essentially a frivolity. Like everyone else, they've been well-conditioned to distinguish between what's important (English, math, science, foreign language, and social studies) and what's not (music, art, gym, media, and theatre). Our culture has regarded so-called actor types and artists in general with suspicion since before Shakespeare's time, so it's safe to predict that these attitudes will hold well into the new century.

I staunchly reject these attitudes. I've watched the kinds of things a rich exposure to theatre can instill in a high school student, and they are as vital to a productive life as mastery of the intricacies of English grammar, the periodic table of the elements, or the fundamentals of algebra:

- the ability to draw vivid emotion from the printed page and arouse instant empathy in an audience
- the growth in self-possession that comes from standing confidently before your peers, parents, and teachers
- the unique jolt of pleasure in drawing appreciative laughter from a crowd
- the gain in judgment and insight that comes from inhabiting the skin of another human being
- the power of holding an audience in thrall

- and most important by far: the heightened sense of community, of sharing in a meaningful act of cooperation
  whose rewards are so instantly visceral

These are ambitious goals for any class to pursue, and it's
tough to deny the difficulty of measuring the outcomes objec-
tively. But few, I think, would challenge the value of the quest or
the intensity of the means for getting there.

Yes, of course, this intensity can exist in a memorable social
studies or chemistry class, but there are few areas in the life of a
school that deliver so immediate a reward for so much hard work
and discipline as the zap of a live audience. That's why a high
school theatre program *must* be rich and exciting: because the
gains to be reaped are so profound.

And that makes the history of prejudice in this area all the
more frustrating. The uneasy parent's reaction to a child's involvement in an acting class: "All those rehearsals are taking time away
from our daughter's more important subjects!" The guidance coun-
selor's dubious motive for including a theatre course in the student's spring schedule: "Between us, it's the perfect route to an easy
A, and Steve's third-quarter average could use a boost." Steve's misguided purpose for signing up in the first place: "I need a break from
all the hard work of the school day, and it's my only fun class."

Right there lies the heart of so much misunderstanding. Theatre *is* fun, and our prejudices dictate that anything fun can't be
worth much. In fact, when any subject is taught with inspiration,
the result is an experience that's fun for the learner. *But in theatre,
as in any disciplined art form, the fun derives from long hours of fero-
ciously hard work*—crafting a scene until it shines, creating a sense
of fluidity and spontaneity in the playing, heightening the actors'
sensitivity to each other, communicating the playwright's vision to
an audience—and *not* from flaunting emotions, hanging with the
"art crowd," or showing off talent.

A strong theatre program is not at all about "showing off talent" (that sorely misunderstood term). Talent is dandy. When we see
it displayed onstage, most of us know who has or hasn't got it, and
of course we all applaud those lucky few. But a strong high school
theatre program isn't about producing the next generation of Meryl
Streeps or Robert De Niros. The result would be a great many unem-
ployed graduates scrambling for work in what is already the single

most oversubscribed profession in the country. It's about growth—personal, intellectual, and emotional. It's about connecting with the inner life of a character, learning the difference between sloppily hamming one's way through a scene and discovering the pulse of something real and true, enlarging the world of the imagination, discovering life outside the bounds of the shopping mall, videoscreen, and cellular phone. It's about going after experiences that teach a valuable lesson: Through hard work, students can sometimes discover within themselves levels of excellence they never imagined existed. And that is the *true* source of self-esteem.

I suppose this sounds a bit high-minded. Can we expect a seventeen-year-old to take it as seriously as all this? Maybe not consciously and maybe not yet. But high school students are ready for the challenge, and by asking them to answer the call we can spark an initiative to instill new respect for acting (to borrow Uta Hagen's phrase), one that with luck may just survive past graduation.

I worry that these objectives will strike some as too lofty and mislead readers into mistaking this book for a theoretical discourse on theatre as the pathway to the essence of a child's inner being. My hope is that *Secondary Stages* much more closely resembles a good cookbook—a practical set of recipes for generating positive results in and out of the classroom. Still, without an overriding vision—a defining philosophy, if you will—pages of lesson plans can't add up to much more than nice ideas for killing time. That's the intent of Chapter 1, to provide a context for instruction that goes to the heart of such questions as:

What is the raison d'etre of a high school theatre program?

Which students stand to profit most from getting involved, and how do you attract them?

How do you deal with outside pressures from administrators, colleagues, and parents?

How can you get the theatre, the school, and the community to coexist happily?

Chapters 2 through 5, the core of the book, comprise the nuts and bolts—a complete course of study for a one-year Introduction to Theatre class designed to provide the foundation for a flourishing cocurricular program. Simply stated, excellence on the auditorium stage must begin with excellence in the classroom.

This view would come as no great revelation were it not for the fact that, until recently, it was a rare high school that offered its students theatre courses of *any* description. Talent in acting was seen as a by-product of pure intuition, and the school play was expected to materialize through a combination of magic and whatever scraps of instruction the director could squeeze into an already busy rehearsal schedule.

Only during the past twenty years or so have theatre educators across the country started to reverse this piecemeal approach by taking steps to initiate a broad-based mainstreaming of theatre programs into the heart of the secondary school curriculum. No uniform nationwide course of study is presently in place, since different communities reflect different needs, and this book makes no case for the imposition of rigidly fixed standards of performance. What it offers instead are well-tested techniques to teach kids the discipline of the craft of acting, followed by a format for exposing them to regular and frequent public performance (see "Theatre Scenes" in Chapter Four).

While *Secondary Stages* is addressed primarily to the first-year theatre teacher, I hope that more experienced staff will find it a helpful resource as well—not to mention the stray speech, English, or music teacher who falls into the curious position of having to conduct an introductory drama course in the auxiliary gym third period.

A Context for Instruction

Foundations of the Course

If you're a high school English teacher new to a district reporting for work your first day on the job, someone in authority will probably give you an officially approved curriculum that outlines, at least generally, what subject matter your students are required to master by year's end. If you've been hired to build a drama program and the class is called *Introduction to Theatre,* don't expect to be handed an officially approved anything. Odds are you're on your own.

What should we teach our students in an introductory theatre class? State education departments, which typically are responsible for providing answers to good questions like this, have a checkered history when it comes to developing practical material for course content in secondary school theatre. So if that's where you're turning for ideas about what to do in class Monday morning, you may well come up empty-handed. Theatre has long been viewed as an educational frill—even, amazingly, at the university level—and many states don't even validate the subject area by granting it formal status in the public school curriculum hierarchy. It may come as no surprise that New York did so only as recently as 1996.

Although the condition is most definitely on the mend, richly detailed, state-approved syllabi in theatre are as yet anything but widely available. That may be a concealed blessing, however, because when they *are* available, you can sometimes find yourself flipping through pages, desperately wondering how to fashion real-life lesson plans out of the tangle of educational jargon (*Aim: to expand the students' understanding of the many and varied theatrical forms of expression that give rise to the enriched appreciation of the many and varied juxtapositions of. . . .)*

My own answer to the question posed at the beginning of this chapter is a minority position: I believe we should use the time to teach students the fundamentals of acting. A great many of my colleagues, probably most, would argue for a more broad-based curriculum, such as units on the history of the art form, literary analysis of scripts, the ABCs of design, the role of theatre in society, and the criteria for reviewing a production. Even for such state-approved syllabi that *do* exist, you can bet your teaching degree that regulations will mandate a traditional survey approach—along with a written final exam in June. I understand and appreciate the driving force behind this trend, which gives the student wider exposure and lends the course some scholastic weight that a curriculum focusing on performance skills alone would arguably lack. I can understand, too, why teachers fed up with the old story of drama programs that "get no respect" might lend their enthusiastic support to this campaign. But I think it would ultimately fail, for the same reasons a physical education class that stresses the historical origins of soccer or requires students to take written tests on the care and maintenance of sports equipment would fail. *It de-emphasizes what is most vital in the subject.* Just as with sports, the key in acting is to get on your feet and do it. And if kids then become hooked on theatre, they can surely move on to the study of history, criticism, technical arts, and analysis of scripts in subsequent electives.

It's important to add here that course offerings vary alarmingly in public schools throughout the country. Most will offer only one theatre class—*theatre*, that is, as opposed to *dramatic literature*, which usually comes under the domain of the English department. But there are also plenty of districts in privileged areas (Great Neck, NY, Beverly Hills, CA) where students can elect classes in directing, scene study, technical arts, and even preparation for college auditions.

The underlying crux of this debate reverts back to the public perception that good acting is easy, and that a student's A in the course can't possibly be worth much on an academic transcript. Sometimes, on quiet days in June, I've raised this question directly with my students. "Oh yeah," they'll say, "most kids out there definitely do see theatre as a blow-off course!" But the theatre students themselves should know better. They've been at the game long enough to appreciate the level of skill needed for performers to achieve excellence—and they know it's a risk many straight-A physics students would never dream of taking.

I can hear the opposition voices chanting, "But *why* make acting the primary emphasis when so many students who may profit from theatre would be excluded from the outset by their terror at having to get up in front of their friends?" Why, indeed? Because *playing* music is more fundamental than discussing it; because *creating* a piece of sculpture is closer to the art form's essence than critiquing one; because *performing* and *writing* stage pieces are the raw materials of theatre, the elements that remain when all else is stripped away.

All these pedagogical and aesthetic questions aside, the hands-on approach is also a hell of a lot more exciting for students. There is nothing sinful in this fact, especially because so many acting skills are attained through hard discipline, concentration, preparation, and attention to detail. And excitement is something kids everywhere have cited as missing from their educational experience.

If you work in a state that spells out the requirements for a deadly Intro to Theatre course, you may have to surrender this vision, especially when the powers that be leave you no choice but to operate by the book. But if the possibilities for a strong, vibrant acting class are good, it will at the very least warm the hearts of administrators to know that the costs and physical requirements are minimal:

- a somewhat larger than average classroom; a small theatre is nirvana, although a standard room will do
- access to a few basic props and pieces of furniture, such as a beat-up couch, table, two futons (highly useful!), a few chairs, and so on
- odd bits of clothing and a closet for storing them
- a terrific luxury: the simplest dimmer board and enough instruments (six, separately controlled, will do the trick) to wash the stage with light

All but the first and last of these can be donated to the cause by generous students.

Nature of the Beast: The Theatre Student in Profile

Nowhere does the coolness factor operate more powerfully than in the life of a high school student. In the area of drama, where public performance usually means high exposure, multiply that pressure quotient by three. Is theatre a cool class to take? Is it cool to get up in front of your friends and start *acting*? These questions, however shallow, are the first ones high school students are likely to ask themselves—if only subconsciously—before signing up for a theatre course.

Yet theatre teachers are usually cautious about discussing this issue, except maybe in private places. Maybe the students are inevitably driven by peer pressure, but are these legitimate questions for the dignified professional? Must the theatre teacher cater to adolescent whimsy by striving to develop a program that's "cool"?

Absolutely and fundamentally yes, for anyone who accepts my premise that a vital program in theatre *must* embrace the broadest possible segment of the student body: wise guys, loners, intellectuals, jokers, scholars, greasers, athletes, mathletes. The gamut.

There are scores of inspired class clowns capable of mastering the discipline of the stage once they realize that acting might finally offer a legitimate showcase for their talents. And many, if not all, of these students are capable not only of turning out memorable performances but also of redefining themselves in the process, of carving out an identity that at last wins them a measure of pride and self-respect in the school.

Only one thing stands in their way—the notion of signing up for a drama course probably strikes them as lunacy! Likewise for scores of jocks, the so-called learning disabled, computer "freaks," and Average Joes who merely want to raise their self-esteem. Why? Maybe some lack the confidence to risk public failure. Others may doubt their ability to submit to the rigors of long and arduous rehearsal. The more likely reason, I think, is that many of these kids have come to associate *theatre student* with a certain personality profile—highly eccentric, brooding, temperamental, artsy. Uncool. This is another form of stereotyping, to be sure. But there most certainly *are* schools—colleges as well as high schools—where that image has been carefully cultivated. It need not be so, and is in fact only the case in high school theatre departments where that kind of "into oneself" sensibility is instilled and nurtured. It is an elitist doctrine that hopes to draw students primarily through the exquisite high-mindedness of its appeal: "My students will be totally devoted to theatre as an art form. They will worship at the shrine of Chekhov, Beckett, Molière, and Shakespeare. They will develop a religious reverence for the craft of acting. They will know of Sarah Bernhardt and Eleonora Duse, Artaud and Grotowski." Indeed! And any theatre director worth a damn would be hard put to raise a hand in protest. But this is not where most high school students begin a love affair with theatre—though we can all hope it's where they'll wind up!

If the above scenario accurately describes the program we are serving up in the name of reverence for an art form, we will in the same stroke lock out that broadest possible segment of the student body right from the starting gate. Any theatre teacher whose instant response is "Right . . . and who needs them? Too many of those kids are only there to cause trouble anyway!" is overlooking an essential and fascinating truth—there is almost no positive correlation between an aptitude for theatre and general academic excellence. Over my thirty-one years of teaching, I have found that a strong concentration of talent in my program did indeed come from students with high scholastic averages. *And* from those with failing grades in almost every subject *but* theatre. There is scarcely any connecting link between the two poles. Some kids were science wizards, others basketball fanatics, literary aficionados, math enthusiasts, journalists; other kids did little else but hang out with friends all day and look for places to smoke cigarettes in peace. From each of these populations *also* came many who were drawn to the theatre program, maybe seeking a quick shot at local stardom, but who became quickly disillusioned as soon as they realized how much good hard work was involved. They rarely stayed the course. When they did, however, the impact could be utterly transforming. The message here is not to shut out those with a serious interest in theatre as art, but to open the doors wide to the rank and file and the casually curious. They will slowly reveal layers of talent and self-discipline no one ever thought possible. Least of all themselves.

But first, they've got to be willing to sign up! For any student with the courage to stick a toe in the door, a program that's cool to check out means just one thing: that it sends out a welcome message to the largest number of potentially interested kids—kids who become gradually conditioned to regard theatre as approachable, free of the familiar stigmas of exclusion and snobbery.

Support for this populist approach is prevalent in the writings of Walter Kerr (*How Not to Write a Play*) and Peter Brook (*The Empty Space*), two keen observers of the qualities that make theatre a vital, enhancing presence in human affairs: "It is always the popular theatre that saves the day," writes Brook (65). "Through the ages it has taken many forms, and there is only one factor that they all have in common—a roughness. Salt, sweat, noise, smell." It is the popular forms of entertainment, including circuses, puppet shows, and traveling theatre troupes *as well as* the works of our greatest playwrights, that at their best have risen to the level of the universal.

So it is that a vital high school theatre program must bring actors into the social studies and English classes, stage scenes in the cafeterias, write their own scripts, bring students with free periods into a small studio setting to attend improvised theatre sports contests or *Star Wars* parodies, present to a film study class a group of prepared scenes from movies about youth during the 30s, 40s, 50s, and 60s. And on and on. That, I'm convinced, is the route to creating a nucleus of students who eventually become capable of rising to the challenge of Shaw, Molière, Williams, Miller, and Beckett. It is further along that path, that kids can eventually open themselves to the shocking discovery that Shakespeare himself is, in fact, pretty cool.

Building Depth and Breadth: Strategies for Drawing Students

Of course nothing is more essential to the creation of a theatre program of depth and breadth than effective teaching, innovative lessons, and, ultimately, the presentation of exciting, dynamic productions. The following list is a slate of techniques—tricks of the trade to supplement those basics.

Get the Guys

That's right. Item One on the list. It's a subject the textbooks are reluctant to address, probably because so few issues these days are as sensitive or emotionally charged. And yet this is, far and away, the *single* most essential task to address if you hope to build the kind of program described here. It is a matter of stark reality that no experienced drama director would deny: Guys, especially most high school guys, are frightened to death of theatre. Yet there is no

Odd Couple without a six-man contingent of noisy poker players, no *Glass Menagerie* without a persuasive Tom and a virile, appealing Jim, no possibility in theatre class of performing scenes from just about any exciting contemporary play or film without the participation of a large, varied population of males. Women are always on hand, eager to participate, possibly because the free expression of emotion in our society has always been more acceptable among females. But if the popular culture is as powerful an influence in the lives of kids as it's usually thought to be, then can't we point to enough examples of young male actors making pots of money in the film industry to hasten the death of that stereotype?

Apparently not. In the mind and gut of most high school males, the prejudice against theatre still runs deep. *Tea and Sympathy* (1953), Robert Anderson's once popular melodrama, got it right: Normal guys play football; guys who sign up for theatre class play around with other guys. The culture of the present isn't vastly changed in that department, as much as we'd like to pretend otherwise. There are still a lot more women pressing to compete on the school soccer, baseball, even wrestling teams than there are men lined up for auditions for the school play. That's why so many of my colleagues continue to echo the cry, "Try as we may, we simply can't draw males to our program."

Here are some techniques for jump-starting your recruitment campaign. All of them work some of the time; a few can fairly be described as cheap pandering. But this is a noble cause, is it not—a case in which the ends surely justify the means? After all, in the long run, the men who break this cultural barrier stand to gain as much through their involvement as does the drama program that welcomes them.

For starters, offer your theatre class a number of scenes that appeal primarily to male actors. Start out choosing excerpts from plays that are relatively easy to cast (*Don't Drink the Water, New York Stories, Mister Roberts, Biloxi Blues, Broadway Bound*) and advance gradually to the tougher ones (*Zoo Story, Ordinary People, Catch 22, Rosencrantz and Guildenstern Are Dead, A Few Good Men, The Grapes of Wrath, Amadeus, True West*). These choices can be balanced out by scenes from plays that cater more to women (*The Children's Hour, I Remember Mama, The Heidi Chronicles, Steel Magnolias,* and *Crimes of the Heart*).

"But how," you ask, "am I supposed to rehearse scenes from

male-dominated plays when I have so few males enrolled in the class?" Easy.

- Begin by asking one or two of the guys who *are* enrolled if they have a friend who's wasting away in the cafeteria that same period.

- Encourage males from your English class or other classes who display some gift for the dramatic—let's say in reading plays aloud in class—to take a stab at theatre. All they need is a willing spirit and a corresponding free period.

- Ask students currently involved in the course and/or productions to recommend males who they feel might be right for theatre class.

- Dare a highly visible jock with an obvious histrionic flair to get involved in a scene. If he triumphs, others will follow.

- In dire circumstances, when I've had a tough time filling a role any other way, I have not been above casting shamelessly to type by approaching someone in the halls who simply "looked right." Guys I've ensnared in this way are often hugely flattered by the request and, more often than not, will say "Sure!" Just as often, they've loved the experience and become theatre regulars.

This practice of darting around the school—chasing down innocent victims in the halls and cafeterias, inviting them to "grab a script and start acting"—might well strike some readers as extreme, not to say undignified. "Is he going to suggest canvassing neighborhood shopping centers next?" Fair point. But remember your goal here: to create a balanced theatre program where both males and females can feel at home. Some of these "early recruits" may indeed be short on acting technique. But they've certainly come to the right place to learn. Remember: if you're standing at or near ground zero, you've got to break the existing cycle and start building from *somewhere*.

Offer the Opportunity for Cameo Roles

Whenever appropriate, incorporate into the scenes brief spotlight appearances, or cameos, by students willing to get involved. This technique works like a charm. Most who say yes—it's a pretty small investment of rehearsal time for a lot of feel-good attention—get smitten by the theatre bug and soon return for more. It has the double advantage of making an acting experience available to a kid who'd normally never think of going out for theatre, and of surprising the student body with some flash appearances by theatre "outsiders"—benign victims, as it were, willing to take the plunge. It's a baby step from there to: "Yeah, I can do that!"

Cameos can be thought of in two distinct ways. There are those already specified by the playwright, such as Hamlet's stroll across the stage at the climax of the "tennis match" scene from *Rosencrantz and Guildenstern Are Dead* and Eddie's brief entrance in the opening Jay/Artie scene from *Lost in Yonkers*. Or, there are those cameos you may decide to interpolate into the action of your own accord. Of course, cameos can't be sprinkled indiscriminately over each and every scene. But in the right spot they can create magic. We found such a moment in the drugstore scene from *Summer of '42*. As Hermie and Oscy were planning their strategy for duping Mr. Sanders into selling them a box of condoms, a teen couple sipping egg creams at the soda fountain turned periodically to express amused disbelief. Their appearance, while not indicated in the script, contributed an extra measure of humor to the scene and gave the lead characters one more obstacle to play on. The students who performed the parts spoke no dialogue, but they had a wonderful time working with the other kids in the class and drew delighted responses from the audience.

One word of warning: Make sure that students who commit themselves to one of these know that they're required to *work* at rehearsals. If they've never before performed in a scene, they may not realize how much discipline is required. It's a trap I've fallen into more than once.

Pick Scripts with Broad Popular Appeal

This simply means that, in a program's early stages, you can gain better momentum by leading off with instantly recognizable titles such as *The Diary of Anne Frank, Dracula, The Miracle Worker,* or *One Flew over the Cuckoo's Nest* and then advancing patiently to *Scapino, Orphans, Only Kidding,* and *All in the Timing*.

Of course a familiar title isn't enough by itself. Before selecting scenes from *any* play, famous or obscure, you'll need to feel pretty confident that the class has the performers to fill the roles. (See "Choice of Material and Scene Partners" in Chapter 4, page 115, for a complete discussion of this subject.) It's also reasonable to argue that these days almost no play is universally known to the general high school population, unless maybe it's been made into a movie. Still, all things being equal, Simon's *The Odd Couple* makes more sense as a source for your first round of presentations than Brecht's *The Caucasian Chalk Circle*.

Bring Theatre out into the Open

Theatrical fundamentally connotes *splashy*; hence it makes good sense for the program to create some splash, at least now and then, so that the school at large can come to know of its existence. Once students in the course have developed self-possession and some basic technique, they should be encouraged to test themselves outside the assigned room. Some English and math classes may do just fine in the same physical setting for the length of a course, but students of theatre should become used to moving about. Think visibility . . . "traveling players" . . . *commedia dell'arte*! I spoke earlier of the kind of program that creates variety by opening up new paths. *Where* you end up is less important than the notion of movement: up and out. In Chapter 5, "Special Projects," a host of these ideas is described in detail. Here is a brief preview:

- thirty- to forty-minute children's plays that may be rehearsed in class and then transported to elementary schools within the district;
- a group of scenes that parallels specific curriculum content in English, social studies, or art classes (for example, *Our American Cousin* or *Oedipus Rex* excerpts prepared for a history class's study of the Civil War or ancient Greece);
- a group of scenes performed for the district's middle school (with minimal scenery);
- a comedy improv show performed in a local hospital, rehabilitation facility, or home for seniors;
- ten-minute scenes, scripted by members of the class, presented during two consecutive periods for invited audiences in the school library; and

- talent exchanges with neighboring school districts (for example, a colleague of mine established a repertory troupe that transported fully rehearsed, one-act plays to other towns, counties, and states, and then, months later, hosted actors for return visits).

Yes, you most certainly do need an enlightened, if not to say free-spirited, administration ready to back you in these ventures, and I plead guilty here to making it all sound a bit easier to pull off than it might be in real life. But that doesn't mean the effort is not well spent, or that patience and perseverance won't win out in the end.

Involve the Staff

Far from being a gimmick, the practice of encouraging the direct participation of the instructional staff can add immeasurable richness to your program. Over the years, I have found a tremendous number of teachers at our high school more than eager to jump in when students asked them to play major roles in scenes rehearsed for class (see Chapter 5, "Special Projects"). To the surprise of all, many possessed pretty sophisticated acting skills and were highly motivated to present themselves in the best possible light. All they need is a willingness to participate and a matching free period.

More important, staff members who worked with us over the days and weeks left the experience with a very different sense of what theatre was all about. They witnessed firsthand how much time and labor went into the rehearsals and gradually began to appreciate the degree of discipline required to get a scene on its feet. The results: a greater respect for student actors, greater tolerance for student burnout during the week of performances, and, best of all, *the opportunity to observe excellence in kids who sometimes do poorly in traditional settings.*

Happy Coexistence:
The Politics of Theatre in the School and Community

A *politics of theatre?* Presumably it sounds bizarre to speak of the politics of high school earth science or calculus. But theatre—because of its capacity to spark public outrage—is never far from the flame of controversy. Outside the walls of academia, just a few short years ago, Terrence McNally's *Corpus Christi* was triggering demonstrations in the New York streets and dissension in the national media for weeks on end. *Theatre Is Not Safe*, as Gordon Rogoff put it in the title of his 1987 volume of essays. Nor should it be. It must remain a hot medium, even in this unshockable age, even within the protected grounds of the traditionally conservative public high school.

Of course the drama program does not stand alone in this arena. When English teachers select books for classroom study these days, they too know that someone outside the door will be keeping watch. The American cultural landscape has never been more heated, so it's easy to understand why society is casting a close eye on the schools. If a chosen novel is not part of the prescribed curriculum—sometimes even when it is—there will be administrators, parents, and occasionally students all too ready to challenge its worth and appropriateness. When that same novel violates the standards of decency of a group of so-called concerned citizens, their voices can cause the temperature in the community to rise sharply. Teachers who think they can shut out the heat by closing the door are kidding themselves.

In the theatre classroom, no great surprise, the air is warmer still. Your kids—once past a reasonable period of apprenticeship—will be performing a broad range of material for their friends, teachers, and parents on a regular basis. There will be plenty to delight and plenty to offend just about everyone. With that degree of continuous public exposure, you, as the drama director, are placed in a vulnerable position. Decisions large and small can mean unfriendly notes in your office mailbox. Granted, there is an upside to this same equation: In years when a memorable group of student actors passes through, when classes seem to click, when audiences jam the studio to check out the latest round of "Theatre Scenes," you can feel like the winning football coach. But fair weather or foul, the high visibility factor remains a constant.

This means—unless you strive for a program of utter tameness, and I know few theatre types who do—that you can always be sure *attention will be paid*. So it makes sense early on to temper your idealism with a touch for diplomacy with students, administrators, colleagues, parents, and board members. Put more cynically, you'd better learn fast to play the public relations game. It's what happy coexistence is really all about.

It's tough to predict when objections will be raised, and tougher still to know who will raise them. I've failed to call the shots any number of times—sure in one instance that I'd be in deep trouble for presenting scenes from *A Children's Hour* (not a whimper—probably few had heard of it!), astonished in another at the volume and variety of elements that could manage to find *someone* to offend (*Biloxi Blues*). From a long history of scenes presented to the high school audience, let me toss out a list of personal examples as a basis for achieving a healthy balance in the war between public relations and artistic judgment.

- objection to rampant sexism in scenes from *Vanities*, *Steel Magnolias*, and *Taming of the Shrew*
- objection to charges of lewdness in the prostitute scenes from *Shivaree* and *Biloxi Blues*
- objection to the appearance of a bare-chested Romeo in Act III, Scene 5 of *Romeo and Juliet*
- objection to the presentation of scenes from *Balm in Gilead* for its bleak depiction of the dregs of civilization (and on lots of other counts as well)
- objection to *One Flew over the Cuckoo's Nest* for its failure to present a major role for a sympathetic female character
- objection to sexual content in scenes from *Carnal Knowledge*, *The Graduate*, *Brighton Beach Memoirs*, *Lovers and Other Strangers*, *Lysistrata*, *Scenes from the Ex-Pat Café*, and countless others
- objection to crude language in scenes from *American Buffalo*, *True West*, *Orphans*, *Burn This*, *My Left Foot*, and countless others
- objection to cigarette smoking in scenes from *Biloxi Blues*, *Alice Doesn't Live Live Here Anymore*, *When You Comin' Back Red Ryder*, and others
- objection to simulated alcohol consumption in scenes from *A Streetcar Named Desire*, *The Turning Point*, *The Last Picture Show*, and others

It's tempting to argue each of these through to a reasonable conclusion, but since your battles will involve different scripts and different standards, what would ultimately be the point? For example, I can appreciate, through hindsight, the hypocrisy of requiring a health teacher to expose students to those grisly photos of tobacco-stained lungs and then granting the theatre director license for them to strut around the stage puffing away on cigarettes. So if a script called for smoking, I'd probably try to find a way around it, given a second chance today. Conversely, I might fight all the harder over *Cuckoo's Nest*, insisting that it's not the playwright's job to represent the sexes fairly, but to show life as he sees it and allow audiences to judge the play's merits for themselves.

What you *do* need is a set of guidelines for preserving your sanity on the one hand and upholding the quality of your program on the other. It's no easy task. For one thing, reasonable discussion rarely helps since these disputes are almost never settled through logical discourse. *Arsenic and Old Lace* is a jolly classic, so it's fine with everyone that its two main characters commit nonstop murder. *Talk Radio*, as everyone knows, is "lewd and subversive," so no amount of scrubbing or scissoring will silence the charges of blasphemy. *The Prime of Miss Jean Brodie* is literature, so few would condemn its allusions to premarital sex (of more immediate concern is the near-impossibility of finding a suitable high school actress for the title role or the difficulty of making the play emotionally accessible to today's kids). *Blue Denim* and *Splendor in the Grass* are "shocking and scandalous," so they must be bad for our children's health.

Of course most parents know that their kids have ventured past the innocence of *Sesame Street* and *Mr. Rogers' Neighborhood* by the time they reach high school. Their objection to certain plays is not meant to deny the existence of sex, drugs, violence, or four-letter words. It's based on the terror of the unknown: What will happen if we allow the schools to sanction such behavior by granting it a public forum? Ten years ago I would have laughed these fears off. Even today, I question the idea that seeing *bad* people represented onstage may incite high school kids to commit *bad* acts or that, once past elementary school, we enter a theatre to seek models of good citizenship. But I understand parents' fears better than I used to. Today's headlines have given them good cause for anxiety, and even if it's misleading to argue that provocative theatre triggers antisocial behavior in a teen, I can still respect the parent who demands that we err on the side of caution.

I'm lingering over these questions because I'm aware, through long experience, of the difficulty and complexity of the issues and of how stubbornly they resist pat solutions. In fact, therein lies the heart of the problem: A whole lot of people out there are sick to death of patient discussions of complex issues. They want a quick antidote to what they perceive to be the "poisons" eating away at traditional American values, and it's convenient for them to target whatever lies close at hand. Such as the drama program. That's why, in formulating the following guidelines, we need to strike a balance between the parent or administrator who would limit your choices to the likes of *Organdy Cupcakes* and *Jessica Goes to the Prom* and the renegade student who refuses to rehearse a script unless it reeks of sex, drugs, and rock 'n' roll.

School Policy

If the regulations are set down in black and white, follow them to the letter. You *can* work to amend an idiotic rule, but choose such battles with care. It's not worth risking your neck over a violation of official policy just because a child wants the kick of saying a naughty word in public. I *don't* believe in sanitizing the text. If a character says "I don't give a shit," that's the playwright's choice, and I'd be the last one to recast the phrase as "I don't give a darn." But I prefer that compromise to the loss of my job. Clear statements of policy also allow for a safe response to the student who moans "Why can't we . . . ?" (". . . pretend to smoke a joint . . . ?" ". . . put on *Marat/Sade* . . . ?" ". . . take off our clothes onstage . . . ?") These kids aren't really after a rational explanation—they just "want to." Yes, I suppose some may read "It's against school policy, that's why" as a cop-out! But it's also a practical solution for getting by in the real world.

> **CAUTION!** Remember that any time you *do* feel compelled to alter the original text, the following warning statement appears on the copyright page of just about every published script in creation: *No changes shall be made in the play for the purpose of your production unless authorized in writing.* Take these words at face value. They don't stipulate that you can't make adjustments—only that you must secure the licensing agent's permission in advance.

I was lucky in that my district permitted me huge latitude in choosing scripts and rarely pressured me to censor them. In fact, there was no written code of any sort, so far as I knew. The administrators seemed to operate on the assumption that, as an experienced professional, I could be counted on to set reasonable limits. But more than a few of my colleagues disagreed, feeling that I took advantage by crossing the line once too often. They argued that a formal written policy was sorely needed. Maybe so, because there's an obvious downside to too much freedom: You risk venturing too far, forgetting, after all, that it's children you're working with.

But I realize that, for the vast majority of drama teachers across the country, too much freedom isn't usually the problem.

Political Correctness

Disputes in this category concern gender, race, ethnicity, and sexual orientation: "You shouldn't do scenes from *Taming of the Shrew* because that play presents an offensively sexist view of women." "You shouldn't cast a black student as Rheba in scenes from *You Can't Take It with You* because it's undignified for an African American to portray a servant." "You shouldn't do scenes from *Our Town* because its perspective is entirely lily-white Anglo American." "You shouldn't do *any* excerpts from plays that feature homosexual characters because an impressionable teen might construe that as an endorsement of the gay lifestyle." These issues pose true dilemmas: If you honor the objection, you must either alter the script (see Caution! on page 15), which is highly presumptuous (think of altering a Monet painting or a Mozart sonata), or toss the selection altogether, which soon reduces you to a handful of insipid choices and robs your theatre of its legitimate power to provoke. If you ignore the objection, you find yourself under fierce attack and risk nonstop bombardment from all sides.

There's no easy escape from this labyrinth except to consider each case on its own merit, weigh the options, and give it your best shot.

Gender

I thoroughly reject the claim that *Taming of the Shrew* presents a sexist view of women or that Shakespeare is urging husbands to find happiness in marriage by forcing their mates into bland obedience. The proof lies in Act IV, when Kate refuses to spar with Petruchio and for the first time in the play ends a fight by deferring to his "better wisdom":

> Then, God be bless'd, it is the blessed sun:
> But sun it is not, when you say it is not;
> And the moon changes even as your mind.
> What you will have it named, even that it is;
> And so it shall be for Katherine.

These are not the words of a dutiful wife but of a mature woman who's figured out that she can manipulate her man into submission by uttering the words he wants to hear and then proceeding to do whatever she damn pleases. William Ball's production of the play for the ACT reinforced that interpretation by having Katherine flash an oversize wink at the audience in the last scene following the words "My hand is ready, may it do him ease."

So you can silence the naysayers in cases like these by doing some homework. Even with plays like *Steel Magnolias*, however, which might fairly be labeled sexist from a contemporary urban perspective, can't we appreciate the humor of the story or pungency of the characters without whining about the condition of women whose only aim in life is to hang out in a beauty shop and exchange local gossip? To do so would be to miss the show's tone and, worse still, to mistake a portrait of small-town eccentricity in the deep South for a weighty political tract.

Complaints like the ones mentioned above can be pretty frustrating. The charges strike me as ill-founded, even silly, despite the best possible motives. If everyone is willing to sit down and talk things through, fine—time well spent, at least from a public relations standpoint. But to withdraw the material afterward means you abandon the power to make the most fundamental decisions for the conduct of your theatre class. The bottom line: some people will discover some cause for offense in *any* scenes you choose to present. And they have every right to air that offense publicly—but not to determine policy.

Race and Ethnicity

Matters of race and ethnicity are something else again. Here you stand on shakier ground. For example, the script for *You Can't Take*

It with You most certainly does specify "a colored maid named Rheba—a very black girl somewhere in her thirties." Now Kaufman and Hart were not, so far as I know, callous, insensitive men. Their play has retained its charm and tenderness after more than sixty years and remains a popular choice among community and high school theatre groups. But these writers were products of another time, so they can perhaps be forgiven for referring to a thirty-year-old woman as a "colored girl." Yet even if we cut the authors some slack on this one, we're still not out of the quicksand. You can assign your kids a scene from the play, you can assign the part to a black student, but you can't assign her to feel comfortable playing it. The history of slavery is real, and scores of African Americans find it difficult to forget that, for generations in this country, servant roles were virtually all that were available to them—on stage *and* screen.

Once again, the rules of logic don't help much. "Well . . . rewrite the dialogue, rechristen the character Rita, and give a white student the part." (See Caution! on page 15.) Even if you feel OK about tinkering with Kaufman and Hart—the character's lines are clearly rendered in 1930s "Negro" dialect—what exactly is the premise behind this argument? That it would be undignified for a black girl to portray a servant, but not a white girl? Alas, there's no easy answer, and sometimes the only practical solution may be to pull the plug. "Reject a scene because of concern over so minor a role?" Well, yes, short of finding a solution that compromises neither the author nor the dignity of your actors.

Modern repertoire introduces other thorny issues of plausibility. Can you cast a superior black actress as Kate Jerome in *Brighton Beach Memoirs*? An Asian American as Cetta DiAngelo in *Daughters*? A woman as Dr. Spivey in *One Flew over the Cuckoo's Nest*? On the opera stage, these questions haven't bothered anyone much since the early 1960s. But in professional film and theatre, cross-racial and cross-gender casting are still close to unheard of today. Presumably those defending the practice would argue that modern audiences couldn't possibly accept such jarring breaches of realism.

In a high school theatre program, there is only one defensible position in my view: Your casting of scenes must be color-blind. It took time and the efforts of some enlightened students to help me arrive at this realization. "How," I'd ask them, "can you expect the audience to believe that Helen Keller's mother had black skin?"

The students' answer made more sense than mine: "If skin color has no place in the story, if Mrs. Keller's *race* has no connection to the theme of the play, then the audience will accept the actress's presence no matter her skin color. Otherwise Asian American, African American, Hispanic American, and a lot of other *American* kids who go to this school have no place in your program! It's an entirely different matter if we're talking about *Othello* or *A Raisin in the Sun*."

Of course, these patterns also operate in reverse. The *Our Town* example cited earlier is indeed drawn from real life, difficult as it may be to imagine a person who'd feel justified in attacking Wilder's classic for being "too white." A friend and fellow drama director was forced to defend herself against such charges a few years back. It was a case of political correctness reduced to its ultimate absurdity: To satisfy her critics, she'd presumably have to have chosen material with equal ethnic representation from all races and creeds. But these arguments aside, if one rejects *Our Town* as being too *white*, one must equally reject *A Raisin in the Sun* and *Fences* as being too *black*, or *Teahouse of the August Moon* and *F.O.B.* as being too *yellow*. We've got to abandon this mad crusade; everyone is ultimately tarnished by it.

Sexual Orientation

The subject of homosexuality raises the steepest of all challenges because here, ironically, it's the *kids'* prejudices that pose the greatest obstacles. Can you hand a sixteen-year-old heterosexual a scene in which they're asked to portray a gay teenager? Can you hand a sixteen-year-old homosexual the same scene? There may be any number of complex answers to these questions, but "Sure, no problem! Why not?" certainly isn't one of them. It's a very fragile issue, however you approach it. If the particular student is highly anchored, highly evolved, and highly courageous, the answer may be a qualified *yes*. But the performance will raise the eyebrows, if not the outright hostilities, of a good segment of the student audience. Homophobia still rules among high school kids, all of whom are at the most tender stages of the formation of their own sexual identities. Your theatre program cannot single-handedly reverse that fact.

I'm in no way arguing here that the homophobes must be appeased—merely that they're present—in large numbers. Nor am

I implying that you can address this matter by ignoring it. There's deep hypocrisy in hoisting the flag of equal rights and equal tolerance in behalf of racial, ethnic, and religious minorities, and at the same time telling gay kids that their situation is, in effect, "just too hot to handle."

The best strategy is to advance slowly. Avoid using a sledgehammer with your audiences, and discuss *all* variables with your actors in the frankest terms well before handing anyone any pages of script.

Finding the right material is the number one prerequisite. There aren't a whole lot of plays suitable for teens that deal directly with this subject. *The Children's Hour* and *Tea and Sympathy* do so obliquely, and these both work superbly with the right high school actors. But Hellman is intentionally ambiguous about whether Martha is driven to doubt her sexuality because of the strain of the trial or the resurfacing of very real fears, and Anderson tells us cheaply in the last scene that Tom simply needed the right time and the right lover to assert his own heterosexuality (read: normalcy). Although *Streamers*, *Boys in the Band*, *As Is*, and *Angels in America* are much more explicit, these pieces contain *bona fide* adult material inappropriate for high schoolers. Take a close look at Rudnick's *Jeffrey*, McNally's *Lips Together, Teeth Apart* and *Love! Valor! Compassion!*, Lane's *Dancing on Checkers' Grave*, and the screenplay for Lucas' *Longtime Companion*, all of which contain scenes that strike a balance between appropriateness and candor.

One cringes to imagine the "PC-altered" versions that could befall future revivals of plays that fall into the wrong "well-meaning" hands: *Oleanna* ("too caricatured a depiction of feminists!"), *Inherit the Wind* ("too caricatured a depiction of rural Americans!"), *Brighton Beach Memoirs* ("too caricatured a depiction of immigrant Jews!"). The solution isn't to cut up or revise the texts of proven scripts, but to welcome the arrival of plays that slowly begin to reverse the old stereotypes. And isn't it finally a bit lunatic decades later to berate Hart or Kaufman or Wilder for failing to observe life from our so-called enlightened perspective?

Sex, Violence, and Obscene Language

Fewer than fifty years ago, high school theatre operated within clear limits: no sexual references, no sexual innuendoes, no "dirty" words onstage. There was no need to waste time arguing over what they were; everyone knew. Even a prolonged kiss might be judged questionable and yanked. At least drama directors in those days knew where they stood. Obviously these standards have shifted, as seen by the slow infiltration of many once-taboo words into the scripts of prime-time TV shows. Kids laugh hysterically when you tell them about the 1939 uproar over Rhett Butler's "Frankly my dear, I don't give a damn!" in the final scene of *Gone with the Wind*. For them, the fuss might just as well have been over *gosh* and *golly*. Or about the rule in TV sitcoms forbidding married couples to be shown sleeping in the same bed. Many out there upset with life in America at the turn of the twenty-first century would probably cherish a return to the standards of 1939. It ain't gonna happen. But I can say one thing with absolute certainty: If, along with the classics, you mean to include in your theatre program contemporary scripts for and about youth, you *will* come upon strong language and sexual references at every turn. I can't name many plays in this category for which that description doesn't apply. You might ask, "Do I cut the section? Change the words? Find something else? Leave everything as is and hope for the best?" It would be sweet to think these problems could be resolved solely through the exercise of your best professional judgment. In reality, you're caught in the same old juggling act—to create a balance among administrative concerns, school policy, parent feedback, the dictates of your conscience, and the best interests of kids (see Caution! on page 15).

Violence

So far scenes with violent content have never been the source of an objection.

Literary Quality of the Script (See Violence)

The Fundamentals of Acting Through Improvisation

Lesson One: The Cornerstone—Believability

> *They're gonna put me in the movies*
> *They're gonna make a big star outta me*
> *We'll make a film about a man that's sad and lonely*
> *And all I gotta do is act naturally.*

> — The Beatles

Act naturally. What could be easier? Creating belief in the circumstances of a scene is the soul of the actor's craft. That's his job—to present himself so that an audience can accept the character as a flesh-and-blood human being, not a windup doll. It sounds simple. Yet we've all attended performances of plays—in schools, in community theatres, sometimes alas even at the professional level—in which one or more of the actors spouted lines in what can only be called their "acting voice." The words sounded forced, phony, and insufferably theatrical. When we encounter this, our unconscious instinct is to think "Why can't they just behave naturally up there?" The answer should be simple, too, but experience demonstrates that the ability to act believably is *not* something all of us possess just by virtue of being human.

Most laymen think otherwise, of course. They believe that, once his lines have been memorized, the actor just gets up there and does it. And in one sense, this is a reasonable assumption. We are all experienced at the business of life, so what's the big deal, we ask, about placing ourselves convincingly in the shoes of another human being? We just need to do so in costume and makeup under the lights. Maybe the director has told us where to enter and where and when to cross, but the rest is left to impulse, instinct, and inspiration. And so is born the myth that good acting requires little or no training and that—unlike mastery of the violin, the painted canvas, or the periodic table of elements—you either have the talent to act well or you don't. People who hold this view regard acting classes as useless by definition, and they point, quite rightly, to the often astonishing naturalness of some screen actors, small children especially, who seem able to pull off miracles with virtually no prior experience or training, forgetting that these performers are invariably playing themselves, or at least close approximations of themselves.

But anyone who has carefully observed the beginning efforts of most untrained performers will soon discover just how misguided this thinking can be. Given the simplest set of circumstances, say two characters meeting on a street, and perhaps a few lines of printed dialogue, many will falter, try too hard to impress, produce arch, strained, or mechanical readings, mumble inaudibly, become tongue-tied. And the list goes on. Now, all at once, dawns the realization: "Hmmm . . . this isn't as easy as I thought!" Even more revealing might be a chance to observe experienced professionals at work on a set. It soon becomes clear just how much craft, attention to detail, and sheer discipline is required to produce that seemingly "effortless" illusion of naturalness. And why the best of those actors earn such generous salaries.

This foundation of truth—of producing behavior that rings true, that is natural and believable—is an absolute. Without it, nothing that happens onstage can ignite the imagination of the audience and set something living in motion.

Let's be sure we've got our terminology straight. The words *natural* and *believable* are easily confused through long habits of misuse. What of *stylized* or intentionally *theatrical* plays, some may ask, where *unnatural*, exaggerated acting is called for? (Masks? Mime? Theatre of the Absurd? Kabuki? Musical theatre?) In fact, no such confusion exists: The need for truth (believability) in performance is unqualified. In the wildest of fantasies, in the most nonrealistic of plays, the actor's stubborn belief in the circumstances of the script must prevail or the audience will sense that something is missing.

And all this applies to the high school setting as surely as it does to the professional arena. When the ring of truth is absent, the playing will be hollow. That's why it's impossible to overstate this believability dictum. It requires so much emphasis as a starting point only because it can be so tempting at the high school level to allow the actors to step gingerly around it. Honesty in performance doesn't come easily. There will always be those who love watching kids behave cutely, come out of character for a wink at the audience, ham it up, strut their stuff. Worse still is the acceptance of phony acting on the assumption that student actors can't yet be expected to approximate the real thing. They're not yet mature enough or experienced enough to pull it off. So we let them resort to their acting voice in the belief that something better will replace it with time.

They may *not* be ready, granted, to carry off scenes from *King Lear* or *Who's Afraid of Virginia Woolf?* But, given age-appropriate material, they are ready to behave believably, and—in practical terms—to bring conviction to the characters in improvisations, scene work, and one-act plays.

Since creating *believable* behavior is a necessary starting point for any acting course, you as the teacher would be wise in the early stages to work exclusively with improvisation and withhold scripts altogether as students master the fundamentals. This is a far better path to truth in acting because, without a sheet of paper or set of memorized lines to focus on, the students will be free to concentrate on acquiring the necessary skills. Acting is a difficult craft—absorbing enough of their energies to dispel thoughts of curtain calls and cameo appearances in upcoming episodes of the season's trendiest sitcoms. But it is eminently teachable.

Orientation to the Activities

It is *important* to note that every member of the class need not perform every activity. Twenty-five renditions of even the most riveting format can prove lethal by the middle of the third day. Below is a guide to the activities in this chapter.

Warm-up Exercises

The assignments are often preceded by warm-up exercises designed to give students the necessary tools to solve particular acting problems. Whenever possible, therefore, the exercises should be taken up first.

Levels of Difficulty

I've indicated levels of difficulty for each activity (basic, intermediate, or advanced) to help gauge student readiness and suggest a possible working order. Remember, however, that students differ subtly in the maturity and skills they bring to a particular task, so these distinctions aren't always airtight.

The Role of Humor Onstage

Although humor and effectiveness are fine if they evolve naturally from an improv, the goal is not to impress the audience with one's cleverness but to become immersed in the truth of the circumstances of the scene. The kids will challenge or plain forget this again and again because everyone, high school students especially, is a sucker for a laugh, and everyone loves the instant feedback that comes from giving pleasure to an audience. That's why adolescents are such big fans of comedy improv, the kind popularized by TV shows like *Whose Line Is It, Anyway*.

It's inevitable, therefore, that the kids' improvisations will utilize humor. But consciously aiming for audience approval is the death of these exercises because "playing to the crowd" will reinforce every bad habit young actors may bring to the course. Whenever their performance seems to shout "Hey guys, check this out!" accompanied by a figurative wink, you must step in firmly. It's no easy task because the inertia is powerful. Kids who are natural hams will protest, saying, "Hey . . . it was funny. The class cracked up, so where's the problem?" The answer is that *funny* is not a problem. Not even slightly. *Check this out!* is a problem.

Believability Onstage

Kids constantly misinterpret what is meant by *natural* onstage, which can be a tough situation. They often take the term to mean *laid back*, recreating an action *literally* as it would occur in a scene from their personal lives. As a result they forget that theatre is a heightened, concentrated form of real life presented to an audience. The problem is not helped by their viewing experiences, which are usually limited to TV and film, two media through which a grunt, whisper, or murmur can be easily amplified through the power of technology. As a result, kids sometimes mumble, utter sounds unlikely to be heard a few feet away, and, worst of all, completely close themselves off from contact with the audience. The solution is obviously not to insist that they face directly front and begin shouting their lines, since that approach will revive precisely the sort of hamming you're trying to discourage. Instead, whenever you find them acting truthfully, but inaudibly, simply say "Good, keep it! Don't change a thing. Just magnify things slightly; pump up the volume so we can share in it out here." For some young actors, the effort to jump this hurdle is long and painstaking. You need to be patient and reinforce over and over again that playing strongly, energetically, and emphatically is not in conflict with playing believably. In fact, since theatre events are usually (we hope) extraordinary events, exactly the opposite is the case.

Focus in the Scene

Since most kids pressure themselves to wow their classmates, you may find them struggling during an improv to create fascinating plots with surprise twists. "Playwriting is not scene improvisation," as Spolin (1963a, 46) puts it, and "some students find it very difficult to keep from 'writing a play.'" Of course the scenes they create will be action driven, and some story elements will always be present. But their focus should not be on inventing cute or clever scenarios. It happens most conspicuously when a single actor in an improv violates the cooperative spirit of the work by suddenly launching into a long, impassioned monologue ("Hey . . . check this out!"), or, with no plausible connection to what's already been seen, takes the action off into uncharted territory just for the sake of shock value. You need to discourage this tendency; instead, fix everyone's aim on achieving the limited purpose of the scene, which is always spelled out in the directions for each assignment. Once that purpose has been reached (and sometimes, when the actors are floundering, even *before*) it's time to yell "cut!"

Grading and Evaluation

"What's my grade?" Students are conditioned to ask this question in all aspects of their school life, so the request should come as no surprise. It's a mistake, though, to evaluate their work formally in the earliest stages of the course because so much anxiety is attached to the business of standing up and performing for one's peers. The first obligation is to instill trust, and only a reasonable grace period can confer that. But the end of the marking period does inevitably roll around, so prior to day one you must face up to the task of formulating criteria for a meaningful grade. Those criteria should be directly spelled out for the class when the time is right. I wouldn't presume to tell another teacher what they should be. I *will* say that intricate point systems make little sense to me—two for clarity of articulation, three for interaction with other characters onstage, six for maintaining concentration, and so on. There's probably no area of the school curriculum less hospitable to a numerical rating system than acting. To pretend otherwise is to think one can meaningfully distinguish between an improv that deserves an 81 and one that deserves an 84! I'm dogmatic, too, about insisting that the group understand how the process of evaluation works to encourage growth. Kids can be hyper-sensitive about this matter since, unlike just about any other school discipline, the target of the discussion is their bodies, their voices, and ultimately their imaginations. That's why I don't believe in bombarding high school actors with lots of so-called constructive criticism. "What might have made this scene even stronger?" That's the golden question, since it neutralizes attack and offers immediate suggestions for improvement. All things being equal, actors need care, nurture, and encouragement.

Feedback and Evaluation

Some guidelines for evaluation sessions are set forth in the beginning chapters. Later on, the process should become automatic. You should carry the bulk of the discussion in evaluation sessions early in the course. Too many conflicting voices from too many corners of the room can invite chaos. I've watched acting classes destroyed by the presumption of students trained from kindergarten to believe that all opinions carry equal weight and validity. The result: kids sounding off too often and too early. As they become more knowledgeable, students should of course participate more and more actively in the feedback process. But the evaluation sessions must always be brisk and to the point. Even you need to know when to keep still and when to move on. No acting class is more deadly than one in which each gesture and each fragment of behavior is analyzed and evaluated ad nauseum.

Warm-up Exercises in Believability

The following exercises are ideal for beginning a class session in believability. They serve the same purposes for the actor as do stretching exercises for the gymnast: to limber up the muscles and allay tensions. The exercises should be performed briskly and with minimal comment from the teacher.

Chair

Place a chair in front of the class. One by one, students walk onto the stage and incorporate the object into the briefest of scenes. For example, Student #1 repositions the object several times for aesthetic effect, much as an interior designer would, exits the stage; Student #2 wipes the seat prissily with an imaginary cloth, exits the stage; Student #3 sits down, crosses legs, uses chair to pose seductively for imaginary character, exits stage, and so on.

For variety, repeat the exercise. This time, each student who walks onto the stage will use the chair as something other than what it is, such as a lawn mower or a vacuum cleaner.

Stick

The class forms a large circle. One by one, the actors carry to the center an approximately two-foot-long stick. Each uses the stick as anything other than what it is and then passes the object to the next actor. Most groups are usually pretty resourceful, inventing endless variations once the obvious (baseball bat, pool cue) have been tried.

Make sure actors avoid *indicating*—in other words, using the object halfheartedly or only sort of doing what they pretend to be doing.

Telephone

The class sits in a circle. The teacher hands a telephone receiver to any one student, who must then hold a brief but believable conversation with an imaginary other character. After a maximum of thirty seconds, the phone gets passed to the next actor.

For variety, repeat the exercise at the start of another day's lesson. This time the actors must play characters other than themselves—weirdos, old people, or little kids.

How Was Your Weekend?

Monday morning. The class sits in a circle. Students spend less than a minute each relating a few of the more interesting things that happened to them over the weekend. Three members of the group, each of whom you've "set up" in the halls during the break between classes the Friday before, are lying (acting) about everything. Once around the circle, the teacher reveals the setup and asks the class to identify the three actors.

Door

An invisible door stands upstage center. Each participating actor stands behind the closed door, and when you call "Action," he or she must open it and step into the "room." Their expression and body language should reveal exactly what they see inside that room—for example, a robbery in progress, surprise party guests, the furniture in total disarray, and so on. No dialogue is permitted.

Where?

Actors enter the stage area one at a time. Each utilizes body and gesture to place a particular character in a particular location. No dialogue is used. This exercise remains tremendously valuable throughout the duration of the course, since the establishment of setting is basic to the performance of any improvisation. It should be repeated frequently at the beginning of any given class period.

Play Ball

Actors form one complete circle. (If the class is large, work in two shifts.) Hand one player a basketball. Ask her to throw a chest pass to whomever she pleases, after which the ball continues to move from player to player across and around the circle. After a time, vary the style of the pass (bounce pass, under leg pass, etc.).

Now put the ball aside and start the exercise over without it. Continue for a while, until the players get the "feel" of the ball, its texture and weight. If their focus is strong, the actors should be jumping high when the ball is aimed over their heads, bending to the floor if it's rolled across the ground, chasing it into the wings if they fail to catch it.

Once this imaginary ball becomes real for everyone in the group, call out "OK . . . it's a ping pong ball . . . a medicine ball . . . a bowling ball . . . a hardball." Again, continue until the actors' belief is secure.*

Assignments

Introduction: Opening Day

The first session of any theatre course is a journey into the Twilight Zone because students will enter the classroom in a high state of nervous anticipation. This is a performance class, and they know their inner resources will be tested and their imaginations put on display. Some may find ways to cover this anxiety, but all minds will be busy with silent questions: What's the story with this teacher? Who are the wise guys in the group? How soon will I embarrass myself to death? Will I have the courage to get up there at all? As a result, almost any lesson plan that lifts tensions and gets the group through to Day 2 is a good one.

Start off by playing the Beatles' "Act Naturally" and ask for their take on the lyrics (it helps to give them copies of the text). Do they imply that the best acting comes from just *being yourself* onstage? Is there truth to the notion that good acting can't be taught? What's the difference between acting that is *natural* and acting that is *phony*? The students' responses to this last question will give new focus to the conversation. Can they remember seeing

---

*This exercise was adapted from *Improvisation for the Theatre*.

performances by professional actors that seemed fake? What are the elements that make a memorable performance believable? There's unlikely to be much unanimity of response at this point, but that's OK because a set of criteria will emerge gradually as the unit unfolds.

If time permits, you can round out the period by briefly discussing some of the concerns that are probably on everyone's mind:

- the aims of the course;
- a description of the daily format;
- a preview of some of the projects that will engage the class—from the briefest improvs in the early weeks to the production of a one-act play at the end;
- some information about the extracurricular program; and
- the types of shows you will be putting on during the coming school year.

Let these informal exchanges place everyone at their ease, and save the full-group participation activities for the second day.

Assignment #1: Take Two (Basic)

Adolescents can usually be counted on to enter a classroom colorfully. There will be some who engage in animated conversation, maybe gossiping, arguing, or joking. Others may slouch in under the yoke of the test they just failed. There will be the two freshman guys practicing karate stunts, the student with yesterday's leftover question for the teacher.

At the beginning of Day 2, allow them to enter the classroom just as they might on any other day. Then, at exactly the moment you'd normally silence the noise and begin the formal lesson, yell "Cut!" The students will be understandably puzzled.

✳ Procedure

Explain that they're about to perform their first exercise in believable acting. Have everyone review together—quickly but precisely—the separate actions that occurred as they entered the class. Make certain that the order is accurate. There will be some disagreement, and obviously every tiny detail can't be included, but before long some consensus will be reached. ("Sherri and Pat entered first, laughing hysterically about something dumb and walked over to the back row, noisily shushing one another. Then Nick came in alone, munching a wad of bubble gum, said 'hi' to the teacher, and so on, and so on, until 'Cut!' ").

Now explain that everyone must leave the room, congregate a short distance away, and—when you yell "Action!"—enter the class a second time, reproducing as exactly as possible the first entrance. As you do this, don't give up if the order becomes scrambled. The group can always more or less find its way to the end.

✱ Evaluation

The discussion that follows this exercise is almost always revealing. The first logical question is "How close to the original entrance did we get?" But once a few people have chimed in with various comments ("Yeah . . . well Chris was supposed to have thrown that ball of notebook paper into the trash can *after* Matt yelled 'What's with your hair, Jen?' "), it's time to ask a more interesting question: "How did it *feel*?" Most kids will say "Weird" or "Strange!" "Why *weird*?" "Because we weren't just doing it; we were *pretending* to do it." An obvious point, maybe, but this could be a good time to remind everyone that *that*, of course, is a piece of what acting is about, and that to get it to feel like the real thing isn't always as easy as it looks. "Who felt the behaviors were as natural and believable the second time as they were the first? Were there phony moments? When? Were there times during the second take when you found yourself trying too hard to be interesting or clever? Did you feel more pressure to be noticed?"

This is a simple exercise that crystallizes something fundamental about acting. *They* are the characters in this case, but to begin by recreating their own actions believably is a meaningful first step.

Assignment #2: Short Takes (Basic)

In this next stage, you challenge individual actors in the class, one by one, to reproduce believably a simple action they've each probably performed countless times "in real life."

✱ Procedure

Start by giving each actor in the group a different item from among the choices listed below (make up additional actions to match the size of the class). The format for the improv is a bogus lecture that you will deliver to the class disguised as the day's lesson—the duller the better. As soon as all the students are clear about what you're asking them to do, give out numbers to establish a running order, and then begin your lecture. "Now as we have seen, the necessity of synthesizing all the elements of the actor's technique must be complemented by a fundamental consistency of style so that the . . . Jamie, are you copying this into your theatre notebook? . . . resulting characterization is an expression of the Stanislavskian interpretation of the blah blah blah . . ." As each student is ready, he or she interrupts and performs the assigned task. The goal is to do so naturally, believably. (No "acting" please!) A brief discussion follows, as outlined above, in "Take Two," after which you resume the lecture until the next actor is ready to jump in.

Sample Actions

1. You enter the class considerably late and have to make up an acceptable excuse. (This actor will begin from outside the classroom.)
2. As the teacher's lecture is in progress, you suddenly realize in a panic that you left your wallet, which happened to contain a $50.00 cash deposit for the upcoming junior class ski trip to Vermont, in your gym locker the period before.
3. As the lecture continues, you grow more and more ill, so much so that you must interrupt and ask the teacher permission to leave the class to visit the nurse.
4. For two actors: As the lecture continues, the person next to you begins some kind of petty fight, very quietly at first. It escalates to the point where there is an outburst of anger and shouting that completely disrupts the class.
5. As the lecture continues, you ask the teacher a complex question concerning its content, designed to earn serious brownie points. You could not care less about the answer, but you must *seem* deeply fascinated.
6. As the lecture continues, you fall asleep and begin snoring.
7. As the lecture continues, you begin "coming on" to the student of the opposite sex nearest you, first by passing notes, and then by whispered conversation. (Avoid the temptation to play for cheap laughs.)
8. As the lecture continues, you interrupt the teacher, complaining

about the mind-numbing boredom of the lesson, and beg to do something else.

9. As the lecture continues, you proceed to remove books and paper from your backpack and begin doing an assignment for another class.

If the classroom setting begins to lose its novelty, you can shift to other locations for the remainder of these:

10. You come home very much past your curfew and have to offer your parents a convincing excuse.
11. A cop has stopped you and a friend. You're an underage, unlicensed driver and you have to talk your way out of trouble.
12. You've been caught cheating on a test and have to persuade the Dean of Discipline that you're innocent of any wrongdoing.

✳ Evaluation

The criterion for success with all of these is the question to the class, "How believable was this? If *yes*, why? What made it so? Did the student appear to be acting, or did she pull off the real thing?" Don't allow their responses to become too superficial here ("Yeah, yeah . . . it was *very* believable."), but don't beat a dead horse either. The feedback discussions should be extremely brief at this point or the momentum of the exercise will be lost.

Assignment #3: Get the Teacher (Basic)

Even the most sweet-natured students have played this game sometime in their past, or at least fantasized about doing so. The format provides a clear-cut model for future work on intention.

✳ Procedure

Inform the students that they are about to perform an improv set on the morning of the first day of classes following summer vacation. The setting is the high school they now attend. The students are to play ninth graders, all of whom have been assigned to your freshman homeroom. Once you've finished the instructions, all will leave the room, assemble in the hall, and prepare to reenter the classroom in full character. Your role is that of a first-year teacher eager to welcome everyone and establish procedures for attendance, announcements, distribution of schedules, locker combinations, and so on. And, of course, to deliver an inspirational message to the kids on this first morning of their four-year stay in the high school. The improvisation begins when you simulate the sound of the passing bell and ends when you yell "Cut!" (This situation parallels the opening scene from Bel Kaufman's *Up the Down Staircase.*)

All actors should pursue the same goal: *to get the teacher,* to subvert his authority and prevent him from accomplishing the items in his agenda. Presumably the students will each choose different ways to achieve this end. If that's the case, so much the better.

Pointers

1. There's a trap your actors will fall into every time if they're not warned about it in advance. Creating believable behavior is the purpose of the exercise. They must not, therefore, succumb to the temptation to overreach the limits of credibility. Everyone will be understandably intoxicated by this chance to "go sick," as it were, on the teacher. If they choose that route, they'll destroy the rich possibilities of this assignment. Make clear that they are to employ subtlety, subterfuge, and indirection rather than overt insubordination (throwing paper airplanes, making loud noise, answering insolently). Demonstrate the difference if necessary. The latter choice results in nonstop silliness and chaos, the former more interesting and realistic behavior.

2. No one is to talk over anyone else. If the actors ignore that rule, the scene will lapse into a blur. (There will be *some* overlapping dialogue no matter how strong your warning, which is fine.)

✱ Evaluation

"Well, how did we do? Were the characters portrayed truthfully? Did they pass as believable ninth graders? Were there moments in the scene that seemed less than realistic? Why? At what points did it seem like the real thing? How so?"

Assignment #4: People Observation (Intermediate)

✱ Motivation

Introduce this exercise by asking who among the students is a fan of "people watching"? Just about every hand should shoot up, since observations of the tics of human behavior are among the most basic of the raw materials actors use in building their characters. A lively and interesting talk will follow: Do you enjoy studying the little mannerisms that people unconsciously display? When you watch two people arguing heatedly, do you notice their gestures, the way their eyes express their emotions, how they stand? If a teacher walks into a room on the first day of class, there is an infinite number of things you can tell me about his personality before he utters a single word, right? (Kids love above all else discussing their teachers' mannerisms. Make sure everyone agrees to leave names out of the discussion!) What are the things that give him away? Without naming names, can you cite a tiny quirk of behavior that is almost a trademark of a particular friend of yours? Something that defines her personality, that makes her *her* and nobody else?

✳ Procedure

Explain to the students that they're going to walk around the world a bit differently for the next several days. The assignment is to study individual people silently and intently, especially to observe their physical behavior—actions that express a lot about the person who's performing them. When they witness something really juicy, something that rivets their attention, they must simply recreate the scene *as believably as possible* the day they're scheduled to present themselves in class.

An example: They're in the supermarket and watch a woman, apparently in her 70s, studying the merchandise on the top shelf. She's examining the fine print on several cans very intently—seems to want to compare prices and ingredients of a few brands. Her movements are slow, careful, but she's having a tough time with her glasses. At long last, she mutters something incomprehensible to herself, makes her choice, and moves on.

On the day they're scheduled to perform, the students simply recreate this scene for the class without changes or embellishments.

Pointers

1. Tell the audience nothing by way of introduction. Just get up and perform the scene without revealing the setting or explaining the action.

2. Feel free to use props or the simplest costume elements to enhance your belief in the scene. If the lady in the supermarket wore a scarf, bring one in, along with a few tin cans. A chair can serve as a shopping cart.

3. Don't feel you need to throw in details to make your scene more dramatic than it was in real life (the cans fall noisily to the floor and you scramble desperately to retrieve them!). Just trust that the same actions that captured your attention will hold your audience.

4. For this assignment, don't consider scenes that involve much, or better yet, *any* dialogue, and—since you're only one person—more than one character. The focus here is on the ways in which *physical behavior* communicates personality.

5. Females in the class should feel free to play males and vice versa. Place no limits on age.

6. Make certain that the scene you recreate takes at least twenty seconds or so to perform. If the running time is shorter than that, you'll leave everyone feeling that the action has ended before it's begun.

7. Avoid for this assignment the temptation to make something up from your imagination. Don't take the lazy route. Observe real people doing real things. Trust that the genuine article will be interesting for its own sake. Every beginning actor knows that people are plenty weird and that that weirdness is what makes the behavior so fascinating to watch.

8. Last, and most important—When you recreate your scene, don't fall into the trap of "indicating" the action, which means shuffling through it, only halfheartedly getting under the skin of the character. Actors who habitually indicate give off an aura of indifference. You watch them and they seem to say: "I can't wait 'til this is over and I can get the hell off this stage!" Reproduce the details cleanly and precisely.

✳ Evaluation

As each of these scenes is performed, the students will probably want to know whether they're in agreement about what they've seen. ("Was she pouring coffee?" "Did he pull a knife out or was that a cell phone?") It's a lot more interesting—and more instructive too—to keep the focus on how the performance revealed the *character qualities* of the person observed. Perceptions will vary and that's fine; the clashes of interpretation will add richness to the discussion. Resist the temptation, though, to turn to the actor and ask, "Well, what was it really?" In bypassing this question, the actor will find out, sometimes to her amazement, exactly how disparately the members of the class processed what they saw in the scene. This is important when one considers that an audience at a play never gets the chance during a show to ask an actor "Well, what was it *really?*" They simply get to watch and to react accordingly. Keep the discussion focused instead on the answers to questions like these:

1. What was the sex of the character? What told you so?
2. What was the age of the character?
3. Where were we?
4. Were other characters present? What told you so?
5. What sort of lady was this? Petty? Considerate? Overly precise? Vicious? Snobbish?
6. When he snapped his fingers that way, what did it reveal about his personality?
7. Is she a domineering type? A pushover? How did you know? (If a student answers, "How are we supposed to answer that? There was no dialogue." remind them that that's just the point. There are important ways to know *without* reference to dialogue.)
8. Would this person be an affectionate parent? What would you imagine her profession to be?
9. He was working in the office, right? What kind of behavior would you expect of him at home? Shopping at the mall? On the beach?

The fact that there may be wise guesses but no definitive answers to questions like these is what makes the discussion valuable for an actor, because it sheds light on a more important truth: Character and meaning on the stage are communicated primarily through physical detail. In life and from the audience in a theatre, we go with what the body, the walk, the tilt of a chin, the attitude of the eyes tell us *before* we go with what is said. This in no way diminishes the importance of speech; it simply reminds us that physical behavior speaks first. (Much more about this in Chapter 3.)

Assignment #5: True/False (Intermediate)

The work thus far has intentionally kept students closely bound to the familiar. If they are to begin to develop the habit of representing believable action rather than posing cutely and falling into their show biz mode, it's essential *early in the course* that they remain grounded in the arena of their experience. That experience, played out on the stage, may be boldly exaggerated, it may be wildly comic, but it should for now avoid entering the world of the French aristocracy during the Revolution or the inhabitants of eighteenth-century Salem. These are cultures alien to the majority of your students and demand a highly-developed sense of dramatic style in order to be rendered believably. This and the next few assignments hold fast to the belief that they will represent well what they know best, although there is some gradual "opening out" as the class moves progressively through the exercises.

✳ Procedure

If the group is large, assign this exercise to only half the students. Each participant, on the due date, must come prepared to spend approximately five minutes in front of the class relating a story from his or her personal experience. The chief requirement is that the experience be as extraordinary as possible: terrifying, hilariously funny, embarrassing, momentous, or bizarre. Students should be encouraged to narrate the events as energetically as possible, with maximum use of gesture, voice, and body.

The twist is that each member of the class, on the day you deliver the directions for this assignment, will receive from you a folded index card containing inside a printed T or F. Who's got what should be recorded in your grade book so there can be no equivocation later on. Those with Ts are honor-bound to relate experiences that are truthful in every detail. In other words, "Here's what happened to me and every word of it occurred exactly as I've described it." Those with Fs must concoct personal experiences that are entirely made up from start to finish, but of course must address the audience as if they were relating the unvarnished truth. This second task is tougher to perform, but the challenge to put one over on the crowd is usually motivation enough.

Pointers

1. Hand out an approximately equal number of Ts and Fs so that the audience remains off balance with each new speaker.

2. Remind students that you're aware how easy it would be to cut corners on this assignment, with holders of F cards narrating true stories simply because they were too lazy to make up false ones. The bottom line here is that the fun of the game is lost unless everyone plays by the rules.

3. It would be just as easy for students to reveal in advance to a friend in the class whether their index card reads T or F. See above.

4. Students often ask "If we receive an F on our index card, is it okay if we relate an experience that is *partly* true?" Again, to keep the fun in the game, the answer should be "No. Exercise your imaginations and make it 100 percent false."

5. Explain that everyone should reject from consideration for this assignment any true experience that a friend in the class will have prior knowledge of.

✷ Evaluation

Since everyone is playing him- or herself, the acting challenge in the assignment lies in the degree of believability present in the delivery of those students holding the Fs. Once an individual has finished narrating the story, members of the class have a few minutes to cross-examine the speaker on the facts in an effort to turn up contradictions or inconsistencies. ("Didn't you say that your parents were in the car at the time? Well then why . . . ?") At the end of the questioning period, ask the class, "OK, hands of those of you who think this story is true? False?" The speaker now finally breaks the suspense by revealing what was on the card. A particularly generous teacher may want to hand out edible treats to kids who con more than half the class with a false story, or convince more than half the class that a true story was in fact true. Appropriate only in Grades 1 through 6, right? No indeed. Be assured that high school kids turn quickly into kindergarten students when candy prizes are offered!

If you're feeling ambitious, a quiz show format would work well for this assignment, too.

Assignment #6: In the Halls (Intermediate)

This can be paired with its companion exercise, introduced in the section "Preserving Believability with Scripts" (see Chapter 3, page 90).

✳ Procedure

Ask students to pair up in groups of two, three, or four (two is best) and to spend no more than fifteen minutes outside the room observing what's out there. The goal is to find a "scene" approximately thirty seconds to a minute long that they will recreate for the class on their return. Coming across something sceneworthy shouldn't be a strain, since human beings of high school age are naturals at producing colorful or outrageous behavior. Caution everyone in advance—they should not bring back a three-person scene if their group only has two people, or a four-person scene if they went out in a group of three; they should not to come back with too short a scene because the performance will have ended before the audience has had a chance to become emotionally involved; and, above all, they should not jazz up or doctor what they've seen in order to heighten the entertainment value of the material. The behavior of real people is eccentric enough.

When the students return to the classroom, have them take a minute or two to review informally whatever it was they saw so that all the actors can feel comfortable with the dialogue and the order of events. Encourage each actor to try to pin down the voice and body language of the person they've observed, but not to over-rehearse. When everyone is ready, the scenes should be performed in succession.

> **NOTE:** If your school administration would be unfriendly to the idea of a class of acting students wandering the halls during an assigned period, have the student groups agree to meet before the start of the school day and use the halls as their field of observation. Either way, insist that the kids not just "make something up." It's contrary to the purpose of the assignment.

✳ Evaluation

Some of the questions in the evaluation section of the "People Observation" exercise are appropriate here, and you can throw them into the discussion whenever they apply. But don't become too concerned with analysis and criticism on this one. The value of the exercise lies in the students' responses to the scenes themselves, which invariably capture moments that could only have found their way to the stage through actors' observations of real life. The audience is usually riveted because they recognize the scenes so easily from their daily experience of school life—a life that rarely bears much resemblance to their world as depicted in television sitcoms.

Lesson Two: Breaking Down Tensions

Just about every basic acting text contains an early chapter on relaxation. It's an indispensable step because students at any level will stifle their best creative impulses if they approach the stage with a knot of tension in their throats. Adolescents who choose to take their first baby steps as actors in a high school theatre class are testing themselves in the single most potentially threatening environment in creation, with the possible exception of a middle school cafeteria. Laughing *at* is an everyday sport among high school kids. We're all familiar with the view that a certain edge of tension helps performers, that a touch of nervousness keeps them focused and alert. True enough. But *anxiety*, in this case the terror of appearing foolish before one's peers, is something else again. It's always destructive energy, and you must work to quell it in every situation.

More than half the responsibility for doing so falls on you, the teacher, and it begins with setting the right tone in class. You want just enough informality in the air to communicate that it's OK for the students to relax and take risks, just enough restraint to signal that they're in school and the teacher is in charge. There's no formula for achieving this balance; it's a matter of feel and it develops over time. *First law of the realm: come down hard whenever a kid openly mocks the efforts of a fellow classmate.* Any teacher with eyes can distinguish between constructive criticism and ridicule. Arrange a private conference with the offender and set the matter straight, briefly and firmly: *"You can't do that here."* If you let such moments pass, they'll heighten rather than reduce tensions. Everyone will shut down—perhaps permanently. Among memories of scores of comfortable, mutually supportive classes of student actors, I can recall a few that just plain got away from me, that were dominated by a climate of meanness that held on to the bitter end despite lectures, pleas, threats, and punishments. Your best hope is to respond quickly at the barest hint of ill will.

The best formats for helping kids limber up physically and emotionally are those that allow them to let go of their protective armor—their sense of cool. If you can get them to risk a little silliness in front of their friends, to chance a few moments of benign foolishness, the result is usually a palpable lifting of tension. After a while, the benefits tend to accumulate from day to day, and pretty soon everybody feels more or less comfortable with everybody else. Watch, as always, that the nonsense stays within appropriate bounds—tougher, I know, to achieve than it sounds.

Pick and choose from among the activities that follow, then invent some of your own. You can begin classes with these every day for a while, then return to them as needed.

Loosening Up Exercises

Physical Warm-ups

Of all the exercises you will present over the course of a semester or school year, these are among the few which typically spark *some* core of resistance from *some* portion of the class. A few kids associate them with halfhearted warm-up sessions in gym class; others refuse to see a link between stretching and acting. Don't respond with a list of exaggerated claims. Try rather to portray relaxation warm-ups as akin to a gymnast's stretching exercises, a necessary first step to feeling energized, poised, and alert.

- After kids find a spot onstage where they're each surrounded by a maximum radius of free space, lead them in stretching exercises, leaning alternately from the waist to the left and right. Arms circling left, right, front, back. Shoulders stretching forward and back. Neck circling.

Wrists and ankles stretching. Shake first the hands, then arms, then legs, then head. Collapse into a totally relaxed position.

- Kids find a free space and stand, legs spread. All raise arms over head and reach as if to touch the ceiling. Hold for count of five. Collapse at waist into a totally loose rag doll position. Repeat the cycle several times.

- The kids stand, legs slightly apart, and shake their hands vigorously. You yell, "Freeze!" Students stand motionless, applying maximum muscle tension. Repeat several times.

- Close the classroom doors! Everyone stands in absolute silence. On your signal, kids in chorus produce a quiet cacophony of sound without words as they jog slowly in place. You then "conduct" a slow, steady crescendo until the sound is deafening and the in-place jogging has peaked. On a visual cue, you then cut the sound and movement output to zero. This pattern may be repeated, at most twice. Be sure you demonstrate in advance how this exercise may be performed without causing injury to the voice.

- Clear the stage space. Start students in their regular seats. On your signal, students rise as slowly as possible from their chairs and enter the playing space in slow motion. They then move through the space, all at the same time, in random patterns, *without* touching each other, and gradually increase the speed of their walk as they go. When everyone reaches maximum speed, you then shout "Freeze!" One person may be tapped to come forward and slowly form human sculptures from among the frozen bodies.

"Check Your Cool at the Door" Warm-ups

✳ Cheerleaders

Students break up into small groups and spend a minute or so preparing a high-energy cheer to root a school team on to victory. They then perform these in turn for the entire group. Make clear in your instructions that the cheers can be comic in tone but not outside the bounds of good taste.

✳ Shadowboxing

Students shadowbox in place at high energy. For variation, have them continue to spar, but in character: as elderly retirees, ambitious stockbrokers, ballet dancers, gas station attendants, or college professors.

✳ Silly Walks

Half the class moves into the wings, stage left or right; the other half remains in the audience. You play music as actors cross stage, one at a time, using Monty Pythonesque silly walks. No student may repeat a walk that's already been used. You shift quickly to new music and the walks change appropriately. Repeat exercise with remaining half of class.

✳ Truth or Consequences

In preparing this game, complete a bunch of index cards equal to the number of kids in the class. Each card contains a description of a "ridiculous action" consequence, such as:

- Put three crackers in your mouth at once and whistle "Here Comes the Bride."
- Get on all fours and bark like an angry poodle.
- Stand on a chair and impersonate a street corner orator delivering a message of doom to the passing crowds.

As a format for the game, conduct a bogus "pop theatre quiz" to punish the class for its poor study habits over the past several days. Questions are directed one at a time at individual students: "Jessica, what is the name of the seventeenth-century French theatre critic who sought reforms in scenic design?" "Alex, what famous nineteenth-century English actress is known for the 'graceful and considerate dignity of her performances and the utter simplicity of her costumes'?" Whenever a student answers incorrectly (hopefully every time!), a buzzer sounds. (You must improvise an appropriate sound effect.) The student then draws a card from the "Ridiculous Consequences" grab bag and performs the action indicated. No cries of "Oh, I can't do this!" are permitted. After the action is satisfactorily executed, that student is out, and the game continues. No need to prolong the exercise until each and every student is out. The point of the game, remember, is to dispel tensions and build group togetherness.

✳ "I'm a Fool, I'm a Fool!"

Here everyone gets a moment to play court jester. Prepare a generous pack of index cards, each of which contains a carefully printed tongue twister, such as:

> Some shun sunshine, some shun sleep.
>
> The sea ceaseth, but it sufficeth us.
>
> She shines city shoes.

A student comes up and draws a card and then pronounces the tongue twister. If he or she falters in any way, a buzzer sounds. Propose an original "jester's task" for the student at the lectern to perform. Once the task is completed, that student is out. He or she takes a seat, and must now call upon another student in the class to come front and take a turn. If this new contestant falters, he or she performs a new task suggested by the student who has just returned to his place in the audience. Students are on their honor *not* to propose a task they wouldn't be willing to perform themselves! Stop when the game has lost its fizz.

✳ Musical Death

Seats in the class are arranged in a circle as for the game Musical Chairs, one chair fewer than the total number of people in the class. Teacher plays a high-energy musical excerpt while members of the class move around the circle at a good steady pace. When the music stops, the student without a seat must perform a brief death scene before leaving the game. Deaths may be serious or comical, but all must be performed with total commitment and conviction—no mugging or indicating. As the game continues, chairs are removed one by one and the pattern is repeated. *No one may perform a death scene that's been used earlier in the exercise.* This one can continue until the last player remains, since the format is surefire and rarely if ever loses its group momentum.*

---

*This exercise was adapted from *The Act of Being*.

NOTE: I am sensitive to the widely-held view, even among some theatre educators, that because activities of this kind encourage silly behavior, they add to a general impression of acting classes as lacking in seriousness of purpose. In fact quite a few *students*, usually cited as desperate for classroom activities that provide an escape valve from the routines of academia, have been conditioned to question the worth of anything that's too enjoyable. ("This is fun, but what's the point?" "Oh, more of this 70s 'get up and feel the space' stuff!") My answer is that this step is an absolute prerequisite in a course in acting. It's the only antidote I know to the anxiety syndrome we spoke of earlier in the chapter. A release mechanism is *essential*. If you have a few students who voice these complaints, ask that they humor you on these fun and games and then reassure them that the serious stuff will not be long in coming.

Lesson Three: Getting Focused

Learning to concentrate on the stage, to free the conscious mind from the distractions that lie outside the events of a scene, is both the easiest and hardest of the tasks a high school actor faces. *Easiest* in the deceptive sense only, of course, because on the one hand your kids may wonder what the big deal is. "Why a unit on concentration? There's no problem. If we find ourselves drifting, you yell 'Concentrate' and we just pull ourselves back in!" *Hardest* on the other because, if there's one safe generalization to be made about adolescents in this period of human history, it's that concentration does not come to them easily. Their conditioning in every segment of our fragmented culture works to undermine what old folks once referred to as *patience, reflection, continuity*, and *sustained attention*.

Motivating Your Students to Concentrate

One of the quickest ways to get beginning high school actors to appreciate the indispensability of focus in a scene is through a sports metaphor:

> You're sitting in the gym at a school basketball game. One of the home team players scores an awesome shot. The fans cheer wildly. When the roar subsides, a boy from the stands shrieks, "Way to go, Aron!" Aron turns from the court as play continues, walks in the direction of the voice, shouts "Hey, thanks, Justin. I was pretty proud of sinking that shot, and I really appreciate your show of support!"

I don't mean this to be funny—it's one of those moments unthinkable in real life. In fact, in an actual high school basketball game, it would be bizarre for Aron to acknowledge the fans' existence in *any* way. To do so would be considered hopelessly gauche. Athletes soon learn, probably without being told, not to allow anything to wrest their concentration from the game. It reduces their effectiveness on the court, and—the ultimate high school insult—it's uncool.

When actors ask audiences to step into a shared reality, the need for absolute focus is even greater, because any lapses in concentration onstage will instantly weaken the audience's willingness to suspend their disbelief. Yet, from the six-year-old onstage waving out front to mommy in the first-grade play to the high school kid who casually slips in and out of character, we show a pretty high tolerance for amateurs who disregard this rule.

In watching your actors learn the ropes, you'll find their concentration wavering in both flagrant and subtle ways. Some may actually burst out of scenes: "Wait, can we start over?" "Hold it . . . what we were supposed to do again?" But most of their slips in focus will be a lot less apparent. You'll watch them perform a basic exercise and notice their eyes drifting off course; sometimes for the briefest second they'll shoot a glance at the audience—or more likely at *you*—as if to ask, "Is what I'm doing up here OK?" Sometimes they'll pull away from the end of a scene so eagerly that every cell in their bodies seems to cry out, "Thank heaven that's over!" (A remedy is to insist they hold for a few seconds before breaking.) Sometimes, when another character is dominating a scene with a long speech, their body language will convey a deep sense of discomfort—"Well, what exactly am I supposed to be doing while she goes on and on?" The answer, "Listening as you would in real life," doesn't help since the discipline needed to replace fake listening onstage with a true absorption is not yet in place.

Sometimes a particularly alert student may ask, "Yeah, but how much of my concentration should be on what the character's doing, and how much on my job as an actor ('I have to project the next few lines so that my words soar above the noise of the crowd,' 'I have to make sure not to throw that glass of water too forcefully,' 'I have to remember to walk front when she finishes speaking')?" This question may come too early in the course for a meaningful answer. My best response would be to admit that there is some overlap, but that the bulk of our awareness must inhabit the skin of the character we're creating, with a small residue held in reserve to attend to the business of the stage.

Warm-up Exercises in Concentration

These exercises will give your actors a start in mastering the art of concentration, but be aware that a deeper, more complete assimilation of this skill doesn't take effect overnight. It's a slow process that takes hold only after the students continue to apply the principles over time—first through improvs, later in scripted scenes and full-length plays.

Lineup

You can get a good start on concentration early in the course with an exercise similar to the one described in Chapter 3 of *Improvisation for the Theatre* (Spolin 1963a, 51). Ask half the class to stand in a straight line along the front of the stage, the other half to remain in the audience. Tell the students onstage that when you say "Begin" they are simply to look the audience over, pure and simple. No words, no gestures, no "acting." The audience must in turn do nothing to distract the performers—just remain silent spectators. Before long, those onstage will begin to show signs of discomfort: smiling nervously, fidgeting, coughing, shifting their weight. After a reasonable lapse of time, ask your actors to perform a small chore, something concrete like counting the number of chairs in the room or the number of students in the audience wearing sneakers. This is Spolin's famous "point of focus." With it, the actors have something specific to engage their attention, the anxiety disappears, and the actors are free to absorb themselves in an actual task. Although this exercise seems simple, what it teaches us is profound: that to shed our self-consciousness when we perform onstage, we need to *concentrate* on something simple, like counting the number of students wearing sneakers, or on something complex, like repairing a damaged friendship. The level of difficulty increases significantly as the work progresses, but the essential task remains the same.

The Concentration Ladder

Announce to the class that you are about to give everyone some practice in the art of concentration. By the time the exercise is complete, all will have had a chance to come before the group at least once to test their ability to stay in focus against ever-increasing odds. They do not in this instance need to create characters outside themselves. The difficulty of the tasks will increase at each new level, which means, in a typical class of about twenty, that each successive plateau will bring approximately three or so students to the front. In short, kids who volunteer early in the game will be assuring themselves of an easier turn at bat. I always increase the "psych" quotient by awarding prizes. Far from trivializing the proceedings, the practice seems to heighten the energy in the room and adds a welcome touch of levity. Gradually increase the value of the prizes as you rise from one level to the next, for example, from a single M&M® for level one, to a whole chocolate bar at level six. ("Oooooohhh!")

Level One
Select a brief but intentionally boring paragraph from, let's say, the introduction to a dry textbook. Try to locate one that contains no more than three or four sentences and a basic enough vocabulary so that most of the words are simple to pronounce. The first few volunteers must each take a turn reading the paragraph aloud to the class in a strong, clear voice, without slurring or stumbling.

Level Two
The next group of volunteers must each read the paragraph in a direct conversational tone, as if imparting intensely personal information to the listeners. Eye contact must be genuine and

frequent. A few members of the class may be appointed to insert gently distracting remarks as the speaker continues. (Nothing beyond agreed-upon bounds of good taste, please!)

Level Three

The next group must each read the paragraph one last time in a tone suggesting that the material is fascinating beyond all description—as if, for example, the words occurred at the climax of a spine-chilling mystery/suspense novel. Again, eye contact must be genuine and frequent. This time the teacher may assign *one* student from the audience to be responsible for the heckling, which is much tougher on the speakers, because instead of a general din, they will be responding to specific barbs from a specific person. The speaker must not respond to the heckler or allow herself to be distracted by him.

Level Four

The next group takes a few moments to put together a brief speech on their favorite pet peeve—The Supermarket Customer on Line in Front of Me Who Engages in Long Personal Chats with the Cashier; Getting a Genuine Human Being in the Wonderful World of Voice Mail; Getting Out of Bed on the First School Day Following a Long Vacation, and so on. Each student must come before the class and deliver a one-minute talk on their chosen topic without once using an intrusive *like*, *uh*, or *you know*. A speaker may say "Most of *you know* someone who . . ." or "We're all familiar with people who *like* chocolate . . ." but not "I hate people who, you know, try too hard to . . ." or "I was, like, at the supermarket one day when. . . ." Kids love the challenge of this one, but have to concentrate so hard to succeed with it that their brains sometimes seem ready to burst from the strain.

Level Five

Two students come before the class and conduct an intense debate on a mutually agreed upon subject. Choose a topic that can be argued without research or great depth of scholarly knowledge, such as "Video Games Are a Harmful Presence in Our Lives" or "American Children Are Growing Up Too Rapidly Nowadays." The speaker who chooses to support the proposition makes a one-sentence opening statement, and the other speaker is allowed a one-sentence rebuttal. (Note that the quality or accuracy of the arguments isn't really the point here.) The debate proceeds for one minute, during which time the speakers continue to advance and illustrate their positions, gradually responding to each other's points *simultaneously*. This sounds like a mental and physical impossibility, but once the players find a groove through intense concentration, they can succeed brilliantly. When it occurs, the class usually looks on in awe. They are, in short, speaking and listening at the same time.

Level Six
Two players stand before the group and spend one minute telling their partner about something interesting that's happened to them between the time they got up that morning and the start of class. If nothing interesting happened that morning, fine, make something up! Something interesting happened, but it wouldn't take sixty seconds to relate? Fine, stretch it! They must be talking simultaneously, as if speaking with each other, but in fact be relating their own separate experiences without any back and forth response. The challenge to their powers of concentration at the end of the minute is to then turn to the class and deliver as detailed an account as possible of the experience *their partner* just narrated.

Assignments

Assignment #1: "But in Life, Things Like That Just Don't Happen!" (Intermediate)

This improvisation requires the actors to establish characters within a specific setting, so as a warm-up, do a simple review of the "Where?" exercise on page 29.

✳ Procedure

Pair up all students in the class. Each is designated as Character A or B. If there is an odd number of participants, a single group of three can work just as well, or you can pair up with the unpartnered actor yourself. Once the directions to the class have been given, allow the pairs of actors to meet privately for a few minutes to agree on the answers to these three questions: Where is the scene set? Who am I playing? What physical activity are these characters engaged in when the scene starts? Remind them to make the setting clear for the audience near the beginning of the scene, much as they did in the warm-up location exercise, and to choose any physical activity other than just "standing or sitting and having a conversation." Dialogue is permitted.

The catch in the assignment is that Character B, as part of the advance planning, must decide to do something during the course of the scene that would be very difficult to imagine happening in real life. This decision is *not* shared with Character A, who finds out what the surprise is only as the scene is actually being performed. Any violation of this trust, such as saying "Oh, don't worry, I'll let you know in advance what *it* is when we set things up!"—completely destroys the fun of the assignment. The point is for those students playing Character A to respond without breaking concentration, reacting believably within the scene as they imagine their characters might if actually faced with such a bizarre occurrence in real life.

It may help to offer the class an example of how two hypothetical students might handle the assignment. Let's say they talk privately and come up with the following answers to the above questions: The scene is set in a downtown restaurant; Character A decides to play a well-dressed, monied businesswoman; Character B decides to play an unscrubbed vagrant; Characters A and B are strangers to each other. They decide that when the scene opens, A is eating lunch, creating the illusion of actual food, interacting with the environment, responding to an unseen waiter, and so on, while B is examining the room, stealing side glances at A. Now Character B decides, without saying a word to Character A, to introduce some odd twist of behavior into the action as the scene is unfolding.

Their preparation complete, the actors set up the stage and take their places. Here's how it might go. They begin the scene exactly as described above. After fifteen seconds or so, B rises slowly, walks over to A, stands over her, carefully observes her as she eats. Now he sits down at A's table, continues to stare at her strangely, smiles a quizzical smile. At length, A says uncomfortably, "I'm sorry, but I don't know you. Could you . . . uh . . . please return to your table?" B continues to stare, smiles the same eccentric smile. A few seconds later, B leans across the table, and in the most polite manner possible, removes a few fries from A's plate and begins eating them. A now reacts exactly as she imagines her character might, without skipping a beat, without breaking concentration. The scene continues until the reaction registers fully with the audience, at which point you can say, "OK, stop!"

✳ Evaluation

The important questions to ask are these:

> At the moment when B reached for and ate the fries, how believable was A's reaction?
>
> Did she appear to anticipate what was coming? How so?
>
> Would you have expected her reaction to be in any way different had this scene occurred in real life?
>
> At the key moment in the scene, was it *Actor* A expressing surprise and shock or *Character* A? Did she break or maintain concentration?

Some students are likely to be satisfied with superficial answers: "Yeah . . . it was pretty good, I guess." Insist that their responses be as specific and well-supported as possible.

Following the evaluation, the remaining students in the class present their scenes, all of them based on different characters and plot lines, but all incorporating the three requirements of the assignment.

Assignment #2: Independent Activity (Advanced)

This is an adaptation of an exercise from the book *Sanford Meisner on Acting* (Meisner and Longwell 1987). Once the students have a clear sense of the exercise's purpose and can accurately complete the preparation steps, they will discover in it a powerful tool for building concentration on the stage. This description, however, omits the word repetition game Meisner uses to force his actors to behave and respond truthfully. It's a method I've found compelling but also beyond the reach of the majority of high school actors, most of whom have not yet attained the maturity or patience to approach it seriously. This adjusted version has its own value in developing focus within a scene.

✳ Procedure

Instead of introducing the activity with a set of abstract directions, begin with the following object lesson.

> Set the stage to simulate a room in a college dorm, the more clutter the better—books spread at random, blankets and sheets cast asunder, two futons, crumbled paper on the floor, empty bags of junk food, the works. Place a copy of the Manhattan telephone directory somewhere among the debris. Check in advance to make sure there's a number listed for a K. C. Smith in the East Seventies. (If not, adjust accordingly the name and address discussed in the next paragraph.) Write the actual phone number down on a piece of paper and place it in your pocket. Ask for two male volunteers, Characters A and B, and explain the given circumstances of the scene so that the class can listen along.
>
> You are freshmen roommates at NYU. Character A, you have recently met a gorgeous girl who's invited you to a large weekend party at her Upper East Side apartment. Mom and Dad are away on a long vacation and there will be no adult supervision. She gave you her telephone number on a bit of scrap paper, but of course you've lost it. Fortunately you remember this much: Her name is Kim Smith (she told you specifically that "Daddy" made her a gift of her own private phone line); She's listed in the phone directory (under K. C. Smith, she said—her full given name being Kim Courtney), and their place is somewhere in the East Seventies. It goes without saying that you are desperate to attend; this girl was a true knockout! Your goal as you play the scene is *to find that phone number*.
>
> Character B, you have been sick to death recently of A's sloppy living habits—his refusal to share laundry and cleanup chores. When the lights go up, you enter the room with a basket of clean wash, determined to persuade him to help you keep the place looking neater and more respectable. You need not make this the one and only topic of conversation in the scene, but it is your overriding purpose.

Caution the actors to avoid creating stereotyped characters and to free themselves of the pressure to be interesting or entertaining. They are merely to interact believably as roommates and to go after their individual goals as the action progresses. However, "to go after their individual goals" does *not* imply that they can't respond to each other naturally, or even actively help each other during the course of the scene. As soon as A has found the *actual* number in the phone book, he then removes the number from his pocket and displays it for everyone in the class to see. If the numbers match exactly, you can then call "OK, stop!"

✴ Evaluation

The important questions to ask are:

> Did these roommates seem to have a shared history?
>
> Did they interact believably?
>
> Did A's pursuit of the phone number appear genuine, or did he appear to be faking it?

The value of the assignment is that the characters become absorbed in a real task—not unlike the act of counting chairs or pairs of sneakers—within the framework of a few new givens, such as a more detailed setting, specific characters, and a relationship. That process of absorption should free them of anxiety and self-consciousness, this time *within* a scene, opening the way for anxiety-free (or at least anxiety-reduced) acting as the course continues. Before you permit others in the class to discuss and prepare their own scenes, make sure everyone understands the three requirements for the independent activity:

1. It must be something of *extreme* importance (finding that exquisite girl's telephone number)
2. It must be something *very* difficult to do (finding the number in a phone book that contains fourteen pages of Smiths)
3. It must be something that can actually be accomplished *during* the scene, not faked.

In other words, Character A was *really* looking up that number in the book, not pretending to! Kids usually stumble over this requirement, so emphasize that it's an indispensable part of their setup. If necessary, remind them that there are a whole range of activities that *can* actually be performed onstage during the scene and not simulated, such as putting something broken back together, practicing a piece of music, memorizing a short poem, drawing something, or solving a monster of a math problem. The scene doesn't end until that process is truly complete—the break restored, the piece of music mastered, the poem memorized. Again, kids who, against the spirit of the exercise, choose to memorize a poem they already know and thus spend the improv *pretending* to learn it are simply robbing themselves of the benefits of a valuable lesson in acting.

Lesson Four: Developing Sense Memory

Introducing the Concept of Sense Memory

Set a futon and pillow onstage and ask for a show of hands from those prepared to come up, one at a time, and recreate for the class exactly what took place in their rooms that morning from the moment they awakened until the moment they got out of bed. You're likely to get more volunteers than you need; kids are strangely willing to enact and witness endless variations on this theme. Why? The scenario essentially lacks any compelling dramatic content. I suspect it's because they enjoy the chance to invade someone's private territory and because they're amused to check out the little quirks of behavior that set them and their friends apart—the way someone's hand gropes the air to silence an alarm clock, for example, or the way another's eyes widen in horror at the thought of having to throw off the covers, or the way someone continues to lie comatose as the morning silence hangs in the air. Or it may be because of the surprise overlaps of experience that trigger thoughts such as "Oh, wow, *I* do that!"—cover the head with a pillow; stretch fiercely, roll over, and go back to sleep; rise to face the day and then fall back helplessly on the mattress. Discuss some of these contrasts and similarities as each new actor takes a turn.

Now try a different variation or two. Tell the class that you're going to deliver a brief lecture on the evolution of performance styles in the theatre of postcolonial America. As you speak, interrupt yourself periodically and announce to the students: "Okay, as I continue talking, pretend that it's 60 degrees in here." "Forty." "Twenty-five." Or travel up the thermometer from 70 degrees. Or ask them to pretend that they're listening after having slept a total of four hours the previous night.

These little volleys allow for a relaxed transition into the practical study of *sense memory*: the actor's ability to recall physical sensations and reproduce them convincingly for an audience. *Practical* is the operative term here, because no other aspect of the actor's training has been the basis for so much ridiculous excess (the lyrics for "I Felt Nothing" from *A Chorus Line* got it right). We've all been there—exercises that position actors in front of imaginary glasses of orange juice for up to thirty minutes, waiting as they summon forth the precise tang of acidity on the tongue. Or confine them to a chair for half a class session, struggling to recall the fragrance of tea roses in an English country garden. These abuses aside, though, skill in sense memory is not one a beginning student can afford to skip over lightly. Plays are staged in theatres, after all, and no amount of detail in the stage setting is sufficient to transport the audience to a beach or a cheap motel or a sports stadium without the help of an actor skilled in the technique of sensory recall. They're not *really* lying on a beach, right? So the actors' faces and bodies have to be able to recreate imaginatively the sensation of the sun's rays, the warmth of the sea air, the smell of the surf. In short, they must be able to bring the audience on location, as it were, through the accuracy of their recall of physical detail.

All this is less apparent to most kids than you'd imagine, so some of the principles of sense memory may need to be driven home during a brief introductory discussion. When a skilled actress sobs over the loss of a precious bracelet, the students may need to be reminded that the stage prop was probably made of cheap glass; that the characters stumbling around during a staged total blackout had to practice ignoring the spill of residual stage light; that only the cheapest of actors would need to down a few shots of tequila in the wings in order to play a drunk scene convincingly. This last example always draws a few knowing laughs. It *doesn't* work to play a drunk scene drunk. There is the small matter of remembering scripted lines, dialogue cues, blocking, stage business. . . .

Once the discussion takes off, the kids will likely chime in with their own memories of ineptly performed sensory moments from popular films and TV shows, scenes in which they couldn't believe for a minute that the character had *really* just awakened from a long sleep, *really* just held a phone conversation with an imaginary party, *really* just swallowed a glass of poisoned wine, and so on. The purpose of this lesson, then, is to learn the ropes. And the skill is, as we've seen, a practical necessity, not just a theoretical academic exercise. Act I, Scene 6 of *Gypsy* begins with all characters onstage fast asleep; Act II, Scene 2 of *The Prime of Miss Jean Brodie* begins with the characters coming home in a heavy downpour; many of the events in *Street Scene* unfold against a background of sweltering heat and humidity.

What, then, does the actor draw upon in order to transfer this sense memory into something concrete and believable for an audience? Sometimes, to be frank, on nothing more than a well-preserved memory of the real thing. You've gotten out of bed every morning of your life and can probably duplicate those actions without thinking about them. So you transfer the experience to the circumstances of the character and the play pretty much by rote, as with the exercises at the beginning of this section. But students are sometimes shocked to learn that this technique won't serve them consistently, that it can fail when they least expect it. They've suffered in the heat time and again, yet, when they find themselves inside a chilly sixty-seven degree theatre having to reproduce the feel of a scorching afternoon outdoors, the sense memory mysteriously deserts them. They *indicate* hot, and the results are clichéd and false—fanning themselves too eagerly, mopping their brows too self-consciously, and so on. When this occurs, they will need to break the process down, observing themselves more truthfully the next time they experience the actual physical state:

- Did my limbs feel uncomfortably heavy?
- Did my eyes droop?
- Did the air seem "heavy"?
- Did my response time slow down?

In reality, your homework assignments notwithstanding, most high school actors will resist so methodical a preparation, finding it too analytical and fragmented. They're more likely to give you a half-remembered approximation of something unconsciously lifted from a film or TV actor's performance—it's easier that way, and high school kids love easy. This process is a dead end, however, encouraging half-baked imitation instead of freshness and individuality. Don't allow them the lazy route. As holds true so often when the actor's instincts just won't carry the day, a believable performance must be obtained through good, old-fashioned hard work.

"What about recreating physical sensations we've never experienced directly?" an observant student may ask. "What if the role requires us to die of suffocation, navigate a minefield, experience child labor, commit murder?" Playwrights, as we know, make such demands on actors all the time. There are three possible courses of action. The first is Stanislavski's *magic if*, the actor's capacity for taking that all-important creative leap and landing at the truth through the power of imagination. "How would I respond physically *if* I were walking in a minefield," or "*if* I were experiencing child labor?" The second is *close observations* of others, experiencing the sensation firsthand (often impractical, alas!). And the third course of action is *substituting a personal experience* that approximates the sensation required in the script—for example, you've never laid foot in a minefield, but you *have* been caught outdoors during a severe electrical storm; you've never endured suffocation, but you *have* known the feeling of acute loss of breath following, let's say, a long-distance run; you've never killed anyone, but you *have* known how it feels to want to! All this experience can be harnessed, or at least a piece of it, to serve actors effectively in a scene.

One final caution: At this stage, your purpose is to isolate the problem of sense memory for your students. But they need to understand at some point that accurate, believable rendering of physical sensation is rarely if ever the *point* of a scene. Some high school actors become so wrapped up in responding to the texture of a fabric, the smell of a perfume, the taste of a slice of pizza, that they forget there are other warm bodies onstage waiting to set the scene in motion.

Warm-up Exercises in Sense Memory

Individual Sense Memory

The items below can be assigned arbitrarily, or you can distribute them among volunteers. Members of the class should select one choice from the list, practice at home until they feel confident that they've recreated the experience believably, and then perform their scenes one at a time in class the next day. To aid them in their preparation, list on the chalkboard the methods discussed above, any or all of which they can use if simple recall fails to do the trick. Remind students to place their sense memory exercise in context so that the scenes have a clear beginning, middle, and end. Using the first item as an example, it helps the audience to watch the actor walk solemnly into the bathroom, open the medicine cabinet, and remove the bottle gingerly from the shelf instead of merely witnessing the swallow and its aftermath.

- taking a tablespoon of vile-tasting medicine
- fighting off a serious cold or cough
- lying alone on a beach blanket, enjoying the warmth of the afternoon sun
- burning your hand while working at the stove
- waiting at a bus stop as it begins to drizzle, rain, pour
- coming home drunk
- experiencing nausea after a large meal
- finding your way through the darkness after a power failure
- listening to a dull lecture when your foot falls asleep
- making your way through a tangle of weeds and under-brush
- taking a morning shower
- walking into a classroom following a fight outside the school
- crossing the finish line after a long-distance run
- waiting for a taxi in 15 degree cold weather
- fighting off extreme fatigue as you try desperately to finish a term paper due early the next morning

Group Sense Memory

Many of the above items can be adapted to serve groups of actors equally well. These exercises need not emphasize plot or depth of character. Simply place five or six students within one of the settings below and have them portray a character appropriate to that setting. The action may make use of dialogue, movement, and conflict, but the primary purpose is to create the sensory elements of the scene as realistically as possible. Once that goal has been reached, you can yell "Cut!"

- a group of strangers waiting in line for more than twelve hours to buy tickets to a rock concert or baseball game
- a group seated outside an apartment building on a sizzling night in July
- a group standing on a subway platform, waiting impatiently for the arrival of the train
- a group of commuters standing in an elevator during rush hour when the power suddenly fails
- a group of hikers lost in the densest part of the woods
- a family seated at the dinner table when a full power blackout suddenly occurs

✳ Evaluation

On completion of the individual and group exercises, the following questions can be addressed by the class as a whole:

Did the actor recreate the sensory elements believably?

Which details of his or her performance were rendered effectively? ineffectively?

Did the sensory elements blend appropriately, or did they seem disjunct and rehearsed?

Lesson Five: The Liberating Element—Intention

On the simplest level, intention isn't a tough concept to teach your students. Using real life as a model, here's how the process works— we *always* want something. Every waking moment. It may be something simple and sedentary, such as I want to read a book in peace, I want to lie down and rest, I want to finish knitting that sweater. In the theatre, characters rarely stay with these wants for long. They're unexceptional, and they're boring to watch. The playwright's focus will probably fall on something more psychologically complex, and one or more other human beings will probably share in the exchange: I want to tease *her*, I want to seduce *him*, I want to control *them*. They almost always demand a response: I want to win Rose's *respect*, I want to destroy McMurphy's *cocky attitude*, I want to build Stella's *trust*. The job of getting under another person's skin, of fashioning a character drawn in depth, then, starts with putting these wants (intentions) into clear, precise, actable language and then finding the *physical means*—the vocal inflections, body language, facial expressions, physical actions—to communicate them. The work isn't nearly as cerebral or calculated as I'm making it sound. Once actors can articulate an intention, the physicalization should follow naturally, not through forcing the hands into a fixed position or the voice into a certain register.

"But what about *emotions*?" I can hear someone counter. "You may be right to say that we always *want* something, but don't we also always *feel* something, and shouldn't the truthful pursuit of those feelings be the actor's central task?" No, in fact, because in life feelings are always the effect, not the cause, of our wants. We never want to *feel* sad: We want to comfort a friend over the loss of her marriage, and so we may feel sad as a result. We never want to *be* angry: We want to punish a lover for breaking a lifelong trust, and so we feel angry as a result. *Want* is the engine that drives us, and the *fight to obtain what we want* is always what makes theatre compelling.

Warm-up Exercises in Intention

It's best to introduce the students to the subject of intention directly through the exercises given below. Definitions and generalizations, the stuff we've been exploring together thus far, won't awaken much interest at this stage anyway. They're too abstract, and the kids will receive them indifferently. Note that while the early focus is on the face and voice, the body will come into play soon enough. Remember, too, that all students need not do every assignment.

Intention 101

Write *Oh, I didn't realize you were coming too!* on the board. From their seats, five or six kids must direct that line of dialogue to you, each in turn delivering it with a different intention (see below). As always, the number one criterion is believability. The lines must be spoken, not cleverly, effectively, or "theatrically," but with absolute naturalness and conviction. No mugging or hamming, which doesn't mean the result can't be funny.

Student A: . . . to belittle him

Student B: . . . to build him up

Student C: . . . to charm him

Student D: . . . to scare him

Student E: . . . to snub him

Now try a second sentence: *Did you say what I think you said?*

Student A: . . . to threaten him

Student B: . . . to discredit him

Student C: . . . to delight him

Student D: . . . to overwhelm him

Student E: . . . to shock him

And a third: *Don't worry; I'll take care of it.*

Student A: . . . to dismiss him

Student B: . . . to reassure him

Student C: . . . to unsettle him

Student D: . . . to terrify him

Student E: . . . to take him down a few pegs

A student may occasionally protest that a certain line can't be spoken believably with the particular intention you assign. For example, pairing the sentence *Oh, I didn't realize you were coming too!* with the intention . . . *to scare.* I disagree—suppose the speaker knew that your "coming too" would jeopardize the success of a carefully conceived criminal operation. I will grant, however, that the lack of context in the setup of this assignment—who and where are these people, and what are the implied circumstances of this one line scene—poses a special challenge: the actors must allow their imaginations to supply the missing links, or the line will lack that necessary ring of truth.

To finish the exercise, make up some additional sentences and combine them with your own list of intentions. Make sure the verbs are strong and active. (See page 67 for more on verbs.)

Intention 102

Use new sentences, those below or a few of your own, but instead of supplying the intentions, have students silently choose their own, which they will reveal to the class only *after* they've spoken. Avoid long-winded discussions following each of these; the point at this stage is to test the waters and advance rapidly from one example to the next.

"I wouldn't lie to you, would I?"

"You probably shouldn't have done that."

"I thought you were my friend."

"I can't wait till tomorrow."

"You're such an interesting person."

"Hello" "Hello"

Position a desk and chair onstage. The setting is an office. Have all the actors choose a partner; one is A, the other B. Each couple decides in advance on a specific character they will portray and the relationship of their characters to each other. Character B *only* decides on an intention she will pursue ("I want to . . .") as the scene is performed, without revealing to her partner what it is. When the scene is in progress, the participants are limited only by what they may say: Character A's only line is "Hello," the same for Character B. Actor A pursues her intention as the scene is played. B reacts, choosing an intention spontaneously from the circumstances of the scene. The idea is to communicate as much as possible to the audience, and to tell a brief but complete story with a minimum of dialogue. What the actors do, then—with voice, gesture, movement, and facial expression—will result totally from their choices of intention. The scene may last five seconds; it may take a full minute or more.

For example, in their quick planning session, A chooses to play an officious supervisor, B a newcomer to the job. They agree that these two characters have met briefly during an interview some days before. B on that occasion impressed A as a rather pompous greenhorn with too high an opinion of himself. A decides on an intention in advance, without telling B what it is: *I want to cut down his ego.* You call "Action!" and the scene begins. B is seated at the desk, struggling with a large batch of documents. A sweeps in, drops an additional stack of papers on the desk, chirps a dismissive "Hello," and without stopping to wait for a reaction, sweeps out. B examines the huge work load, sighs, looks offstage, utters a weak "Hello," puts head down on desk. Curtain.

As another example, the actors choose to set the scene in a large stockbrokers' office. A decides to play an ambitious young account executive, B an experienced division supervisor. Against company policy, they've enjoyed a discreet dinner date the previous night. A decides on an intention in advance, without telling B what it is: *I want to kindle her affection for me.* You call "Action!" and the scene begins. B is seated at the desk, talking on the phone. (The limits of the assignment permit her only to utter an occasional "Mmmm" or "Uh-huh.") A walks over to her, glances quickly left and right, finds the coast clear, and smiles broadly. He sits on the edge of the desk, still smiling, whispers "Hello" sweetly in her ear. B frowns, pushes him firmly away, scowls, responds "Hello" between clenched teeth, continues her "Mmmm" "Uh-huh" phone conversation. A waits there patiently, finally leans in and winks at her. She refuses to meet his glance, jabs him in the ribs. Finally he rises, shrugs lightly, and exits the stage. Curtain.

These are descriptions of ways the exercise *might*, not *should*, go. Preplanning the "moves" would produce exactly the kind of stilted, artificial behavior you're training your kids to avoid.

What these assignments, and those that follow, hope to teach is that the text itself is only a starting point for the actor. It's not a matter of looking at the dialogue and figuring out "the right way" to say the words. Many kids will come to the course conditioned to this erroneous belief, and you may have to beat it out of them. It's a matter of choosing viable intentions and then allowing those choices to dictate the physical actions of the scene. As long as the intentions are well-founded and clearly articulated, good actors can render a page of dialogue from a script in any number of different ways, all of them true and compelling and *right*—and that principle applies whether the script is "Hello" "Hello" or *Death of a Salesman.* That's why portrayals of Willy Loman by Dustin Hoffman and Brian Dennehy can contrast so markedly and yet in their separate ways remain faithful to the text. It's also why there is no definitive interpretation of Beethoven's Ninth Symphony.

Phrasing Intentions

Once the class has begun inventing and responding to simple intentions, it's time to attack the job of phrasing them more precisely—choosing powerful verbs. Executed with care, this crucial step will make every bit of difference in the playing.

✳ Focus on Verbs, Not Nouns

A playable intention is something actors can *do* in a scene, not a thing they hope to obtain. Why? Because plays spring to life when they are propelled by physical action—not by things, feelings, or thoughts. You're always safe with "I want *to* . . . ," never "I want *a.* . . ."

No	Yes
I want a new computer.	I want *to persuade* Mom to buy me a new computer.
I want a date with her.	I want *to charm* her into accepting a date with me.
I want a promotion.	_____
I want revenge.	_____
I want a loyal friend.	_____
I want power over him.	_____

✳ Focus on Verbs, Not Adjectives

Focus on what is *doable,* not on how you feel. For example:

No	Yes
I'm very upset with him.	I want to *set him straight.*
I feel so bored.	I want to *energize* those around me.
I'm really ashamed.	_____
I'm so embarrassed.	_____
I am fed up with her.	_____
I feel very impatient.	_____

✳ Focus on Strong, Not Weak, Verbs

The more vigorous the actor's choice of verb, the more playable the scene. For example:

No	Yes
I want to obtain what belongs to me.	I want to *fight* to get back what she took from me.
I want to comprehend his reason for lying to me.	I want to *demand* his apology for lying to me.
I want to think about our future together.	_____
I want to discuss her lazy behavior.	_____
I want to figure out where he's coming from.	_____
I want to remain her friend.	_____

✳ Keep Your Eye on the Prize

What we usually seek in our dealings with other characters in a scene is a desired reaction, regardless of whether or not we succeed in getting one. In fact, it's the drive to obtain what we're after that keeps a scene humming, not the ultimate victory or defeat. Consequently, intentions that name the other person(s) and the hoped-for response are always the most eminently playable. For example,

> I want to inspire the men's confidence. (McMurphy, *Cuckoo's Nest*, Act I)
>
> I want to win my father's respect. (Catherine, *The Heiress*, Act II)
>
> I want to regain Al's trust. (Tom, *Tea and Sympathy*, Act II)

_____

_____

Silent Movie

Select a brief two-person scene from the videotape of a classic film. If the students are unfamiliar with the movie, so much the better. Play the scene with the volume off so that none of the dialogue can be heard. When the clip is finished, have the students tell you, one role at a time, as much as they can about each character's intentions. What do they learn in being able to pick up so much without being able to hear the words?

Assignments

Assignment #1: Improvising from an Intention (Basic)

The setup for these two improvisations should serve as a benchmark whose example you can return to again and again as the course progresses. Their structure parallels that of the simplest as well as the most complex of scripted scenes and demonstrates how the actor's pursuit of an intention remains the driving force that holds a scene together.

Bedtime

Select two volunteer actors, A and B, and privately prep them on the givens of the scene. A is a teenaged babysitter, B a child of perhaps six or seven. Mom and Dad have left for a movie, giving A strict instructions that B is to be in bed by 10:00 P.M. It's 9:55. A's *intention* during the scene is *to get B into bed*. B's *intention* is to manipulate A into allowing him to stay up as late as possible. Now instruct A privately that you want her to use every weapon at her disposal, *to flatter, to sweet-talk, to browbeat, to threaten, to punish,* in order to realize that intention. Instruct B simply to pursue his intention, responding to A's lead. If the actors follows these guidelines, the scene will have forward momentum as well as high entertainment value.

When you determine that the action has essentially run its course, call "Cut!" In reviewing the improv, aside from rating it for believability, discuss whether or not A remained consistently focused on her intention. Then ask, "What were the different ways in which A went about trying to achieve that intention?" The answers should come pretty close to the verbs listed above: "Well, she tried early in the scene to butter him up (to sweet-talk him) then later on she actually threatened him."

In this way, you're sneakily and effortlessly introducing the concept of *scene beats*, which are nothing more than the pivot points, the moments when actors change strategy and take up other means for obtaining their overall intentions (also called *beat intentions* and *super-intentions*).

Don't Jump!

The format is precisely the same as for "Bedtime." The setting this time, though, is a city street. A, returning home after a day's work, is suddenly riveted by the sight of a man, B, standing on a fire escape several stories up, threatening to jump to his death. Her intention in the scene *is to help A to safety.* B's intention is *to win A's sympathy for his plight.* As before, instruct A to break this super-intention down into beat intentions, the one difference being that the actor, instead of following your lead, will now determine these choices for herself—first I'll try *to reason*, then *to cajole, to reassure, to plead,* and so on. Steer the follow-up discussion so that it covers the same ground, making sure that the class isolates and names the individual beat intentions.

Note that for these early exercises, I am not addressing the question of beat intentions for the B characters. Since A in both cases drives the action, the scene can progress spontaneously so long as B has a clear, playable intention and responds believably to A's lead. (More about this subject in "Intention and the Script" in Chapter 3.)

✳ Additional Scenarios for Improvising from an Intention

Make certain as you set these scenarios up that the A characters understand they are responsible for breaking each super-intention down into beat intentions.

Lawn Boy

A is a sweet but lonely old lady, the sole occupant of a small cottage in a rural community. B is a friendly high school student who stops by each week to mow her lawn. The scene begins as he comes in to collect his money. A's intention: *to convince B to stay and chat awhile.* B's intention: *to get A to pay him his money so he can take off.*

Good Taste

A is a big shot in town, wealthy and influential. B is a generally cheerful newcomer to the community. The two have met in the supermarket and struck up a cordial conversation. A has invited B to her house that afternoon for coffee, to show her around the house, and generally to welcome her to the neighborhood. The scene begins with A doing some last-minute straightening up as B rings the bell. A's intention: *to win B's admiration for her superior taste in home furnishing.* B's intention: *to conceal her disdain for A's gaudy taste in interior design.*

The Interview

A is a candidate for a position as secretary. B is a successful, well-respected executive. She has been interviewing applicants for much of the morning. The scene begins with B making some random notes on a previous candidate's résumé. A knocks and enters. A's intention: *to charm B into accepting him for the job.* B's intention: *to test A's composure by throwing him curveball questions.*

Reunion

A and B are middle-aged, both well-established in flourishing careers. They meet at A's house a few days following a surprise encounter on a street downtown. Although both were quite friendly in high school, especially during the acting class they both attended fifth period during their senior year, neither has seen the other since graduation. The scene begins with A setting out refreshments as B knocks. A's intention: *to ignite B's memory of the good old days.* B's intention: *to challenge A's memory of the way things were.*

Assignment #2: Telephone Directory (Intermediate)

Copy several of the white pages from any handy telephone directory and distribute them among four or five students who volunteer for this exercise. One at a time, ask each actor to stand and read the page to the members of the audience, connecting with them emotionally through the choice of a clearly articulated intention. The actors will not need to get through the whole, or even most, of the page before they sit down. The assignment is not unlike the gibberish exercises we're all familiar with, the ones that require actors to use nonsense syllables in place of conventional language. It merely substitutes names, addresses, and phone numbers for the meaningless sounds, which in my experience beginning actors often find uncomfortable to work with. Most kids will be astonished at the wealth of meaning that can be conveyed through the choice of powerful intentions, minus the "crutch" of normally intelligible language (especially if the volunteers attack the material fearlessly).

Student A: . . . to whip the new cadets into shape

Student B: . . . to share with the children the wonders of a magical kingdom

Student C: . . . to dazzle the fans with an exciting play-by-play

Student D: . . . to persuade the jury of my client's innocence

Student E: . . . to frighten the campers with a terrifying ghost story

✳ Variation

The same exercise can be done with pages from a particularly dull preface to a particularly dull textbook.

Assignment #3: Poetic Intention (Advanced)

For homework, have students find one line of poetry to bring with them to class the next day. They must then, one at a time, come to the stage and deliver that line five times, each with a completely different intention. The chosen intentions must pass the test of believability—even if some convey meanings never intended by the poet. If an actor finds this difficult because of the lack of context, allow her to bring a second character to the stage and deliver the lines to him.

Lesson Six: Energy, Voice, and Projection

When I ask students to evaluate their fellow actors' scene work, the most frequently recurring criticism tends to be, "We can't hear them!"

What's at the root of this problem? Beginning actors are often unaware of how to place their voices in order to fill a large room. You may have to dust off your ancient elocution text and teach them to support the breath from the abdomen rather than the chest.

Sometimes it's not the actors' volume level that's the concern but lazy articulation. A quick demonstration should help; when you introduce this lesson, address the class using intentionally mumbled enunciation. Don't try too hard. Just allow the words to turn to mush. Hopefully before long someone out there will yell "What?!!?" Repeat yourself *at the same volume level* with clean, unforced articulation. That example, plus an occasional follow-up reminder—"Bite into the words a bit more. Open your mouth wider and let the sound through. Get the teeth, tongue, and lips to hit the consonants more crisply."—may be all that's needed.

Most of the time, though, what comes off as slack energy or poor projection is not lack of technique at all but rather insecurity in disguise. The kids aren't yet sufficiently grounded in their work, sufficiently focused on the goals they're trying to achieve in a scene, to think "projection." That's why this problem is properly addressed *after* the other fundamentals are in place. The remedy is to interject an encouraging "Great! Now share it with us out here!" or "Pursue your intention with double the intensity!"

Warm-up Exercises in Projection

You Won't Believe This!

In *Audition* (1978), Michael Shurtleff amasses more practical wisdom on the craft of acting than most other texts in the field. Make an effort to get this book; the material is accessible, pragmatic, and, while addressed to theatre professionals, has much to teach adolescent performers. In Chapter 2, he introduces the concept of *the moment before*:

> Every scene you will ever act begins in the middle, and it is up to you, the actor, to provide what comes before.
> This is true if you do a scene at the beginning of a play or the middle of a play or the end of the play. Something always precedes what you are doing. I call it *the moment before*. (67)

Ask for four or five volunteers. Explain that as soon as you've finished instructing them, all must step outside for a few moments. When they're ready, each bursts in one at a time to share news of something extraordinary that's just occurred outside the classroom. Actors are required to begin their "scene" with the four-word quotation, "You won't believe this!" The events must be related at fever pitch, with maximum intensity and conviction.

This exercise forces reluctant performers to open up and hear the sound of their voices resonating inside a small space. Sometimes that tiny step is all that's required as a permanent antidote to shyness. As you continue the unit, repeat this activity with new volunteers at the beginning of class each day.

✳ Variation

Repeat the exercise with four or five new volunteers. The directions are the same, but this time the actors must achieve the same energy without resorting to high speed or volume.

Tongue Twisters

These are old-fashioned, to be sure, but also useful in their way, especially for kids determined to tackle the classical repertoire later in the course—Molière, Shakespeare, Sheridan, Shaw, Wilde. One possible drawback—students who can toss these off expertly often go right back to speaking mush once the fun of the game is past. Follow up vigilantly to ensure that the gains are not sacrificed a day or two later.

> Such slipshod speech as she speaks.
>
> Some shun sunshine, some shun sleep.
>
> A shot-silk sash shop.
>
> The sinking steamer sank.
>
> Buy blue broadloom rugs.
>
> Put the cut pumpkin in the pigskin.
>
> Old oily Ollie oils old oily autos.
>
> Chop shops stock chops.
>
> The sea ceaseth, but it sufficeth us.
>
> The moth's mouth closed.
>
> Bill bought Bettina a black back brush.
>
> Red leather, yellow leather, pink leather, light yellow leather.
>
> Shingles and single, shave a single shingle thin.

A lonely lily lying all alone along a lonely lane.

Round the rough and rugged rock a ragged rascal ran.

How much wood would a woodchuck chuck, if a woodchuck could chuck wood? A woodchuck would chuck all the wood, if a woodchuck only could.

Four frantic flies furiously fought forty fearful fleas.

The silent sun shone severely on six slick sailors sleeping.

Kate hates tight tapes.

Theophilus Thistle, the successful thistle sifter, sifted a sieve full of unsifted thistles and thrust three thousand thistles through the thick of the thumb. Success to all successful thistle sifters.

The big black bug bled blue-black blood.

Rubber baby buggy bumpers.

She shines city shoes.

Assignments

Assignment #1: Overacting (Intermediate)*

Most associate this term with melodramatic, hammy, or fake. The actor produces emotion that is out of proportion to the needs of the scene, or worse still, lacks true internal conviction. I'm using it here in another sense—as a viable technique for bringing fresh life to a rehearsal that's low on energy. Sometimes when actors are sleepwalking their way through a scene, I'll ask them to begin again, this time *overacting* the intentions—overplaying them, taking them to the limit. They usually resist, afraid of sounding fake. I insist and they take the plunge. The first effort is almost always too timid. "No," I'll say. "More! Much, much more!!" The second try invariably comes closer to the mark, surprising the actors with results that begin to sound not forced or melodramatic but alive with an energy that was entirely missing the first time through. The lesson: That this last version works only because the intentions are finally being played with full vigor, rather than tentatively, and halfheartedly, as they were early on.

---

*Adapted from *Impro* (Johnstone 1979)

✳ Procedure

You can introduce overacting to the students through improvisation first. All actors choose partners, A and B. Once onstage, A begins by making a dull observation. Anything will do: "It's cold in here." B reacts by overaffirming A's statement. "Cold?! Yeah . . . you could say it's cold. My arms feel like they're ready to fall off! You'd think our big-hearted landlord could afford to keep the building thermostat a few degrees over thirty-six! I can see my freakin' breath. Look!" He demonstrates, then paces the room, hops up and down on each foot, rubs his hands together, and finally says, "Maybe it's time we called our lawyer." Now it's A's turn to overagree. "Hey, there you go! That's the best idea you've had in weeks, man. We'll be rich! Wasn't he the one who represented the woman who sued McDonald's in that hot coffee incident? We'll just bleed this guy till he drops, that's all, and then we can afford to move to Florida. . . ." And so on, for as long as the actors can continue to produce steam.

It doesn't matter here how witty or original the dialogue is, only that the actors respond *hugely* throughout the scene, continually affirming and reaffirming each other. The gains from this exercise become fully apparent later in the course when the class begins work on scripted scenes.

Assignment #2: Intimacy Improvs (Advanced)

For this exercise, the class must be conducted in a large auditorium. Actors pair up, A and B, and decide privately on a location for the scene, the characters they will portray and their relationship to each other, character intentions, a physical activity, and a landing point for the improv. The "twist" in the assignment is for the actors to choose a situation that requires them to speak in *soft tones*—a young man decides to propose to his long-time girlfriend in a crowded restaurant; a married couple packing for a vacation discuss how best to discourage their son from trashing the house in their absence (he is reading in the next room!); two friends in a movie theatre watch a film and can't resist commenting about the onscreen action; and so on. The actors must meet the challenge of adjusting the placement of their voices so that the dialogue can be consistently understood and at the same time seeking a volume level appropriate to the intimate character of the scene.

✱ Evaluation

Scatter the audience throughout the auditorium for these improvs and, following each one, allow students to report on the actors' audibility from various locations in the house. Everyone consequently experiences what it's like to speak from the stage *and* listen from the audience within the same class period.

Lesson Seven: Character Work

Thus far in the course, the students haven't had to step too far outside their own skins. For the early exercises in believability, they've played variations of themselves, and only for "People Observation" (page 35), "In the Halls" (page 41), and a few subsequent assignments have you asked them to experiment with taking on the voice, mannerisms, and physical qualities of others. In Chapter 4 they'll take on their first roles. That's why this is a perfect time for some concentrated work in character improvisation. The assignments below will supply the juice to energize the kids just prior to picking up their first scripts.

What's the best starting point for this work? *Not* with a whole lot of theoretical discussion and written analysis. It's in the act of performing these exercises that you lay the necessary groundwork, encouraging the actors to try on and shed a wealth of identities in rapid succession. Try them as listed—they range roughly from easiest to hardest in the order given—and by no means feel obliged to have every student perform every assignment.

Introducing Students to Character

Show and discuss the scene from *Tootsie* in which Dustin Hoffman coaches Terri Garr prior to her audition on a soap opera set. The excerpt gives a striking demonstration of how to whip oneself into character when nervous energy threatens to take over.

Warm-up Exercises in Character

Me and My Shadow

This exercise works best in a large space; a full stage is ideal. Choose five or six volunteers. Ask one member of the group, preferably the student with the most distinctive walk, to cross the stage as if strolling down an empty sidewalk. The others simply watch and study his stride. After he travels the distance once or twice, the group forms one single line behind him and crosses the stage again, all trying to duplicate his walk as precisely as possible. Let everyone go back and forth a few times, until you sense that all are moving as one. Ask the audience which actors seem to have captured the "soul" of the leader's walk the best. Repeat the exercise a few times with the remaining students in the class, substituting new lead walkers each time.

Kids sometimes feel weird being asked simply to pace across the stage ("You just want me to *walk*?"), but after some hesitation the resistance invariably melts and everyone seems to have a good time. The pleasure, of course, is in discovering the degree to which a mere walk can stand as a personal signature, a unique way of presenting oneself to the world.

✳ Variation

Have two volunteers, Characters A and B, stand before the class. A begins a brief talk on the subject "One Thing I'd Like to Change About This High School" (or any other topic that doesn't require serious research). The style of delivery must be strong and sure. At any given moment B breaks in, continuing to develop the material using A's voice and body language, as simultaneously A fades out. In other words, it's as if the presentation were the work of a single speaker. The two alternate back and forth this way until the speech reaches a conclusion of some sort.

Have the class evaluate, afterward, how convincingly B seems to have stepped into A's skin. In what parts has she most succeeded? Where did she fall short?

Grab Bag

Put a large black plastic bag on a table in the front of the classroom and before the class convenes fill it with ten to fifteen different hand props (a hairbrush, an umbrella, a stapler, a necklace, a medicine bottle, a music box, or whatever else). The students choose partners, and one actor from each pair removes a prop from the bag. Each couple decides in advance on a location for a scene, strong characters to portray, a relationship between the characters, a physical activity the characters are engaged in, and some landing point for the improv. The object is for the actors to play the scene so that, during the course of the action, both use the prop in a way that reveals *as much as possible* about their characters' personalities. The physical handling of the prop must be central, not incidental, to the plot of the scene.

Costume Piece

All actors select an article of clothing from the theatre's costume room (neatly, please!). The item should stand out in some way—a loud sports jacket, a feather boa, an unusual hat—and should communicate as much as possible about the personality of the wearer. All are placed in a large black plastic bag which is set on a table in front of the classroom. The students choose partners, and everyone removes an item from the bag. Each couple decides in advance on a location for a scene, a strong character suggested by their costume, a relationship between the characters, a physical activity the characters are engaged in, and some landing point for the improv. The object is for the actors to *create vivid characters* through the power of the item of clothing to inspire a complete identity.

Assignments

Assignment #1: Thanksgiving Dinner (Basic)*

Five or so volunteers rise and walk onstage. Ask them to recall their last big family gathering, a time when all the grandparents, aunts, uncles, cousins, nieces, and nephews were together under one roof. Each actor will choose from among these a relative who stands out from the rest in some way—they're either a bully, a glamour queen, a mischievous eight-year-old, a joker, a mother hen, a loud mouth, a wise guy, whatever. When you say "Begin," all participants start a slow, meandering walk through the stage space, moving *as themselves*, simultaneously and in random patterns, without touching each other. As the movement continues, ask them to form a

---

*The exercise is adapted from *Improv Comedy* (Goldberg 1991).

mental picture of the person they have in mind—their walk, their manner of moving and speaking—and then gradually, gradually, to transform themselves physically and emotionally into that person. The walk continues, only by now they have taken on a completely new identity, staying in character for the remainder of the exercise. Encourage everyone to greet and perhaps exchange a phrase or two with the others as they pass. After about thirty seconds elapse, call "Stop," and ask everyone to line up across the front of the stage.

As the interviewer, you will now address all characters one at a time, spending a minute or two in the company of each. Some possible questions:

How are you enjoying the company tonight? The food?

Who are some of your favorite people here? Least favorite? Why?

What do you do for a living? Enjoy it?

Anything interesting happen in your life recently? Tell us about it.

What were some of the hardships you've had to endure in your life? Some of the highlights?

If a student in the audience is so inclined, they may take over the questioning for a while. Much of the conversation can obviously be adapted to fit the person being interviewed. The actors must respond completely in character, through the voice and body of whomever they're portraying. They should be able to do so without too much strain, since presumably this is a person whose life history is accessible and familiar.

Assignment #2: Switch! (Intermediate)

Choose a day when there are an even number of students present in the class. Ask the kids to pair off with someone of approximately the same size, girls with girls, guys with guys. The couples find some convenient spot in the room and spend three minutes or so privately studying each other's walks, mannerisms, way of sitting and standing, speech habits, and body language. Assign a simple topic they can use for practice, such as what each has gotten out of the course so far, the best or worst parts of their school day, what they have planned for the coming weekend, a recent outrageous experience, or whatever. At the end of the three minutes, allow a brief recess while the actors find a nearby bathroom and exchange clothes—at the very least a shirt or jacket, items of jewelry, shoes, simple accessories. There may at first be some awkwardness among the group, but that quickly fades if your tone is straightforward and businesslike. Instruct everyone to make their return entrance to class in the person of their partner and quietly take a seat.

When everyone has reassembled, have each student take a turn onstage sharing with the class the gist of whatever information they gleaned from the interview with their partner. The kids in the audience can then pose brief follow-up questions. *Highly personal questions are off limits!* Each actor must remain completely in character for the length of the presentation, at all times answering as they feel their partner would, speaking in their partner's voice, using their partner's mannerisms and body language. When a question is asked that the actor is at a loss to answer, he or she must fake an appropriate response. This is not an easy exercise, but it is eye-opening to discover, as just about everyone always does, how much easier it is to assume another person's identity when wearing their clothes.

> CAUTION! In the end, I suspect students feel less anxious about the clothing switch—after all, you're not asking women to swap outfits with men—than they do about the fear that someone may portray them unflatteringly in front of their friends. I try to avert this possibility by citing the old Golden Rule. That's usually all that's needed. But proceed with care, since no one is more familiar with the personal dynamics of a particular class than you are.

Assignment #3: Talk Show Shrink (Intermediate)

The day before you plan this exercise, ask the students to create for homework a character with a personal problem that will become the basis for a call to a radio psychologist. It is important to emphasize that neither the callers nor the problems they create should be cartooned in any way, nor should the content border on tastelessness. This is important because there's a current fashion for outlandish excess in both radio and TV talk shows, and that approach will encourage students to resort to caricatures and stereotypes—*not* the tone you want to set for this assignment. Give them appropriate examples if necessary, or tape a few minutes of an actual show. There *are* some that can serve as appropriate models.

The next day, place two chairs stage right and left center. Position them facing slightly away from each other so that there is no temptation for the actors to establish eye contact. You will play the talk show host, introducing guests at random, spending a minute or two with each. They will present their personal dilemma in a nutshell, and you will engage them in conversation long enough to bring the problem into focus and suggest some possible solutions. If these exchanges are vivid and entertaining, so much the better. But the point of the exercise is for the students to create believable human beings who speak in voices of their own and are able to respond without hesitation to your questions.

Assignment #4: Against Type (Advanced)

Actors often rail against the tyranny of typecasting—the tendency of many directors to select an actor for a role who in real life seems physically and emotionally close to their vision of a character in a play. Questions like the following are guaranteed to produce some heated discussion in class:

> Why do directors practice typecasting?
>
> Are there good reasons for doing so?
>
> Can a person who *types* meek and submissive convincingly portray an arrogant, domineering character? How about vice versa? Other examples?
>
> If yes, why is typecasting so popular?
>
> Do people in general and directors in particular tend to type you in certain ways, as, for example, a class clown, a lover, a jock, an older woman?
>
> If so, does the habit annoy or please you?

A subject as controversial as this isn't likely to reach a consensus. One provocative way of channeling the discussion is through the following exercise, which has a refreshing tendency to turn everyone's expectations of each other inside out and upside down. It also answers the tasty question: Can Josh, who always seems to gravitate onstage to smooth-talking, self-assured, hip characters, possibly be convincing to an audience as a shy, self-effacing loser?

Hand each student a pen and an index card. Everyone numbers from one to eight and folds the card in half so that there are two columns. Now ask your actors to respond personally to the following questions and to record their answers in the left hand column:

1. In general, do you tend to think of yourself as sloppy or neat?
2. Conforming or rebellious?
3. "Above the crowd" or "just plain folks"?
4. Outgoing or shy?
5. Uncoordinated or athletic?
6. Hip or square?
7. Slow- or fast-moving?
8. Quiet or loudmouthed?

Some students will react with legitimate confusion. "Well, I'm sloppy about some things, neat about others." "Of course," you answer. "But, in general, *do you tend to see yourself as an Oscar or a Felix?*" And so on with the remaining questions. Others may need help understanding what you mean by *conforming* or *rebellious*.

Once all eight items have been completed, the students are to examine each response individually. If they wrote *neat* for number one, they are to write the word *sloppy* directly to its right. If they wrote *rebellious* for number two, they are to write *conforming* directly to its right. And so on through to number eight. Once finished, everyone circles the eight answers listed in the right hand column.

The students now choose partners. As usual, each pair of actors decides privately on a location for a scene, characters to portray, a relationship between the characters, a physical activity the characters are engaged in, and some landing point for the improv. The hook lies in the act of *creating* these characters. Everyone is to check out his or her index card and carefully peruse the list of eight circled words. The aim is to invent someone who incorporates as many of these traits as possible, who in other words has a personality about as different as can be imagined from that of the actor himself. The audience will thus get to see that actor diametrically transformed.

Be sure everyone understands that there's no pressing need to incorporate *all* eight items on the list. The larger goal is for each actor to reveal a formerly undisclosed side of themselves. In fact, this should be the primary criterion for evaluating the scenes.

Finally, emphasize that stereotypes are off-limits for this one. For example, if an actor's card has the words *square* and *uncoordinated* circled, his tendency might be to jump instantly to the classic nerd, taped glasses, pigeon-toed walk, scrunched features, and all. A logical way of avoiding this trap is to remind everyone that since the traits in the left column don't necessarily add up to a stereotype (they were describing *themselves*, after all!) neither should those in the right column.

Assignment #5: Diner (Advanced)

This exercise reinforces the actor's connection with the physical surroundings. Clear the stage, and then use chairs, small tables, music stands, or whatever else is handy to create a carefully defined environment for the students (in this instance a greasy spoon diner). Describe the setting for them in minute detail, placing the furniture as you go: "Up right an antique jukebox filled with 45 RPM records from the '50s and '60s; off right the moldy rest rooms; up center a counter of badly chipped formica; above it shelves of mini-cereal boxes and less-than-appetizing pastries; down left a corroding cigarette machine. . . ." Don't spare the details! By the time you've finished your description, the actors should feel thoroughly familiar with the space.

Now accept volunteers to portray various characters who will fill the setting during the course of the improv: a grill man, a waitress, a cop, a village postman, two out-of-towners, several business people on their way to a convention, a few kids cutting out of school, a motorist whose car has broken down, and so on until everyone in the class has been assigned a role. If time permits, allow the cast to select an appropriate item of clothing from the costume room.

The plot of the improv will develop spontaneously as the action proceeds. There are only three rules:

1. The scene begins with a bare stage. Once the waitress and the grill man have come on, the other characters stagger their entrances by approximately one-minute intervals, walking in either singly or in related groups.
2. Focus in the scene goes to whoever is making an entrance, which means that characters already on the set continue with

whatever action they're engaged in at the time, only less conspicuously. It also means that characters who enter do so strongly, seizing the spotlight. *Without an understanding of this process of give-and-take, the scene will quickly fall apart.*

3. The characters should find reasons as the action progresses to connect physically with every object on the set—the jukebox, the grill, the cigarette machine, the counter, the tables, and so on. Whether they succeed or not is unimportant. The effort will add interest and energy, so long as all actors take their time and adequately justify each action.

If the students find it tough to observe these three rules, you can call "Cut!" once or twice to regain focus. My experience is that the actors usually respond more and more like an ensemble as the scene advances, gradually discovering how to give and receive focus as they go along. The object of the assignment is less to develop a fascinating plot than it is to create believable characters inhabiting a believable environment.

Assignment #6: Weekend Retreat—Part One (Advanced)

This assignment will consume two class sessions and entails some advance preparation from the students, so fill them in on the particulars about a week in advance. The premise is that all characters have responded to an ad appearing in a current issue of a magazine and signed up for a singles retreat at a nearby mountain resort. The ad has promised recreation, comfortable accommodations, delicious cuisine, privacy, and a weekend of social interaction with others who wish to "forge new relationships and a fresh start in life."

All actors in the class are to construct at home a life history for the character they are soon to become. Every aspect of that character's makeup and disposition must be etched into their imaginations in advance. To this end, the students will prepare a written questionnaire that includes answers to the following (the list may be altered or extended):

What is your character's name? Age? Religion? Ethnicity?

What are his tastes in books, music, movies, television, food, cologne?

What are his speech patterns? His accent, if any?

What is his daily routine?

What occupation does he hold and how effective is he on the job?

How does he dress on social occasions? At home?

How much self-confidence does he possess?

What is his general disposition? (Kind? Gentle? Sarcastic? Nervous?)

What sort of temper does he have?

How would you describe his relationships with friends? Coworkers?

What is the history of his romantic relationships?

What is his educational background?

What sort of family does he come from?

What are his hobbies?

What is his income?

How much of a sense of humor does he have? What's funny to him?

What kind of posture does he have? Ways of moving? Mannerisms?

What is the state of his health?

What is the level of his wit? Intellect?

What kind of politics does he have?

What is he attracted to materially? Is status important to him?

What difficult experiences has he had to face in his life?

What are his greatest fears?

How does the outside world generally regard him?

What does he want in life?

Does he have children? How many and of what sex?

The actor, if he enters into the spirit of this work, is piecing together an image of a fairly complex human being. That person may be inspired in part by someone from real life or totally imagined. Either way, the actor must come in *knowing* him thoroughly. Answers to questions like those above, and to especially "What does he want in life?" must come automatically, because once the actor appears in class on the assigned day, he can't pause to ask himself "Hmm . . . how *would* my character react in this situation?"

The day before the performance, remind all students to bring their outfits to school. The first five minutes or so (no more!) of class time the next day are spent getting into costume. *When the students enter the class, they are in full character.* The transformation should be so complete that in a few instances the kids won't honestly be sure about the identity of some of the actors.

As teacher, you'll portray the hotel's social director, whose job it is to greet the guests, gather them together in the "conference room," and lay out the agenda for this "get acquainted" meeting. It's your character who sets the tone, so the right costume, voice, mannerisms, and body language are essential. Here's a practical format for the session:

1. The social director greets the characters, asks their names, introduces himself.
2. He directs the characters to take seats and form a circle.
3. He takes a minute or so to welcome everyone, to remind them of the purpose of the retreat, and to say a few words about the hotel facility.
4. The social director now asks the individual guests a series of questions as he works his way around the circle. This is the heart of the session. Only the person addressed may respond.

   > Can you introduce yourself and tell us a bit about your background? In other words, your life in a nutshell?

   > What circumstances in your present life caused you to answer our ad?

   > What positive qualities do you have to offer the group?

   > What do you hope to get from this weekend?

   If this structure becomes at all monotonous, the social director can vary the questions slightly.
5. If time permits, the director offers the members of the group a chance to pose a single question to any individual of their choice, which the person addressed may then answer. (The questions should not overstep the bounds of good taste.)
6. The director wraps up the session, thanks everyone for their time, and wishes everyone an enjoyable stay.

A few false steps can derail this exercise, so considering all the advance preparation required, it's worth everyone's time to review the following short list of guidelines the day before the performance.

Pointers

1. Attitudes

Kids, as you might imagine, love to portray strong, mean, bitchy, nasty, domineering, aggressive types onstage. Everyone enjoys an angry outburst now and then. It's fun, it's "out there," it gets noticed, and frankly, it's relatively easy to pull off. The problem is that, left with total freedom of choice, almost everyone in the class will gravitate to these kinds of characters. The presence of one or two in your singles group will add spice to the mixture; more is almost always a liability, since the conversation—despite your repeated efforts to subdue the antagonists—will descend again and again to bickering and negativity. The result: Everyone shuts down! Share this cautionary note with the students and ask them to give it some serious thought.

Worse still is when students are drawn to characters at the other end of the emotional scale: brooding, withdrawn, alienated "lost souls." The problem is that such people characteristically refuse to interact. The result: everyone shuts down!

2. Interruptions

Make sure the kids are clear in advance about the rule forbidding characters to break in on or shout over one another. If this happens once, even twice within thirty minutes, good enough. Sparks fly, and everyone enjoys a moment or two of high drama. More than that results in an atmosphere of uninterrupted static, with cross-conversations and side noise canceling out the whole purpose of the assignment.

3. Keeping Character

Place great emphasis on the importance of remaining inside the scene. Nothing kills the spirit of this exercise faster than the student who, amused by a funny response from a member of the singles group, suddenly steps out of character and destroys the illusion.

Assignment #6: Weekend Retreat—Part Two (Advanced)

By the second day, the students should begin to feel more at home with their characters. As soon as everyone has arrived in class and before they've changed into their costumes, set up the following improv:

1. All actors pair off with the character of their choice. One is A, the other B.
2. Assume that these individual couples decide to spend some time together at a particular setting somewhere on the hotel premises—the tennis courts, the card room, the dining room, the lake.
3. During the improv itself, the separate couples interact on location. The director and the other actors become an audience for each scene.
4. As the action progresses, the director calls out an intention for A to pursue (*charm him, flatter her, humiliate him, intimidate her*). She does so, incorporating the intention seamlessly into the scene. B reacts spontaneously.
5. The scene ends whenever the director feels the action has run its course.

The Transition from Improvisation to Scripted Material

Preserving Believability with Scripts

You'd think that, having acquired a grasp of the fundamentals of the craft, your actors would now stand ready to pick up their first script and transform it into a living, breathing conversation of unforced naturalness and vitality. The day finally arrives when you summon the courage to hand some volunteers a brief dialogue, maybe an excerpt from a contemporary play whose characters speak the kids' language, and what happens? Where's the product of all those days of intense labor? What became of the relaxation, concentration, and sense memory skills you've worked so hard to instill? Why do they speak without shades of intention or a sense of belief in the words they're mouthing? Has the class accomplished absolutely nothing all these weeks? Worst of all—there it is again, the beast you've labored long and hard to exterminate: their *acting* voice!

Some high school courses in the fundamentals of performing, even some at the college level, never do get around to script work. I suspect that's because teachers who begin finally to detect the emergence of something authentic in their students' work after weeks of improv training are understandably reluctant to sacrifice all the hard-won gains. But the decision to delay the use of scripts indefinitely is a mistake. A few special formats aside—mime, comedy improv, an occasional stand-up routine—acting eventually means learning to develop facility with the printed page. With plays, films, TV shows, even advertising spots, the script is always the jumping-off point. And the goal, ironically, is always to make that script disappear.

So why then the disaster scenario I describe above? The answer is complex. A part of it lies in the act of reading itself. Working for the first time from a text, your actors must now deal with the task of decoding written symbols and rendering them as speech. No big deal. They've been doing that since first grade, right? But from what I've observed over the years, both as English and theatre teacher, progressively fewer students feel secure reading aloud these days. Maybe it's because we've been asking them to do so little of it. Secondly, unless they've mastered the trick of taking in large chunks of text at a single glance, their gaze is now directed downward most of the time, which means the exchange of eye contact, body language, and tone of voice becomes at least twice as difficult to sustain. Thirdly is the curious fact that kids who have been around theatre for a while, who have maybe done some community theatre work or a few elementary and middle school plays, often register a conditioned response the instant they pick up a script. They look at their lines and break unconsciously into a canned, affected delivery style that has always impressed adults (a second cousin to the so-called acting voice?). Finally, there's the matter of assimilating the playwright's language—*owning the words*, as it's called. To do so takes practice.

None of the above is cause for serious concern because it is usually no more than a false alarm. The data has been duly recorded in the memory bank. It's just that with the sudden appearance of the script, it all seems momentarily to have vanished. Relax. As you work through these exercises day by day, the skills will reemerge all the more strongly. Like clapping, walking, and chewing gum, the students will soon enough learn to read, act, and react believably—all at the same time.

Assignments

Assignment #1: In the Halls—Scripted (Basic)

This assignment is set up in precisely the same way as for "In the Halls" from the believability section in Chapter 2 (see page 41).

The only difference here is that when the teams of actors return to the theatre classroom after finding a good thirty-second to one-minute scene, they'll spend the remainder of the period not rehearsing and performing those scenes but gathering in their separate groups to prepare a script that records exactly what they heard and saw. One person writes, the others help to recall the details. The script should be in standard form, free of spelling and usage errors, and include all dialogue and stage directions. It should be so precise that other actors, picking up a copy at some future time, would be able to use it to prepare their own production of the scene. At the end of the period, have the writer in each group present you with the finished text.

Before the class meets on the following day, duplicate enough copies of the scenes so that each student can have a complete set. Then, on the second day, begin class by distributing the packets. The actors once again split up into their groups, turn to the script in the packet for their individual scene, and spend no more than five to ten minutes rehearsing. Just going through it once or twice should make the work of line memorization unnecessary.

As soon as everyone is ready, the groups give their performances of the individual scenes—without using scripts, of course. The rest of the students observe and may at the end offer some quick feedback.

Everyone in the audience now turns in their packet to the text of the scene they've just finished watching. The actors perform it again, exactly as before, only this time the audience follows along in their scripts. It may require two class sessions to get through the entire packet.

The value of this exercise is in the watching more than the doing. There's much to be learned, especially if the quality of the acting is high. Although the material being performed is intentionally simple, the principle it teaches applies just as surely to *Romeo and Juliet* and *Ah, Wilderness!*: Spontaneity with scripts begins when actors learn how to breathe life into those black marks on paper. That's the quality test you want to apply to these one-minute in-the-hall scenes. The script is there, and the actors must succeed in making it disappear.

This is one of those self-evident truths of which everyone is thoroughly aware—so much so that some kids may wonder about the point of the assignment. Like the small child who may need to be reminded that the monster under the bed isn't real, it's occasionally worth the effort to reaffirm the obvious.

Assignment #2: Get the Teacher—Scripted (Intermediate)

As with "In the Halls—Scripted," this second assignment parallels an exercise in Chapter 2 (see page 34). The Dramatic Publishing Company has available a play version of *Up the Down Staircase* that is based loosely on the Sandy Dennis film. Obtain enough copies of the script in advance to accommodate the entire class. To save time, cast the parts the night before. Because this assignment is designed as a companion piece to the first one, you should again take on the role of teacher. The cast of characters is large, so some kids may have to take on two roles.

✱ Procedure

In class the next day, explain the purpose of the exercise: "You will be doing a replay of the *Get the Teacher* assignment, only this time the dialogue will be scripted." Give a quick thumbnail sketch of each character as you announce who's playing what. Actors should either *highlight* or *underscore* their lines so that there are no awkward pauses or shouts of "Oh, hang on a second. I lost my place!" once the scene begins. Warn the students in advance which characters begin the scene from outside the room.

The object is to hold the scripts and at the same time make them disappear; in other words, to look ahead so that whenever someone's cue is spoken there's no need for them to refer to the sheet of paper. To pass the test of quality, the scene would have to resemble the real thing—a believable recreation of a first day of school, New York City, circa 1964. If a few kids complain that the dialogue isn't very realistic, you can remind them of the play's publication date.

Challenge the actors before you start: "Remember, if we're doing our job, someone from outside the class who happens to walk in during the read-through should assume they are witnessing something real—not a rehearsal of a scene in acting class. And although you'll be using the scripts, try not to let them be seen. OK, let's start."

Invariably things will go wrong. Despite your warnings,

actors will miss cues. Some will be shocked to see how quickly a certain line comes up; others how long it takes to get to their part. Overlaps will occur, which is fine, but in the process a cue for a subsequent line may be swallowed up. There may be a total absence of background noise, which means characters without lines may forget they're supposed to be as alive in the scene when they're *not* speaking lines as when they are. Or the undercurrent of noise and disruption—kids throwing paper airplanes, leaving their seats to scrawl graffiti on the blackboard, having side conversations, and so on—may be so intrusive that it all but obscures the scripted lines.

If you find things falling apart, stop the action once or twice, incorporate some corrections, and try again. And again. And, if necessary, still again. Hopefully, the changes will bring improvements, so that what came off initially as plastic or wooden now feels believable. The period will end before you arrive at a *take*, which is fine. The more important point is the process your actors are undergoing here: *it's called rehearsal.* That process should offer a powerful demonstration to students new to the theatre game of why most shows take a few months to prepare.

Assignment #3: Vignettes (Intermediate)

The purpose of this assignment is to reinforce the gains of the last two. Find and bring to class a variety of two-character scripts, all of them brief and relatively easy to perform (suggestions for appropriate sources follow on page 107). As you assign the scenes to specific actors, give each duo a description of the setting, a one-phrase summary of the situation the characters find themselves in, and maybe a word or two about their relationship. Allow the actors no more than a minute or so of private time to skim the lines silently.

They will then attempt a cold reading of the scene in front of the class, almost as for an audition, aiming as always for three things: maximum believability, appropriate use of movement, and high energy. (A second couple can use this time to prepare themselves outside the classroom as Couple #1 performs, and so on.) The object is to improve the actors' ability to give and take, act and react, with script in hand. Becoming comfortable in this work is usually just a matter of frequent practice, and this first shot will give everyone a good head start.

For reluctant readers especially, there is a technique that can tone down much of the anxiety in this process. Remind everyone that *cold reading* does not mean *finished performance*. That's what rehearsal is for. Consequently, it makes little sense to try for a brisk rhythm. Aim instead at slowing the scene way, way down, and refer to the script only when the other character is talking. That allows the reluctant reader to fix the words in his head, which frees him to look his scene partner in the eye every time he speaks. (Spencer Tracy's definition of good acting was "Look the other fellow in the eye, and say your lines like you mean 'em!") If the reader can't find his place when he returns to the script, remind him to simply pause, saying nothing until he does. The audience will wait.

Because students are usually driven by nervous energy when they try this for the first time, their tendency is to race ahead no matter how many times you caution them to slow down. Keep at it. Once they appreciate the freedom that comes from mastering this technique, they'll find the right rhythm and take off on their own. Eventually some kids discover a flow that seems to defy gravity; the script does almost appear to vanish from their hands.

This skill has enormous practical value, too, for any of your students who pursue professional careers. The actor who in auditions relates meaningfully, establishes good eye contact, and makes his scene partner rather than the printed page the object of his focus, will compel the director to look up and take notice.

Intention and the Script

If the students have acquired a strong basis for understanding intention through their work in Chapter 2, they should experience this next stage of the course as a baby step. Ideally the introduction of scripts should pass virtually unnoticed—a minor adjustment to a new way of working. Instead of taking off from a given situation and improvising their own dialogue, actions, and reactions, the students are now turning to the playwright for a clear set of boundaries. The setting; the age, vocation, and physical description of the characters, and their relationships to each other; the words they speak—all are for the first time laid out on the printed page. Many students will receive this change as a welcome relief—

"Finally, something to work from!" But there's a trap: Just as the map is not the territory and the score not the symphony, so is the script not the performance. Choosing intentions and playing them with conviction are the true building blocks of the actor's craft. The script is simply the essential starting point.

Confusion on this subject can bring back a problem we spoke of earlier. It is the kids' unconscious assumption that the writer invests every line with one correct interpretation, which the actor must then work to discover through careful process of elimination. ("Yeah, but is that the *right* way to say this line?" they'll ask all too frequently in rehearsal.) It's probably more accurate to argue that the playwright composes his dialogue without giving the characters' intentions much deliberate thought whatsoever. That's a decision for the performer, and it's the decision that more than any other enables him to act without falseness. Choice A colors the scene with one palate of tints and shades, Choice B another. If the students seem puzzled with any of this, show them brief excerpts from the two available versions of *Inherit the Wind*, the first featuring Spencer Tracy as Drummond, the second Jason Robards, and they will instantly absorb the key point: For any well-written script, there will be a range of valid choices of intention for the actor to pursue. Of course that doesn't mean that all options are defensible in all contexts. It would be a bit silly for an actress playing Laura in *The Glass Menagerie* to pursue *I want to get Amanda to teach me her tricks for attracting gentlemen callers* as a super-intention for Scene 1. The script offers a latitude of defensible choices—not infinite license.

Let's return for a moment to that lightweight babysitting improv from Chapter 2 (see page 69) and recall its structure. A's *super-intention*, we remember, was *to get this child to go to sleep for the night*. Her *beat intentions*—different ways to go about achieving that super-intention—were *to flatter, to browbeat, to sweet talk, to threaten, to punish*. The big news is that every scene in every play written by our most sophisticated playwrights—Shakespeare, Molière, Chekhov, Shaw, O'Neill, even Pinter and Ionesco—are structured in precisely this way. Each character is after something (their super-intention) and fights to discover different ways of achieving that something (their beat intentions).

Okay, let's bring the discussion back down to earth with a practical illustration of all this theory. Suppose we take a look at more challenging material and see how an actor can build a performance from a close study of the character's intentions. Let's go to Shakespeare's *Much Ado About Nothing.* If we can successfully apply the process to a script at this advanced level, no material appropriate for high school actors can possibly daunt us. We'll take an excerpt from a single scene and test the criteria we've been examining thus far:

1	BENEDICK:	If Signior Leonato be her father, she would not have his head on her shoulders for all Messina, as like him as she is.
	BEATRICE:	I wonder that you will still be talking, Signior
5		Benedick. Nobody marks you.
	BENEDICK:	What, my dear Lady Disdain! Are you yet living?
	BEATRICE:	Is it possible disdain should die while she hath such meet food to feed it as Signior Benedick? Courtesy itself must convert to disdain if you
10		come in her presence.
	BENEDICK:	Then courtesy is turncoat. But it is certain I am loved of all ladies, only you excepted; and I would I could find in my heart that I had not a hard heart; for truly, I love none.
15	BEATRICE:	A dear happiness to women: they would else have been troubled with a pernicious suitor. I thank God and my cold blood, I am of your humour for that. I had rather hear my dog bark at a crow than a man swear he loves me.
20	BENEDICK:	God keep your ladyship still in that mind, so some gentleman or other shall 'scape a predestinate scratched face.
	BEATRICE:	Scratching could not make it worse, an 'twere such a face as yours were.
25	BENEDICK:	Well, you are a rare parrot teacher.
	BEATRICE:	A bird of my tongue is better than a beast of yours.
	BENEDICK:	I would my horse had the speed of your tongue, and so good a continuer. But keep your way, i'
30		God's name; I have done.
	BEATRICE:	You always end with a jade's trick. I know you of old.

Let's consider Benedick's behavior during this brief dialogue. What exactly is he after here? *What is he going for?* (The latter phrasing works miracles with student actors when you're trying to get them to pin down their characters' intentions.)

He wants to berate Beatrice. Absolutely. But that's a weak choice. It's too intellectual, too general, and it gives the actor no incentive to enter into the fun of this spirited exchange.

He wants to ridicule Beatrice in front of her friends and family. There's more truth to that. Much of the reason he continues to come back at her is for the entertainment of the onlookers. But the phrasing is too wordy. And *ridicule*, while it's a strong and playable verb, is too nasty a choice for this banter. There's a pretty obvious subtext of flirtation here that makes his verbal barbs not just stinging but playful.

Here's a more promising possibility: *He wants to one-up Beatrice for the crowd's pleasure.* Not only is there fun in one-upping a former lover for the amusement of the onlookers, but being forced to summon his wit to top her with each fresh volley will add a flicker of whimsy to the actor's playing. It's a juicy choice, and it gives him a want he can pursue zestfully.

With even so brief a scene as this, there's a need to break the super-intention (to one-up Beatrice for the crowd's pleasure) into beat intentions. An actor lazy about taking this step risks monotony. For example, at line eleven we might say that "he wants to one-up her by gloating," at line twenty-eight that "he wants to one-up Beatrice by dismissing her," and so on.

This is the way that intention works for the actor. It frees him to adjust his tone, his body, his gestures, his facial features, his everything to achieve that intention. The rest of the play, of any play, goes by in much the same way. There are new beats, new super-intentions, new beat objectives. Finding the most viable, those that seem to work best for the character, may sometimes be a slippery task. But it is eminently doable. And your students will be amazed at how reassuring it is to know that they don't have to cast about blindly or rely on their instincts to carry them through a scene. Their playing will be specific, it will have shape, definition, and—most important—forward momentum.

I'm making everything sound a bit more pat than it turns out to be in real life, of course. Identifying a character's drives is not as linear a process as solving for x in an algebraic equation. To one-up, as we've seen, is only one possible direction for the actor playing Benedick to pursue; there's also the matter of how his choices of intention affect the playing of other characters in the scene (more of this later), and of finding the physical behavior to complement the chosen intentions. But each of these steps, taken in turn, brings the student closer to performance level and lends method to what may otherwise become an arbitrary and piecemeal approach to acting.

Assignments

The above material should form the basis for one of the few formalized chalkboard lessons in the course. It's important enough to merit a two-pronged attack: deductive and inductive. You can use *Much Ado* or any other script of your choice, but make sure the kids have copies of the text so that they can follow along. The aim of the lecture should be to teach them how to isolate possibilities for a single character's super-intention in a scene, and then to break that super-intention down into beat intentions. For a while it will all strike them as so much abstract speculation. But later, as you apply the principles through these exercises, the practical skills will seep in by osmosis.

Assignment #1: "Well?" "Well?" (Intermediate)

This is the best exercise I know for applying the theory of intention to an entry-level script. Be careful not to explain too much in advance. Lay out the directions, perform the scenes, and wait for the evaluation step to demonstrate the full potential of the assignment.

Exercises like these are sometimes referred to as open scenes, contentless scenes, or *Chekhovians*. They're perfect for building a bridge between improvisation and script work because, although a text is provided, the work of creating the setting, the situation, the characters, and their relationships remains—for the moment—the actors' responsibility. This particular example, really an extension of "Hello" "Hello" from the section on intention (see page 65), has the added advantage of requiring maximum physicality. Kids generally find it puzzling until they grasp, through repetition, what it tries to teach: *Even with the script as blueprint, the actor is still required to make infinite choices.* Of course these open scenes are rigged to underscore the point in somewhat exaggerated terms. But through repetition and practice, they do train the students to understand just how much of the burden for making things happen onstage lies on their own shoulders.

ONE: Well?

TWO: Well?

ONE: Well, here we are.

TWO: That's right.

ONE: Shall we get started?

TWO: All right.

ONE: Are you sure you know how to do this?

TWO: Of course I'm sure.

ONE: I don't think that's right.

TWO: This is the way it's supposed to be done.

ONE: You're wrong; that's not right.

TWO: Okay, how would you do it?

ONE: Like this.

TWO: That's definitely not right.

ONE: Yes it is.

TWO: If we're going to do it like that, I'm leaving.

ONE: All right.

TWO: I'm going.

ONE: Good-bye.

✳ Procedure

The first part of this exercise may require up to one full class session. Ask all actors to pair up and find a convenient spot to work in. It makes no difference who plays One or Two. If there is an uneven number of students in the group, an unpaired actor may participate in one of the scenes as a silent character, reacting without words to the other two. Explain that they are to use the scripts for rehearsal only, and then perform the scenes for the class that same period. No more than fifteen minutes of preparation should be necessary, including time for staging and line memorization. Props, if they have any on hand, are optional.

Just before you distribute the scripts and everyone breaks up to begin work, announce that you anticipate questions about how to approach the assignment but would like them this time to proceed without your help. One or two kids may still insist on asking:

"Do we have to perform an activity when we present these?" Smile reassuringly, but otherwise resist the temptation to respond.

When rehearsal time is up, seat all the Ones together on one side of the room, the Twos on the other. Conduct a rote rehearsal of the dialogue choral style, repeating it as many times as necessary until everyone in the room feels they've mastered the lines. Remind them too that once the performances begin no actor is to break from the scene. They should have enough improvisational skills and/or sense of the general outline of the script at this point to find their way to the finish line without stumbling.

Perform all the scenes in succession without pausing for comment or feedback. Although contrary to the usual procedure of the class, this change of format will ultimately pay off. Take your own notes during the performances so you can use them as examples to refer back to, then have everyone take a seat and proceed to the evaluation step.

✳ Evaluation

The evaluation step for this exercise should aim at opening up possibilities in the script for acting choices that the students may have missed the first time through. Use examples from their work as a continuing point of reference.

1. *Most important*: Did each of the actors pursue a definite super-intention? That's a vital decision, since it affects every move they make in the scene, every inflection of the voice. It's not enough to say, "My super-intention was to make the pancakes," or even "My intention was to show him the right way to diaper the baby." The choices become more playable as the phrasing becomes more specific: "My super-intention was to show her the way a Cordon Bleu–trained chef would make the pancakes." Or, "My super-intention was to get him to diaper this baby with true love and affection."

2. Did the actors divide their super-intention into beat intentions? If so, those choices will color their playing every step of the way and obviate the need for any canned stage business. For example, the choice "to get him to appreciate my expertise as a safecracker" might lead Character Two to:

- shush Character One for making too much noise during the entrance before the scripted lines have even begun;
- speak his first "Well?" in a superior, impatient tone;
- push One dismissively aside before positioning himself professionally in front of the safe at "Of course I'm sure";
- laugh derisively after watching One perform his demonstration following the line "Like this";
- pause generously after "Yes it is" and stare pitiably at One; and
- say "I'm going" before One has even finished the line "All right."

These details will give the scene richness and texture, but they should *not* be the result of preplanning or marking the script *laugh mockingly* on this line and *pause indignantly* on that. They should grow organically out of the initial choice of super-intention.

Because there is so much to discover in working with this exercise, I always repeat it the next day, choosing new partners and new activities, and then proceed with one or more of the variations in subsequent sessions. The growth in the sophistication of the students' choices as the work progresses is always striking.

✳ Variation I

ONE: Well?

TWO: Well?

ONE: Look, could we hurry it up a bit please. I'm trying to be patient, but . . .

TWO: Almost through.

ONE: Hey, this is ridiculous.

TWO: I'm sorry . . . these things take time.

ONE: I know that, but . . .

TWO: Just be patient a few more seconds, okay?

ONE: A few more seconds?

TWO: That's right . . . a few more seconds. So . . . what do you think?

ONE: What do I think? It's tough for me to say what I think.

TWO: I know but try.

ONE: Can't you see it in my eyes?

✳ Variation 2

No guns, fake or real, permitted in the scene. [Too obvious!]

ONE: Well?
TWO: Well?
ONE: You're late.
TWO: I know. I couldn't help it.
ONE: I understand.
TWO: I thought you would.
ONE: I have something for you.
TWO: Really?
ONE: Yes. This.

> **NOTE:** You may find the students gravitating to takeoffs of episodes from TV action/adventure shows, spy thrillers, and crime dramas with some of these variations. It's a natural enough tendency because their own entertainment diet is so saturated with hackneyed variations on these clichés. Try to discourage the trend, though, first because it stifles their originality and second because ten or so lines aren't exactly enough to earn the audience's empathy for a character shot to death in the space of forty-five seconds.

Assignment #2: Pulling Rank (Intermediate)

In a revealing chapter from Keith Johnstone's classic *Impro* (1979), the author gives a fascinating account of human beings engaged in continually shifting *status transactions* as they go about the game of pursuing their wants. All of us know people who travel through life "playing high"—sending out an "I am superior to the rest of you. Give me what I want because it is my God-given right" message to the world. Such people strong-arm their way through business deals, refuse to wait on lines, dominate conversations in social settings, expect their opinions to be taken as fact, assume haughty, aristocratic airs on the job, and require friends to defer to their every wish. Their direct counterparts are those who "play low"—sending out a message of infinite humility: "I am not worthy of your attention. Give me what I want because I am so helpless and unassuming." Such people constantly kiss up to others, win favor through excessive flattery, play on people's heartstrings, and demand that their friends forever stroke and nurture them. Of course, most of us work both ends of this spectrum and all degrees in between: by raising or lowering our status levels as the situation demands (playing *low*, for example, with a customer about to make a substantial purchase and *high* later that same day with an unruly child); or adjusting our status during a single encounter when a fresh strategy seems more promising (playing *low*, for example, when you want a teacher to agree to a request for a higher grade on a term paper and shifting into *high* when that teacher resists).

Johnstone goes into eye-opening detail, recording countless ways in which the eyes, body, and voice adjust to express overt and subtle shifts in status. It can be fun to spend some time with the kids demonstrating the various signals. They'll find themselves on familiar ground here, having practiced most of these "moves" expertly—though perhaps unconsciously—since kindergarten:

High status

moving effortlessly

sitting back with arms behind head and legs spread

checking extraneous body movement

donning sunglasses

maintaining strong eye contact

Low status

stumbling

scraping

stuttering

fidgeting with hands or feet

speaking in unfinished phrases

saying "er" before each sentence

whining

pleading

constantly breaking and restoring eye contact

The implications for them as actors are profound, since making detailed status choices in a scene allows for a much more richly shaded playing of intention. The result, according to Johnstone, is that "everything feels *easy*, and [one] doesn't experience himself as *acting* any more than he does in life, even though the actual status he's playing may be one very unfamiliar to him" (46).

Kids who grow adept at this become much better improvisers in the process, but I introduce the concept here because I've watched open scenes like these work wonders in teaching the basics of status to young actors, and at the same time training them to handle scripts more securely.

Try these dialogues three different ways, repeating them with new actors as needed: One plays high, Two plays low; One plays low, Two plays high; One and Two play either high or low, but find reason to shift status during the course of the scene.

✳ Variation 1

[A motorist has been pulled over by a cop.]

ONE: [Gets out of car and approaches motorist.] Do you have any idea how fast you were going, [sir, ma'am]?

TWO: No, I'm very sorry officer. How fast was I going?

ONE: A good twenty miles over the speed limit.

TWO: Oh . . . was I? . . . really?

ONE: Yes you were. Can I see your license and registration, please?

TWO: That may not be possible.

ONE: Not possible? I don't understand.

TWO: Maybe this will help . . .

✳ Variation 2*

[In "Sir's" Office. Two knocks on door.]

ONE: Come in. Ah, sit down Smith. I suppose you know why I sent for you?

TWO: No, sir. [One pushes a newspaper across the desk.] I was hoping you wouldn't see that.

ONE: You know we can't employ anyone with a criminal record.

TWO: Won't you reconsider?

ONE: Good-bye, Smith.

TWO: I never wanted your stinking job anyway.

[Exit Smith.]

---

*Adapted from *Impro* (Johnstone 1979)

✳ Variation 3

ONE: Did you go into my room sometime today?
TWO: Yes. I had to.
ONE: But you promised you wouldn't do that.
TWO: I know, but this time I had a good reason.
ONE: Something's missing from one of my drawers.
TWO: Really?
ONE: So you have no idea what I'm talking about?
TWO: An idea? Yes, I have an idea . . .

Assignment #3: Object Lesson (Intermediate)

This exercise allows you to demonstrate to the class in the most practical terms how to lift the energy, focus, and momentum of a scene by applying the principles of intention to the rehearsal process.

1. Select a brief scene for two characters, something that is age-appropriate and relatively easy to perform. (Suggestions for appropriate sources follow on page 107.) At the end of the period, hand copies of the script to two actors to look over at home. The next day, ask them to perform the material for the class, script in hand.
2. Evaluate the first reading. Did it feel believable, fresh, spontaneous, natural? Did it need work in particular areas? (It always does!) Now ask each actor to express what they consider to be the character's super-intention for the scene. If the answer feels murky or imprecise, continue to press for a more accurate wording—something maximally *playable*. (Weak: *I want her to know that I'm an OK kind of person.* Strong: *I want to win her admiration.*)
3. Once you and the actors have agreed upon a convincing statement of the super-intentions, spend the remainder of the period helping them to nail the beat intentions, in other words, to find the physical behaviors (blocking, stage business, attitude, use of face, voice, body, and so on) that allow the scene to *happen*, moment by moment, and then cumulatively.

   CAUTION: This exercise has its risks. It's true that sometimes, serendipitously, the most convincing, unforced results ensue when we attempt little or none of the kind of fine-tuning described above. When that occurs, the best stuff will come out of the first reading. And then what? Horrors! It means admitting to the students that there are indeed moments when the muse is on hand to provide inspiration free of charge. When the chips fall this way, it's best to offer an honest explanation. More often—*much* more often, the improvements will be inescapably apparent and the kids will be forced to acknowledge the superior quality of the results.

This assignment requires the majority of them to learn through watching rather than doing, so I usually find it unnecessary to require it of every student in the class. The purpose, remember, is *not* to model directing skills (although as a secondary benefit, that's perfectly fine) but to equip students with a method for rehearsing independently.

Sources for Scenes

Basic sources include:

Voices from the High School by Peter Dee (Baker's Plays, 1982)

University by Jon Jory (Dramatic Publishing Company, 1983)

Fables for Friends by Mark O'Donnell (Dramatists Play Service, 1984)

And Stuff by Peter Dee (Baker's Plays, 1985)

Voices from Washington High by Craig Sodaro (Dramatic Publishing Company, 1998)

Choices (Dramatic Publishing Company, 1991)

Love, Death, and the Prom by Jon Jory (Dramatic Publishing Company, 1991)

Snap Judgments (Dramatic Publishing Company, 1992)

Voices 2000 Peter Dee (Baker's Plays, 1994)

More advanced sources include:

Table Settings by James Lapine (Samuel French, 1980)

Short Plays and Monologues by David Mamet (Dramatists Play Service, 1981)

The Dining Room by A. R. Gurney (Dramatists Play Service, 1981)

Improvisation as a Rehearsal Tool

Improvisation is an umbrella term for three very different kinds of performance formats. Because they're often referred to interchangeably, it's worth taking a moment to reexamine the differences. The first type provides structures for teaching basic acting skills, such as the exercises found in Chapter 2. The second is used to develop original material for presentation to an audience (Comedy Improv, Theatre Sports, Story Theatre), a form I touch on briefly in Chapter 5. The final function is strictly utilitarian— rehearsal techniques to heighten the fluidity, spontaneity, and believability of the actors' playing of scripted scenes. It's the possibilities in this last application that we as theatre teachers too often fail to explore. We do our improv unit, gradually free the students to respond imaginatively on their feet, and then permanently shelve the work the moment they pick up their first scripts. These exercises are included as a reminder that improvisation and script work are not mutually exclusive disciplines, and that they can operate hand in hand to achieve dynamic results.

Assignments

Assignment #1: Missing Page (Basic)

Select a brief, fairly simple two-person scene—use those at the end of the previous section or any others of your choice. Give two actors a description of the setting, the situation, the character relationships, and the overall intentions, and then ask them to perform a cold reading, precisely as they did for "Vignettes" (see page 94). The sole difference in the setup for this assignment is that the last page of the script will be missing from their packets. This means that the actors must improvise their own conclusion for the scene, starting from the moment immediately following the last scripted line. The challenge is to manage the transition seamlessly, so that the audience perceives no awkward hesitations or breaks in the action. (Of course there will be no hiding the fact that they'll no longer be referring to the text!) After they've finished playing out the scene, hand them copies of a second packet, this time containing the complete original script, and ask them to pick up the reading ten lines or so before the start of their new last page. The audience can thus satisfy their curiosity by comparing the improvised version with the writer's own resolution for the scene.

These directions may seem at odds with my earlier warning against making playwrights of your actors (see page 26). But the measure of their success with this assignment does *not* lie in the cleverness or ingenuity with which they resolve the plot, but rather with the ease of their transition from scripted to improvised dialogue and the level of conviction in the give-and-take of the characters once the playwright's voice drops out. For this reason, resist asking the class which of the two endings they prefer. The point, remember, is to soften the line of separation between improv and script work.

You might think the students would have a tough time managing this format, or that they'd at least need to tackle a few rounds before becoming comfortable with it. In fact, they adjust quite easily, often improvising endings that come uncannily close to those of the playwright.

Here's the question to address in evaluating the results: Does the actors' work with the *script* have the same quality of give-and-take, overlap, spontaneous action and reaction, lurching rhythms, and moments of hesitation and fluency, as does their work with the *improv*? In other words, does it possess the same flicker of invention? This question does not imply that you want their treatment of the script to be all stumbles, *likes*, *uhs*, and *you knows*. Merely that it breathe.

✳ Variation

After a few couples have worked through the exercise, pick out a new scene and try the following variation with two volunteers who feel up for the challenge. Organize everything precisely as before, with one small difference: You will privately direct the actors, when they arrive at the bottom of the last page, to pretend to continue reading from their scripts as they improvise an ending for the scene. It is a harmless form of deception that afterward allows the class to take a stab at guessing the exact location of the playwright's last line, which—if the actors do their job expertly—the audience will be at a loss to identify.

Assignment #2: Parallel Scenes (Intermediate)

Gather together copies of a handful of short two-person scenes, again similar to those listed at the end of the last section. Select a script, call up two volunteers, and provide them with all necessary background information: a nutshell description of the setting, characters, situation, and overall intentions. Allow them to improvise the scene from start to finish *before* they've had any opportunity to examine the script. Then hand them copies of the actual text and ask them to perform a cold reading. Repeat with new scenes and new actors as needed.

Despite what are likely to be significant differences in content between the improvised and scripted interpretations of these scenes, the first try is almost certain to have a greater edge of vitality and freshness. That is the special by-product of a well-improvised scene. And it's the hoped-for purpose of this exercise to allow the spontaneity of the improv to infect the actors' subsequent work with the script. It's a delicate operation, to be sure, hardly a simple matter of cut-and-paste. But if you can highlight for the students the improvised moments that felt especially honest and vibrant, they're frequently able to transfer that energy directly to the playwright's lines.

I've sometimes experimented with the reverse form of this technique, trying to resuscitate a stale or tepid performance of a script by having the actors substitute improvised lines for those of the author. Once in a while the experience will help them connect emotionally with material that has for whatever reason failed to catch fire. More often they'll get stuck trying awkwardly to paraphrase the playwright, or worse, slide repeatedly into and out of the original dialogue, despite all efforts to the contrary.

Scenes for Class Study and Invited Audiences

Heart of the Program: Theatre Scenes

The moment arrives in the training of any group of actors when growth is no longer possible without the stimulus of public performance. An impartial audience becomes the actor's ultimate teacher; through them he learns over time what does and doesn't work. At some point the kids seem to sense this need to open the studio doors and test themselves beyond the safety of their fellow classmates. If you don't suggest bringing in outside audiences, it's a good bet they eventually will.

The first acting class I taught founded the twenty-year tradition of Theatre Scenes at my high school. About halfway through the course we hit on the idea of breaking into small groups, rehearsing a handful of ten- to fifteen-minute scripts using minimal sets, costumes, and props, testing the scenes in class for criticism and feedback, and then performing them for invited audiences during the school day according to a fixed schedule.

The project caught on. Within a few years it had become a once-or-twice-a-semester feature of the school's calendar of special events. Audiences consisted of teachers willing to accompany their subject classes plus students with a corresponding free period. We felt as if we'd discovered the perfect vehicle for translating classroom theory into practice.

The setup carries important secondary benefits as well. By bringing theatre into the open, by granting it regular and frequent public exposure, the program is put on the map. Kids will be more tempted to sign up because they'll realize after watching the scenes that yeah, they can do that, while others will simply want in on the action. It's a way to make theatre a popular, as opposed to an elitist, presence in school life by drawing kids from every social stratum to both the classes and—most important—the audiences.

Theatre Scenes benefits you as the teacher too because it establishes an immediate goal for your students—a reason to cut the nonsense and get down to work. Nothing motivates kids so well as the realization that, before the lapse of a few weeks, a rush of their peers will come stampeding down the halls to become an audience for their work, that the room will go dark and the stage lights come up, that all eyes will face front, curious to check out whatever they have to put before them.

Adolescents as a group aren't known for their foresightedness, so even these realities won't always ensure you three weeks of intense, highly focused rehearsal. But they will certainly help jump-start the kids, who'll know from the second they're assigned a scene that their moment of reckoning lies a fixed number of days ahead.

A few students may momentarily freak out from the tension of having to get out there and perform for an outside audience. But most, so far as I can tell, do not wilt from the pressure; on the contrary, they become far stronger players because of it. And the audiences are exposed to a hell of a lot more theatre than would normally touch their lives: Molière, Shakespeare, Williams, Miller, Pinter, and Wilde on the one hand; excerpts from TV sitcoms, teen flicks, SNL sketches, and soap opera or movie parodies on the other; and a generous helping of Simon, Allen, Wasserstein, Lucas, and Durang in between.

The plan is ambitious but worth the effort. It's the best format I know for turning fledgling actors into seasoned troupers and for awakening audiences of television addicts to the crackle of live theatre.

Theatre Scenes Logistics: Setting Up Shop

The Administrative Nod

There's no point in passing go on any of these preliminaries unless you first secure the principal's support for the project. *Theatre*

Scenes means introducing change, and as any teacher who's been around the system for awhile knows, principals by and large resist change, especially when it involves adding to the size of their daily workload. That's why it makes sense to have thought through every detail before you request a meeting, complete with Alternate Plans B, C, and D, to accommodate any and all contingencies—none of which, you promise, will impinge on the administrator's time or work schedule. Two days and six periods of performances are way over the top? Fine, you'll manage everything during two periods of a single day. Acting students missing subject classes to perform scenes is out of the question? Fine, you'll arrange it so that kids perform during their lunch or unassigned periods. Only English and social studies teachers will be permitted to bring their classes? No problem. You can work with that.

If you're a teacher who has *not* been around the system for awhile, your rookie status can be your greatest bargaining chip. Passion and commitment are always irresistible—or nearly always. Make them work in your favor.

Student Readiness

If your pitch gets the administrative green light, you'll next need to decide on the best time to set the wheels in motion. It means everything to the success of the project to choose that time wisely. Expose your actors to the roar of the madding crowd before they're ready and the results can prove fatal. In a full-year course for beginning students, I generally start work on the first round of scenes just after Christmas vacation. Four months—September through December—are the absolute minimum required to make any substantial headway with the basic skills (see Chapters 2 and 3). At the end of that period, the group should be champing at the bit. If for any reason they're not, the unit can be postponed indefinitely until you feel comfortable that all systems are go.

Never lose sight of the fact that, for some of your students, this venture will mark a major event: their acting debut before the public. And a very tricky and unpredictable public it is. Many students will be nervous, even terrified. They'll need lots of stroking and positive reinforcement, probably the most valuable of which is your assurance that everything will be laid out in carefully measured steps:

- preliminary rehearsals
- dress rehearsals for the class alone
- constructive feedback from classmates and teacher
- polishing sessions
- performances

The bottom line is your promise that their preparation will be so complete by the time those performances roll around that, apart from the trace of nervousness all actors depend on for heightened alertness, they'll enter the stage tuned up and ready to go.

Rehearsal Space

I was lucky in that the auditorium, which lay a few steps away from our usual home in the choral room, was almost always available during the four weeks of preparation for Theatre Scenes. This meant a space big enough to accommodate six or seven separate rehearsal groups, each with its own assigned area. For the duration of the unit, everyone observed the same daily ritual: arrived in class, met up with their partner, got their copy of the script, arranged some skeletal furniture in their work space, rehearsed. We used every available spot—a piece of stage floor, a portion of the orchestra pit, a square of carpet adjacent to the exit doors. Tensions soared only when the room was set up for upcoming concerts or full-stage productions. That required an extra sharp warning of *"Hands off!"*

This arrangement, if you can obtain it, is ideal. It means having everyone physically present at the same time and place, and being able to monitor the kids' progress in all parts of the room, even if from afar. Although a few may occasionally take advantage of your involvement with other students to slack off and formulate plans for the weekend, usually after the first five minutes or so they'll begin work in earnest.

Setting up rehearsal furniture is important because it allows the actors to practice inside a fixed environment, however makeshift, and thereby greatly enhances their belief in the scene. So their first job is always to lay out whatever substitute furniture is at hand—a music stand over here to represent a table, three side-by-side chairs directly upstage of it for a couch, and so on. The addition of a few useful props is better still.

Sometimes the actors complain that they can do just as well without all these trappings, but I consider the point worth pressing. Without benefit of a bare bones set, they'll invariably find themselves sitting on the floor day after day, scripts in hand, using class time to memorize dialogue. "What's the deal, guys?" "Oh, we're just going over our lines." And there they'll remain until the bell.

If you're conducting these rehearsals in a typical classroom, the whole effort is obviously made a lot more difficult. You may have to petition the superpowers to grant you special dispensation for a few weeks' use of the auditorium. But if that's simply not to be, it's better to concentrate on one group each day and allow other groups to run lines or discuss staging than it is to abandon the effort altogether.

Choice of Material and Scene Partners

Which scenes and which actors for which roles? This is a critical step because the kids' feelings about what characters their friends in the audience will get to see them play, whom they're working with, and what kind of material you feel is right for them will obviously run high. It would be nice to be guided in these choices by a handy set of objective criteria. Unfortunately, no such convenient checklist exists. Here are a few guidelines:

- Choose age-appropriate material.
- Try, especially with the first round of scenes, to match actors with characters not too distant from the world of their experience—for that reason, naturalistic rather than stylized choices work best.
- Avoid characters with accents, unless the actor has an excellent head start with the vowel, pitch, and rhythmic patterns of the specific dialect.
- Find scenes that, if performed expertly, stand a good chance of engaging a high school audience (that would probably eliminate Eliot's *The Cocktail Party* and Racine's *Andromache*, though not necessarily Wilde's *The Importance of Being Earnest* or Anouilh's *Antigone*).
- Remember that there is material beyond the ability range of even the best high school performers (O'Neill's *Mourning Becomes Elektra* and Ibsen's *The Master Builder* qualify nicely).

These are commonsense items, but I can't name a single one I haven't violated—more than once. It comes down in the end to a simple knack for casting, for matching actor and role so that each student in the class is ultimately revealed in the best possible light.

I spoke earlier of the dangers of playing into the hands of kids who press exclusively for crowd-pleasing, hot-from-the-multiplex, surefire hits. A tiny dessert portion of these is acceptable. But don't allow the mix to become disproportionately skewed. You'll sacrifice the spirit of the program over the long haul and cheat your audiences in the process.

One practice I've found helpful in the tricky task of selecting the right material for the right actors is to ask everyone, about three weeks prior to the start of rehearsals, to fill out an index card containing the following information:

Name _____ Homeroom _____

Unassigned Periods _____

1. Can you name a specific role and/or scene that you'd enjoy working on? _____

2. If no, can you describe a type of character you'd feel comfortable playing? _____

3. Can you name a student in the class you'd feel comfortable working with? _____

There are risks involved here, and serious questions can arise. What happens if kids write down suggestions for roles unsuited to their abilities? Or ask to rehearse movie scenes that encourage imitation of other actors' performances? What if they expose themselves to embarrassment when the friends they *haven't* requested as scene partners somehow find out they've been passed over? Three good questions, and here are three good responses, all of which need to be announced loudly, slowly, and clearly—twice!—the day the cards are distributed:

1. This request for preferences is *not* a guarantee that students will get what they've asked for. It's being made to help the teacher formulate ideas she may not otherwise have considered. (In reviewing their preferences, I've often looked at a student's card and thought: "Oh, of course. Definitely. I

would never have come up with that character choice for Jessica. But sure . . . why not? She could pull it off!" When a student's suggestions are inappropriate or unrealistic, it's understood in advance that I'll simply ignore them—respectfully and discreetly, of course.)

2. There is a rule for approving requests for film scenes: The students are all honor bound to assign someone else the task of transcribing the dialogue to the printed page—a friend or a parent. An ideal arrangement, if two groups in a class are performing scenes from films, is for one to agree to type up the script for the other—for example, the *Rainman* cast prepares the transcription for the *Diner* cast, and vice versa. That way, the actors start rehearsals with only a distant memory of the original. To bypass this requirement means that the students, as they pause to record the dialogue from a rented videotape—line after line after line—are virtually forced through osmosis to assimilate and then copy the intentions, gestures, inflections, and characterizations of the original performers. Many screenplays, of course, are readily available in published form, and when that's the case, it's the way to go. Incidentally, I've sometimes gotten surprised reactions from colleagues when they learn that I allow students to attempt film scenes. Apart from the danger of copying the original, I can't see a reason for the objection other than snobbery. When a scene is inherently cinematic, in other words, when it shifts location constantly from car, to restaurant, to living room, it can usually be adapted with minimal effort for the stage. If it can't, I'm often able to locate a scene from a play that features a character close in temperament and spirit to the one originally requested by the student.

3. The idea of pairing up actors who express an interest in working together seems to me a reasonable enough accommodation, and the students understand that I will arrange it whenever possible. If not, no hard feelings. They also have my assurance that, without exception, these requests will remain strictly confidential.

Calendar

As soon as you've finalized the script choices and cast the actors, it's time to prepare an itinerary that can be copied and distributed.

This sheet, a sample of which appears below, gives everyone a sense of what's planned for a particular day and how much time remains before the scheduled performances. I also append a list of tips—helpful reminders, if you will. The work process itself, the ten steps that guide the actors as they rehearse the scenes in class each period plus the guidelines for the feedback session, is described in detail in the next section of the book (see pages 121–143).

Four weeks from start to finish, beginning with the first organizing session and ending with the two days of performances, is the maximum time frame for this project. Any more is a sure invitation to boredom. If you can swing it, a three-week schedule is optimal for a possible second round of scenes scheduled later in the school year. The students, already feeling the heat of the audience breathing down their necks, will be pressed to take their scripts in hand and get down to business.

THEATRE SCENES CALENDAR				
JANUARY				
MON	TUE	WED	THU	FRI
6 Preliminary rehearsals	7	8 Teacher works with two scenes per day	9	10
13	14	15	16	17
20 No more scripts	21	22 Dress rehearsals in front of class: two scenes each day (no regular rehearsals)	23	24
27	28 Polishing rehearsals	29	30	31 Performances

Tips are printed on the reverse side of the calendar sheet and distributed among the students.

- Your partner is absent one or more days? Use class time for line memorization and schedule extra rehearsals at home after school.

- Need help gathering props, costumes, sound and light

cues? Ask the teacher or friends who may be able to supply what you're looking for.

- Have trouble with line memorization? Try assembling the cast and taping the scene on an audiocassette—OR—try the index card method—OR—have a friend sit down and read through the scene with you (see pages 137–138).

- Need help because you're not sure about your character? Try using a real-life model whose vocal and physical mannerisms seem in your imagination to match those of the character.

- Forgot your script? Two extras are stored in folders on top of the filing cabinet. Return it at the end of the period. Once they're gone, you're out of luck.

Dress Rehearsal, Feedback, and Last-Minute Concerns

The dress rehearsals should be performed, two scenes per period, following the last day of preliminary rehearsals. It may help to assign grades, if only to underscore the seriousness of this stage of the process. Everyone must be clear about their turn at bat; time is short and there's no room for reshuffling the schedule ("Oh, we thought we were supposed to go Friday!"). Make it clear that absence from school that day is out of the question.

Dress rehearsal means that the actors come to class with their lines memorized, their props and furniture fully organized (I usually keep a beat-up couch, a few chairs, and two futons on hand—the rest the kids know they have to provide themselves), and their costumes, sound cues, and light changes, if any, at the ready. A quick, efficient setup is crucial because the minutes pass quickly and *must* in fairness be shared equally between the two groups.

In real life, this description applies, oh, maybe once in ten times. These are still high school kids, and many will have their litany of excuses lined up. It's important, though, to set a precedent of requiring everyone to proceed with the dress rehearsals as scheduled. To do otherwise is certain death. The slackers, unfortunately, lose more than grade points; they miss a chance to build confidence on the success of the first public exposure of their work.

Conversely, the groups who've "got their act together" enjoy instant returns. I try to anticipate which scenes these might be and make sure to place them at the top of the running order, since the examples of preparedness have their psychological impact on the scenes to come. The greatest benefit for beginning actors in this whole process is the effect it produces: "Oh, so *this* is what it feels like to go through the whole thing nonstop with other people watching!" It's a healthy adrenaline rush!

The feedback session follows immediately (see pages 142–143). Since so little time is available, I take the lead in giving notes, much as I would after the run-through of a full-length play I was directing. The audience, because this is a classroom setting, can then add their observations. I ask them to make their comments clear, constructive, and most of all brief—to contribute only those points the actors can *use* to their advantage.

I have a standard speech that I deliver at the end of the final day of preparation, just after the last polishing rehearsal and before the good luck send-off: "Any last-minute needs must be addressed now. Don't approach me tomorrow during the frenzy of performances about digging up an extra script or lending you the keys to the costume room. I'm here for you today. Tomorrow I'm on automatic pilot."

The Big Day

No amount of well-meaning advice will stave off the unexpected. I can only share a few commonsense strategies that have helped in the past to clear away distractions on "the big day" and inspire kids to perform at their best. Some items are best arranged in advance:

- Set up large rectangular tables offstage, if feasible, where props for all scenes scheduled on that day can be conveniently organized and stored.
- Make sure a changing area, if available, is accessible.
- Check to be sure the lighting or sound effects equipment is in working order.
- Set up enough chairs to accommodate the audience.
- Try to have at least one other adult (a school aide or monitor) present during performance periods.

- Give your audiences a thirty-second intro to each scene, filling them in on necessary background information. I used to assign this task to the kids, but it distracted them from getting into focus for the scene.

- Remind all actors that they need to strip the stage bare in preparation for the next group and that, because of time pressures, this needs to happen quickly!

A Ten-Step Approach to Scene Rehearsal

In offering this ten-point list, I'm not suggesting that actors in the real world create life onstage in stepwise progression, through a graduated, paint-by-numbers approach. But there are some important differences about this first "big" assignment that you can't forget to figure into the equation—first, that most of your students have never been down this path before, and second, that they're working without benefit of a director. This last fact is crucial. It's true you'll be spending portions of class time with the individual groups, but that's not the same for them as having a full-time observer on hand each day to monitor progress and make the big decisions. They'll need solid footing, and this sequence of steps, while no guarantee, will give the kids a course to steer by and a means to function independently of the teacher.

For most of the ten days of preliminary rehearsals, you'll be using the first few minutes of class time to demonstrate the purpose of a new technique, so that when they break up to work on their own, the actors will have a specific point of focus to pursue for the period. It used to infuriate me when students in a particular group did not obediently follow my demonstration of Step #5 with thirty minutes of concentrated rehearsal on Step #5. Don't sweat this one—I've learned over time that everyone moves at a different pace and that it's pointless to insist on any uniform rate of progress. Your students may honestly be stuck at Step #3, or busy inventing steps of their own.

Use the annotated descriptions that follow as a resource to shepherd them along. Make copies of the list for the kids, too, so they can refer to it as needed.

Step #1: Organizing Sessions and Read-Through of the Script (Day 1)

Any rules about the conduct of rehearsals should be announced at the beginning of the period—absence policy, calendar concerns, what to do if you forget to bring your script to class, and so on. Keep it short; everyone is impatient to get to the good stuff.

Next, run down the list of who's working with whom, seat the groups separately, and hand out copies of the scripts. You'll want an orderly first day, so it goes without saying that this mound of paper should be collated and stapled in advance.

Start with a straight oral read-through—no more, no less. I specify *oral* because now and then a group will misinterpret my directions and begin with a silent reading; that's a deadly way to experience the scene for the first time. Kids will usually pass over an edited introduction, so make sure they read that aloud too. If none exists, make the rounds and relay the necessary background information individually.

There's only one essential point the students must absorb before taking this initial step: *Don't pick up the script and start "emoting."* Most of them have never seen the material before; they're in the early stages of a growth process. Encourage everyone to relax and enjoy this first reading. It's not an audition. To try for clever inflections, dramatic pauses, impressive climaxes at this stage is to build a false foundation that will only need to be dismantled as rehearsals progress. So the instructions are simple: Just read aloud together. That doesn't mean consciously striving for a flat, toneless delivery—just avoiding a display of effects.

Invariably a group will arrive at the end of their last page and volunteer a quick capsule review: "This scene sucks." Comments like these no longer throw me. I just ask that they trust my judgment and wait patiently for the scene's riches to be revealed through rehearsal. Some years back I'd have gone home and fished out a few alternate choices. I didn't want to disappoint anyone. The kids would usually thank me. "Some of these are better," they'd say, "but we still haven't made up our minds. Bring in a few more tomorrow and we'll let you know if anything looks interesting."

As a follow-up to this first reading, is it an absolute must for the students to get hold of and study the complete text of the play? Unless the scene is self-contained, the answer must be *yes*. How can the actors represent the characters fully without a complete knowledge of their relationships with other characters in the play, their development from first scene to last, their actions before and after the events of the piece they're rehearsing?

That said, I will admit there have been times, even many times, when I've been forced to waive this requirement. A majority of the plays will not be available at local libraries. Obtaining them through interloan may take too long. Others will be purchasable only through catalogues or specialty bookstores. I always hope the students will *want* to go out of their way to hunt down these scripts, but money, time, or expediency may be a legitimate concern. When any of these conditions apply, I try to fill in the blanks when I sit down with each group. But, I admit, this is a poor substitute for the real thing. One way to avoid the problem is to select and cast the scenes a good two months in advance, then distribute copies of the plays weeks prior to the start of rehearsals, permitting the kids to read and study the texts on their own. However, I don't know too many teachers with either the time or the budget to afford this kind of luxury.

Step #2: Production Elements (Day 1)*

I press the students to get through these first two steps on day one. In fact, if one or two groups don't finish them, I'll ask that they get together that night, complete the job for homework, and hand everything in at the start of class the next day. I set a brisk pace here because I want to downplay the fancy tech stuff and place the greater emphasis on the power of their acting to carry the scene. Here are the minimum essentials:

- Take paper and pencil and sketch out a crude approximation of your set (a small dresser over here, two futons center, a night table LC, a foot stool DR, etc.). Some or all of these details can be amended later on.
- Include on the back a complete prop list.
- Explain any special lighting needs and sound effects (the chirping of birds at the opening, a wash of bright light

---

*All *day* references are offered only as suggestions.

when the dialogue begins, a pool of concentrated light stage center just before the blackout).

- Find someone in the class outside your cast who will agree to run tech for all performances—bring up the lights, operate the tape recorder, etc.

I collect the sheets and keep them on hand for easy reference.

Don't make too much fuss over any of the production elements. It's not a catastrophe if fluorescent light is your only source of illumination. The lack of theatrical equipment is not going to mark the difference between success and failure on a project like this. Technical wizardry is beside the point. Some kids, those with a strong aptitude for design, may go home and sketch an elevation of their set in full color. I'd give them every encouragement, but I wouldn't penalize those who stuck with the basics. Something I do insist on is the actors' promise to bring to school as many rehearsal props as possible—anything to help further their belief in the scene.

Step #3: Reading for Communication (Days 2 and 3)

This is a critical stage in the work, the more so because the instructions are so deceptively simple: *Reread the scene with your acting partner(s), but this time make the script disappear.* There is no urgent need yet for character transformation, analysis of intentions, or scene beats. You want the kids merely to sit facing each other and use the dialogue as the basis for a believable conversation between "Brian" and "Jackie." The acid test is one I described in the last chapter: They must be so well connected that a person walking casually through the room would assume, were it not for the scripts, that the two were engaged in an actual conversation, not rehearsing a scene for their acting class.

What this does, if the actors really begin throwing and receiving the ball, is to trigger the start of some genuine communication between them. The change, when and if it comes, can arrive as a delicious shock to the actors' nervous systems; they'll feel a bit giddy, like jazz musicians improvising in perfect synch. A volley of action and reaction will take hold, and they'll internalize the scene in a whole new way. (A more detailed explanation for achieving this flow can be found in the "Vignettes" exercise in Chapter 3, page 94, and in the Action/Reaction step late in this chapter, pages 139–141.)

This process of give-and-take is more than a happy addition to the students' technique; it's part of the foundation. Without it, we get that off-key effect so typical of bad actors, even some potentially talented ones, who seem to inhabit an invisible bubble, never *truly* listening, waiting patiently for their turn to speak but lacking the familiar response signals—the encouraging nods, shifting of features, surprised pauses, disbelieving glances, involuntary body movements—the whole inventory of responses that register not only when we're speaking but actually *hearing* what others say. In life we do this all the time, never consciously thinking, "Oh, she just acknowledged my point since I notice she's shaking her head *yes*." It's all part of an unconscious exchange. In the theatre, because we don't yet own the words or the circumstances, we must begin by creating these conditions deliberately, but *without* letting the technique show.

If the students seem lost in all this, advise them to spend one full day observing real-life conversations more closely; the light-bulb over their heads will pop on, and they'll understand the simple act of conversation in a whole new way.

So much for the theory; here's the application. Begin by asking a couple of students to bring their scripts to the front of the room, and set their chairs directly facing each other. I find that they can usually get off to a decent start, allowing their faces and voices to interact convincingly for a few lines or so, but they invariably lose the thread by the middle of the first page and revert to old habits, without even noticing the lapse. To allow all this to sink in you must stop them, many times if necessary, and point out where they've strayed. It's when they pause to acknowledge the derailment *themselves* ("Hold on a second. We lost it!") that you know they're getting somewhere with this.

Following the demonstration, all students should sit with their scene partners, select a single page or less of dialogue, and work on this skill for a good fifteen minutes. You don't want any line memorization to be taking place just yet. If it does, the actors aren't really on task. At this point you *want* them to use the scripts and at the same time, of course, *not* to use them.

Give all the scenes a turn in front of the class, and if necessary extend the exercise into part of a second day. But the process doesn't end there. The ability to give-and-take, once acquired, always seems ready to slip away. Keep on top of it—and your students.

One afterthought: I assume with a group of beginners that the vast majority of the pieces you choose for this first round will be naturalistic in tone. Stylized scenes, scenes of heightened lyricism, romanticism, verse, fantasy, and so on, are more challenging and don't yield as easily to this approach. They should be taken up later in the year, or—depending on the course offerings in your school—in an advanced acting class.

Step #4: Creating the Character (Day 4)

As soon as "Brian" and "Jackie" can employ the script to carry on a believable conversation as themselves, they're ready to slide ever so gently into the body and voice of their characters. Keep in mind that, to help make the transition easier, I've already consulted their index cards and chosen scripts with characters close to these actors in age and temperament. That way I've made sure that their first public acting experience is a hop off the diving board instead of a grand leap. Shameless typecasting? By narrowing the possibilities in this way, do they end up hardly having to act at all?

I remember a first-timer who had a tremendous success on our stage as Joseph Wykowski in *Biloxi Blues*. "Still," someone commented to me after a performance, "he wasn't exactly acting, was he? That was just Phil up there." The implication was that he deserved only minimal credit for skillfully recreating someone so like himself. I don't buy this line of reasoning. In addition to the mechanics of line memorization, the mastery of stage business and blocking, there's the challenge for the neophyte of internalizing the lines and making them convincingly his own (he was *not* Wykowski), and interacting truthfully with the other characters in the cast. Should we take off points because he and Wykowski shared certain traits?

Inexperienced actors gain confidence onstage by degrees. A shy junior might show an intuitive understanding of Adrian in *Rocky*; later in the semester, she could be ready for the greater complexity of Laura Wingfield; toward the end of her senior year, for the brashness of Saint Joan or Annie Sullivan. I've witnessed this phenomenon countless times. But the process can't be rushed.

I'm not saying that exceptions, even *many* exceptions, can't be made for kids already prepared to take that giant step outside themselves. Lots of students stay with theatre precisely because they love the chance it gives them to shed their identities and become whomever they least resemble. We rehearsed a scene from Osborn's *Morning's at Seven* a while back. The student who played Homer was a hulking kid, captain of the wrestling team. He portrayed this endearing schnook with a sweet, innocent edge and not even a trace of winking sarcasm. The audiences were understandably won over. Any time an actor is able to transcend his presumed limits, everyone—teacher, actor, audience—is enriched in the process (especially in a high school, where kids guard their public images so fiercely). To stretch is important, even for beginners. But only when they're ready and only when you, their teacher, say so. (One hint of that readiness, by the way, is to recall which students responded most comfortably to the "Against Type" improvs in Chapter 2 [see pages 82–84]).

This same graduated approach applies to the preparation of an assigned role. The average high school theatre student is not ready for the full Stanislavski treatment; many (not all) lack the emotional maturity and seriousness to plumb the full depth of their characters. I've tested this proposition over the years, assigning them lengthy character diaries that trace family background, political leanings, career descriptions, relationships with offstage characters, and so on. I've required them to analyze closely in writing and through class discussion "what the character says . . . what the character does . . . what others in the play say about the character . . . what he says about himself . . . what he probably eats for breakfast. . . ." The kids generally do the homework. But most grow impatient when they can't find the means to manifest all this newly acquired knowledge onstage—in both physical and emotional terms.

Where, then, do your actors begin their all-important search for a sharply etched character? With a mental picture of a human being that can only grow out of their imaginations as they read and reread the script. This is the one element of the craft that I agree can't be taught; the image rises from mysterious places inside the performer's consciousness. The drooping chin, sloping shoulders, shuffling gait, and birdlike glances that together seem so appropriate in a portrayal of, let's say, Miss Gaunt in *Jean Brodie* don't emerge as items compounded from a textbook checklist. Clearly the process is organic, and it's never finished in a day.

What's needed at the onset is some kind of Open Sesame, a

shortcut if you will, into the heart and soul of the character that will set the internal engines running. Almost any introduction is better than analytic discussions. They may yield insights, but not enough of these are transferred directly to the actor's nervous systems. Start with the physical and the rest will fall into place. I've found leading the students through some explorations of walk and voice to be a perfect beginning. So the day before the class is set to move ahead to step four, I ask the actors to spend some time at home experimenting, trying on and discarding a few possibilities in private. Then in class the next day we perform two exercises, "Three Chairs" and "Vocalise."

Three Chairs

Set three chairs in a row, leaving maximum space between them. One student goes onstage and walks from chair A to chair B as herself, then—as she moves past B to C—begins to take on the walk of the character. The transformation can be gradual rather than immediate. You can watch and afterward suggest appropriate changes. (If the room is small, you can use two chairs and have the actor make the transition as she doubles back from B to A.) Repeat with the remaining students.

Vocalise

Have the students in each scene choose a page or so excerpt from their script and then come before the class, one group at a time, striving—as in step three, "Reading for Communication"—for maximum communication. This time, though, they start the reading as themselves and then perhaps halfway through gradually slide into the voices of their characters. If they feel no need to assume a vocal quality hugely different from their own, don't force some artificial sound on them just for the sake of novelty. If, for example, actresses performing a scene from *Steel Magnolias* feel terminally awkward about mastering the southern dialect, it's preferable for them to retain their own speech patterns and adjust their voices to the *personalities* of the characters than to butcher the dialogue with an off-key version of a Louisiana accent. In short, it's better to use something close to one's own voice than to fall into something fake.

Again, follow up on the readings with your suggestions and

observations. Let me reemphasize that for this work, most of the choices should spring from the imaginations of the actors; intuition will be their most reliable guide. It's when intuition fails that I fall back on the bag of skills we explored in the character improv section (see Chapter 2, pages 77–79):

- using a prop to suggest a character (a clipboard for Kathy in *Vanities*);
- using a costume element to suggest a character (Thelma's housedress in *'Night Mother*);
- suggesting that an actor seek inspiration for a character in the mannerisms of someone she knows personally; and
- suggesting that an actor find within himself qualities of personality that seem appropriate for the character.

None of this material, though, is reviewed formally. It's all pulled out as needed. I also hit hard the point that these exercises in voice and walk aren't the beginning and end of their study of character. It's scarcely the business of day four alone. There should be fresh growth each day. I really do find, though, even among high school students, that after a brief exploratory period performers develop what I can only describe as a proprietary relationship with their characters. It's by far the most important work they do and, ironically, the part for which they should least require the teacher's intervention.

Step #5: Finding the Intentions (Days 5 and 6)

This is an ideal time in the rehearsal schedule for the students to begin breaking down the intentions. Regardless of how many days the class spent on "Intention and the Script" with their work on the exercises from Chapter 3, you'll need to take some additional time at the start of this lesson to review the basics (see page 95). The excerpt that follows will stand as proof that the principles that apply to an analysis of a scene from a repertory classic like *Much Ado About Nothing* remain essentially in place for an analysis of a scene from a good sitcom: studying the character's behavior for the length of the scene and then asking, "What basically does he want here?" (the answer gives the super-intention), and "How does he go about getting it?" (the answer gives you your beat intentions).

A simple way to review the material is to reproduce copies of the following script and distribute them among the students. It's a brief excerpt from Baumeister's early one-act play *Bachelor Pad* in which the main characters, Tom and Alex, meet up with their blind dates at the local Grease Pit. Have four volunteers perform a cold reading in front of the room, seating them as if at a table in a seedy restaurant. Then ask members of the audience to collaborate on naming the super and beat intentions as if they were playing the role of Tom. Once all the students feel satisfied with their individual responses, they should each pencil them directly onto the script.

Their likely response when they share these in discussion: "He wants to impress the girls." Sure. That's a reasonable choice of super-intention. But knowing just this much may not give the actor the spark he needs to ignite the scene. Suppose at a given moment we decide he wants *to dazzle them,* or *to wow them with his sophistication,* or *to destroy them with his sex appeal?* Struggling to find the right verbs will make for a world of difference in the playing of the beat intentions. Demonstrate this for the class by having the volunteer actors apply these newly phrased intentions to their reading of the scene.

The next step is to explain that the activity they've just completed is the one they are now to apply to their assigned theatre scenes. Allow them the remainder of the lesson to do this, but make sure everyone finishes the assignment by the end of class so you can collect the scripts and spend some time overnight (a weekend is best) sifting through and commenting on their choices. Complications will crop up. A few students may be puzzled over how best to word the beat intentions; or they may be at a complete loss to phrase the super-intention. No sweat. This is a first shot, and you're on hand to help.

[The Grease Pit. GUYS are still seated in the same position as the GIRLS, age fifteen or so, enter.]

JULIE: [Near the entrance. To TAMMY.] Now remember . . . act sophisticated and normal. [THEY arrive at the table.] HI!! [A stupid, obviously fake voice.] I'm Julie and this is TAMMY!

TOM: Oh, like Tammy Baker! [Long pause. No response.] Jim and Tammy Baker? [HE shifts nervously in his seat.] Well . . . anyway . . .

ALEX: How ya doin'? I'm Alex.

TAMMY: [To TOM] What's your name?

TOM: It's classified.

TAMMY: What?

TOM: It's classified. You see, I could tell you, but then I'd have to kill you. [Long pause as the two girls look at one another in total disbelief. HE smiles.] *TOP GUN?!* Tom Cruise says it in *Top Gun.* [Another pause as ALEX buries his head in his hands.]

ALEX: Anyway . . . so . . . uh . . . how old are you guys?

JULIE: Twenty.

TAMMY: [Almost simultaneously.] Twenty, too.

ALEX: What?

TAMMY: I'm twenty, too. You know . . . she's twenty, and I'm twenty, too! Uh . . . ALSO?!

TOM: You guys go to college?

JULIE: Yeah . . . uh . . . Albany.

TAMMY: [Again, almost simultaneously.] Yeah . . . we . . . uh . . . Albany too!

TOM: That's good. You guys major in anything yet, or . . . [Pause.]

TAMMY: History.

JULIE: General studies. You know . . . a little bit of everything.

TOM: [Gestures ". . . a little bit of everything . . ." She returns the gesture with a lightly mocking smile.]

TAMMY: So . . . what do you guys do?

TOM: I'm a sanitational engineer.

JULIE and TAMMY: Oh . . . garbageman!

TOM: Garbageman! [THEY exchange knowing smiles.]

ALEX: [To save the situation.] So . . . you guys about ready to order?

JULIE: Sure . . . okay . . . cool. [THEY all look over menus.] Oh, Tammy, wanna split a Greek pizza?

TOM: A pizza?! Why come to a nice restaurant like this and order pizza?

TAMMY: You call this a nice restaurant?

ALEX: Hey, the Grease Pit is a *very* nice restaurant.

TAMMY: I'm sure.

TOM: There's nothing wrong with the Grease Pit.

ALEX: I think I'll have one of those, too. [TOM gives ALEX a look.]

TOM: Anyway, I'm gonna have the chicken cutlet parmigiana.

JULIE: Ooooh! There's an original order. [ALL but TOM laugh.]

TOM: You can't get that at a school cafeteria!

JULIE: Yeah, you can!

TOM: You can *not*!

ALEX: Tom! I don't think she needs your sarcastic answers, okay?

TOM: You want answers?! YOU WANT ANSWERS?! I want the truth! YOU CAN'T HANDLE THE TRUTH. [Pause. He smiles.] *A Few Good Men*, remember? Jack Nicholson? [No reaction.]

In editing what the kids have designated as the characters' intentions for their own scenes, focus each and every time on making certain that they've chosen active, playable verbs—choices they can lean into both physically and emotionally. There will be a few students in the class—those who've always had an aversion to English grammar—still unclear in their understanding of the term *actable verb* or, for that matter, any kind of *verb* at all. You'll find on the pages of their scripts notations like "He's being a flirt here." or "She's very upset with his attitude." or "He wants a ton of money." Keep pulling them back, again and again, to the phrase "I want *to* . . ." or "I want to get her *to* . . ." or "I want *to* make them . . ." until it becomes a matter of habit. Actors love throwing out adjectives and nouns and will try at every turn to wriggle out of committing themselves to a good, solid actable verb.

When you return the scripts to the kids the next day, spend a few minutes with each group, answering their questions and helping them to interpret your comments, suggestions, and corrections. Then proceed to step six.

Step #6: Intention and Staging (Days 6, 7, 8, 9, and 10)

It's the middle of the sixth day of preliminary rehearsals, and someone in the class is bound to have noticed that there's been no talk yet about staging these scenes. Even kids who haven't given the subject much conscious thought will probably be impatient by now to get up from their chairs and begin working out the "moves."

And that raises a good question: What's the best way, exactly, to proceed with the formidable task of blocking the action—figuring out crosses, stage business, positions of characters in relation to each other?

For anyone in the class who's had a role in a formal production, the realistic answer is, "Easy. You do whatever the director tells you." And that's true. Whenever a show is being mounted on a large scale with a large cast, the director *must* dictate most or all of the blocking. The success of the play depends on it. And not just in order to avert collisions among aimlessly drifting actors. Effective blocking is one of two principal means at the director's disposal for communicating the *interior* action of the play to the audience. It's the way he uses the actors' bodies to *say* the text—to "turn psychology into behavior," as Elia Kazan put it.* (Working with the actors to pin down the intentions is the other way.) Staging a play is a slowly acquired skill, one that's filled the greater part of several full-length textbooks. So offering the students a detailed unit in the fundamentals of focus, movement, composition, and picturization makes little practical sense at this point. What does make sense, since these are mostly two- to four-person scenes to be mounted on a small stage by the kids themselves, with only intermittent help from the teacher, is to keep your presentation simple and direct. I stay with four basic principles, described below.

Create Appropriate Action Onstage to Physicalize the Character's Intentions

Actions may include, but are not limited to, the slam of a phone receiver, the serving or consuming of food, a shuffling through papers, a cross to examine the contents of a letter, an embrace, a turning away, and any of an infinite number of other possibilities. That is the way to make visible what the audience is already processing verbally. These movements should not be painted over the surface of the scene just to create visual variety and keep the

---

*From the *Streetcar Named Desire* Notebook of Elia Kazan. Quoted in *The Passionate Player*, George Oppenheimer, ed. Viking. New York, NY. 1955 p. 342.

audience from falling asleep, but to express the *inner* action of the scene—the wants, feelings, relationships of the characters—in physical terms. It boils down to this: If you've nailed the intentions and then really play them, really get behind them, the staging will almost take care of itself. You'll be using your body, the set, and the props to do whatever the pursuit of those intentions demands.

Here's a quick and effective demonstration of this principle: Ask two actors to perform a brief improv as mother and son. She's in her thirties, he's a middle school eighth grader. It's 3:15 in the afternoon, and he's just arrived home from school. His report card came in the mail that morning; the grades were less than splendid. The mom's intention is to persuade her son to take his schoolwork more seriously in the future. The son's intention is to get his mother off his back.

The two walk onstage and begin playing the scene. Immediately following the son's entrance and the mom's angry display of the report card, they generally develop the action along similar lines—by bickering back and forth until an impasse is reached, at which point I yell "OK, cut!" They may argue wittily, forcefully, sarcastically, abusively, whatever, depending on the level of invention of the volunteers. But despite all the weeks of improv training, where the emphasis on physical expression of intention has been reinforced time and again (see page 53, "Getting Focused" in Chater 2), they invariably revert to old habits, staging the scene as two characters standing in an empty space, facing each other, talking.

As quickly as possible, I reset the stage, placing a small table with comic book and chair DC, and a counter UR (we always used the top of a rundown upright piano for this) on which are set all props necessary for preparing an after-school snack: a delicious peanut butter and jelly sandwich and some cold milk. Then I ask the actors to "take it from the top."

They need no further explanation to get the point. When the scene is repeated in this way, the staging is infinitely varied, incorporating crosses to and from the table to the counter, use of the comic book to express the son's intention to dodge his mother's questions (one resourceful actress actually snatched it from her son's grasp and hurled it to the floor), inventive handling of the food items to express the mother's intention to telegraph her rage and impatience for the son's benefit, and so on.

I remind the students, just before they break up to begin staging their own scenes, to keep in mind the contrast between the
first and second versions of this improv and then I recap for them
the principle it teaches:

> Whenever appropriate, use hand and set props, the stage
> furniture, or your own body to physicalize the inten-
> tions for the audience. It's not enough to be able to
> mouth them or record them in the script. You've got to
> *play* them.

Weed Out All Extraneous Movement

It will take a day or so, despite all these months of training, for
your actors to get comfortable on the set. Until they relax and
transform the few chairs and music stands into an environment
their imaginations can accept as real, you'll notice all sorts of
symptoms of their uneasiness: fidgeting of hands and feet, needless
shifting of body weight, random wanderings on the set, hiding
behind furniture for protection. The antidote is to force them
repeatedly to shift their focus away from themselves and onto the
character's intentions. "What are you going for here?" "What is
your character after?" "What does she want at this moment?" It's
amazing how quickly those questions relieve the actor's anxieties
and redirect her focus where it belongs—in a theatre scene or in
life—on the pursuit of an intention. The point, then, is

> *don't move without a purpose.* Any movement that does
> not further an intention is wasted movement that can
> only distract and confuse your audience.

Consider the Playwright's Stage Directions

Lots of celebrated acting teachers turn apoplectic at the mention
of this subject. Should stage directions be observed or ignored?
Sanford Meisner, in his book *Sanford Meisner On Acting*, does not
mince words: "Cross them out immediately," he thunders, insisting that they predetermine emotions ("angrily") and movements
("taking her in his arms") that should be arrived at spontaneously (191).

This makes sense on one level, especially when we consider

that many so-called acting editions of plays contain loads of stage directions never included in the author's original text—all set down by an assistant who recorded the blocking for a different staging by a different cast.

But there's also a convincing rebuttal for this argument. Whenever we *can* determine that the directions were the playwright's own, what is our basis for demanding that actors categorically ignore them? It's akin to insisting that a conductor ignore all the composer's phrasing and dynamic markings in an orchestral score. What law of the stage dictates that the playwright be limited to providing only the *words* his characters will speak and nothing else? (The dinner table scene between Annie and Helen from *The Miracle Worker*, to cite just one perhaps unfair example, would play mighty strangely were the actors forced to obey Meisner's injunction.)

I resolve this issue in my own classes by telling the students to look the stage directions over and use the ones that feel right— that make comfortable the playing of their chosen intentions. It seems idiotic to reject stage directions that further the plot, such as *taking the poison* or *opening the letter*. Those that suggest specific stage moves, such as *crossing DL* or *sitting on the sofa*, are more problematic. Once the actors say "yes" to positions one and two they're almost forced to follow the dotted line with the remainder or become hopelessly entangled among those they do and don't choose to observe. As to the naming of specific emotions, such as *furiously* or *with a trace of sadness*, proceed with caution. The bottom line is that when when stage directions work for you, there's no statute on the books to prevent you from using them.

Plan Your Blocking to Allow All Actors Optimal Visibility

I know. Easier said than done. As teachers, we take for granted that even beginners will have the common sense to position themselves for maximum contact with the audience. But that's the paradox of life lived onstage. We keep badgering students to act naturally, truthfully, and believably, and in the same breath remind them that they must be concerned, when they sit down at a table, about remaining visible to the people seated in rows out front. Your best hope for an effective crash course in these blocking basics is to hit a few main points strongly and swiftly. If this minilesson takes more than ten minutes, you know you've gone on too long.

- Using kids as models, quickly define C, UC, DC, L, R, UR, DR, UL, DL, DLC, DRC, ULC, DLC.

- Demonstrate, again using kids as models, why upstage is stronger than down ("Please don't 'upstage' me!"), center stronger than left or right, high (atop a chair) stronger than low. That would mean, for example, that important words from one character to a second character seated C on a couch should be delivered from upstage, not downstage, of the couch.

- "Never turn your back to the audience!" Well no, that's not entirely true, especially if it's for an expressive purpose, at a moment when the character is not speaking. If it's for an expressive purpose at a moment when the character *is* speaking, make sure to compensate with a boost in volume.

I make no claim for thoroughness with this quick tour of the blocking ABCs, but for the relative simplicity of the staging needs of most theatre scenes, these few items do cover the minimum essentials. When other specific problems crop up, they can usually be addressed easily enough during feedback sessions.

Step #7: Mechanics—Memorization and Projection

I'm calling this *Step #7* not because it's important to set aside any specific day for focusing on memorization or projection, but because it's only around now that the students will have attained a strong enough footing to give this work the attention it needs.

Learning the Lines

The majority of the kids are still young and retentive enough to memorize their dialogue and cues without having to sit down to learn anything. Just going over the scene day after day is all they'll need to commit the lines to memory—theirs and everyone else's. I always insist that they study the lines exactly as given, or with at least 99.93 percent accuracy. The playwright has not chosen the words arbitrarily. Presumably there's a reason for a character saying "I'm real scared of him," as opposed to "That man terrifies me." If, in asking the class whether anyone is having a rough time of it, a few students do raise their hands, I offer them their pick of three options, explaining that different methods work best for different kinds of learners:

- Place a blank sheet of paper over a page of the script. Uncover your first line and study it until you feel you've got it down accurately. Continue moving down the page in this way, taking it from the top each time you mess up.

- Assemble the cast of your scene and hold the scripts as you feed all the dialogue into a tape recorder. This allows kids who learn best aurally to replay the tape as many times as needed, memorizing the words painlessly, as they would lyrics to a recorded song. The obvious danger in this method is that the actor may remain a prisoner of the rhythms and inflections preserved on the tape and so lose much of the flexibility that should always remain part of the rehearsal process.

- Sit down with any friend(s) willing to go over the script with you. Because you're working here with someone other than your acting partner(s), make no effort to emote—just run the lines.

Whichever method the students use, it's important to designate a particular day as the memorization deadline and mark it clearly on their calendars: "No more scripts." Otherwise they will continue forever to cling to them for security, often long after the lines have been fully mastered.

Projection

Two projection problems tend to emerge at this stage of the game that rarely surface during the improv phase of the course:

- You'll notice some of the actors rushing their lines unmercifully. This is almost always a function of nerves, a voice inside their heads that keeps chanting "If I get through this thing *real* quick, I'll be able to leave the stage and put an end to all the misery." The phrase *Slow down!*—shouted impatiently and repeatedly from the wings—can only be counted on to exacerbate the situation. Two suggestions may help, though I'll admit this disease has a way of resisting treatment.

1. "Remember, Danielle, that you're up there to pursue your intentions. Make sure the other characters in the scene have heard every word you've said. You've *got* to get your message across to them."

2. "Okay, Danielle, I want you to speak your lines as if addressing a not particularly sharp elementary school child. He just doesn't seem to get what you're saying. Be firm but patient. *Make* him understand." Danielle may hesitate to comply, but if she can conquer her resistance, she may for the first time find herself speaking at an intelligible rate. (I've found that the use of this tactic has *not*, surprisingly, resulted in a stilted, schoolmarmish tone.)

- Still more widespread is the students' habit of trailing off at the ends of lines. They attack each thought with a quick burst of air, leaving too little breath for the end of the sentence. This fault is more easily corrected. "Hit the *ends* of the lines, Craig! Remember: People retain best what they hear last." The application may result in an artificial-sounding delivery at first, but all that disappears once the technique becomes automatic.

Step #8: Action/Reaction (Days 11 and 12)

By week's end, the kids will have had three to four days to work out the blocking for their scenes, just about right if they've followed their calendars (see page 118). The groups should shoot for their first nonstop run through on the final day of preliminary rehearsals—all staged in the separate rehearsal areas, scripts in hand for the last time, minus sound and light—a kind of halftime trial run to determine where things stand.

And that's my lead question the next day in class: "So . . . how do things stand?" The classic response: "It's sooooo boring."

No surprise. The students just need your reassurance that what they're experiencing here is par for the course. Along with all the added layers of discovery—new intentions, bits of stage business, character revelations, blocking—something else is certain by now to have vanished: the spontaneity that flowed so effortlessly during the first read-through. That's a built in by-product of rehearsal, routine to you but new to most of the kids, many of whom have forgotten through daily repetition whatever it was they once found immediate or compelling or funny in these scenes.

I struggled for a long time to obtain a cure for this syndrome. It had always felt a bit odd to spend two days dispensing instructions on how to be spontaneous. I knew the addition of an audience to be the best hope for restoring this lost vitality to the scenes, but I didn't want the kids to sail into the homestretch thinking their performances were doomed to put the audiences (and themselves) to sleep.

The solution came from a student who one year asked, "Okay, you tell us to prepare all our intentions, then to come to rehearsals with our scene partners and play those intentions to the hilt. But how do we incorporate the *effect* of whatever signals our partner is sending out? In other words, if I'm really listening to her, she's going to force me to react in unexpected ways. But in one sense, I feel I'm no longer free to do this. I have to go with whatever I've *preplanned* in the script as my next intention. Doesn't that cancel out any possibility of responding spontaneously?"

This question hits on something fundamental: Drama is conflict. No one in the cast of characters is after the same things. As in life, the battle is ongoing, and what keeps the gears turning are not just the characters pursuing their intentions but their struggle to tear down the *obstacles* to those intentions. It's the constant pressure of want against want that fuels the conflict and creates the friction that keeps the audience caught up in the action. And therein lies the path to renewed energy and spontaneity: to walk into the next rehearsal with full emotional preparation, having carefully completed all the homework on intention and character, and then to forget everything—to just *let it happen*. Put another way, they've applied the technique; now they must make the technique disappear.

This is a tough one to convey to your students, because by *forget everything*, I'm not advising them to trash all the hard work they've done on their characters' voice, walk, mannerisms, and wants, just to remove all impurities from the mix and freshen things up a bit.

The germ for letting this happen lies in the Spolin "Play Ball" exercise (page 30) and in Step #3, "Reading for Communication" (page 124). Remind everyone of the aim of those exercises—to destroy canned responses so that the performers are once again free to act and react, affect and be affected, as if for the first time. There's so much talk in acting texts about being *in the moment*, of producing the *illusion of the first time*. The best hope your actors have for capturing it at this point is not to enter the stage stuffed with scores of details that they must walk out there and remember. We don't want the audience to see the homework. But we want the actors to know that they're unlikely to achieve spontaneity without it.

If, during the last two days before the scheduled dress rehearsals in front of the class, some of the groups still complain that their scenes won't ignite, try one or more of the following exercises.

Overreaching the Intentions (Basic)

This is by far the most forceful approach: You require the actors to rehearse the scene by "overacting" the intentions, taking them beyond what they may consider to be reasonable limits (see "Overacting," page 75). The kids must understand that this is not an invitation to get silly. Those who risk taking this direction literally will find that it delivers *not* the corny or plastic results they fear but the shot of adrenaline the scene needs just prior to dress rehearsal.

Invisible Script (Basic)

If the lines still sound stiff or forced, if one or more of the actors in a particular group sound as if they're still carrying around an invisible script, try asking them to *think* their lines as they say them. It doesn't help to add extraneous *hums, you knows,* or fake pauses. The eyes should be searching for the words, reaching to phrase the thoughts as we do in life. That way, if pauses occur, they'll emerge naturally.

Sex Change (Advanced)

This suggestion does wonders to restore lost energy. Rehearse the scene using scripts, but allow the female to play the male role and vice versa. (If all the characters are of the same sex, simply switch parts.) The actors are on their honor to resist camping it up. If they're mature in approaching this exercise, they'll discover a wealth of new possibilities, many of them usable.

Left Hook (Advanced)

The actors rehearse as usual, but are encouraged, every so often, to insert an improvised line in keeping with the tone and style of the rest of the scene. The other actor(s), without dropping a beat, must react in character—spontaneously, seamlessly, and believably. If they can get back to the script and then, later in the scene, depart still again from the scripted lines, so much the better. There is no expectation of transferring these improvised moments to the finished performance. In fact, as teacher, you will propose this exercise only when the students know their blocking, lines, moves, and intentions *so* well that the scene feels terminally limp, soggy, and predictable.

Step #9: Dress Rehearsal and Feedback (Days 13, 14, and 15)

We've already examined the logistics of dress rehearsal and feedback (see page 119). The only new concern important to address here is the matter of slowly advancing jitters—stage fright. It's a very real phenomenon, likely to reach peak intensity just before dress rehearsals, the moment the kids realize they're actually about to test themselves in front of their classmates (and soon enough the school at large) for the first time. If you decide to assign grades to these run-throughs, the pressure increases proportionally. It's a rare high school actor who will verbalize his fears directly ("I'm so scared!"), which is why it's always preferable if you take the lead. "Things will go wrong. It's inevitable. We're human beings. These rehearsals are set up so that if anything does misfire, you can fix it. Even if you forget a line or two, keep in mind that you've developed enough improvisational skill at this point to cover the blank moments." What they need from you now is a light touch—combined with assurances that, in the end, it's all this careful preparation that will safeguard their self-respect. Least helpful to the kids is to share the burden of any anxieties *you* may be dragging around. I've gone that route once or twice and know the contaminating power of such destructive energy. Swallow it.

An occasional actor will become seriously rattled as dress rehearsals approach. This rarely occurs, but when it does, the trouble can usually be traced to insecurity over learning the lines. For some this task is truly demoralizing, inspiring fear that can *itself* become a crippling force. Unless I suspect laziness—always a real possibility, in which case I feel justified in coming down hard—I will do everything possible to bolster the student's confidence, even if it means finding spare time for extra help with the script.

Step #10: Polishing Rehearsals (Days 16, 17, and 18)

Your calendar sets aside three days for polishing the scenes, but the vagaries of real life are certain to swallow up at least one of them (unanticipated snow day? extra period for raiding the costume room? sudden absence of key student?). The actors should use them as they see fit, to sharpen the rhythms, go over lines, organize the tech elements, and complete at least one, preferably two, nonstop run-throughs.

Remember to mention that when the scene feels limp the trouble usually lies not in the pace of the dialogue but the sluggishness of the cues.

Sample Performance Schedule

Make sure in setting up a performance schedule for the scenes that you check to make certain that

- students give you a list of periods during the school day when they *cannot* be scheduled to perform
- there is enough time in the period to accommodate all the scenes you've selected
- the program for each period offers a balance of comedy and drama
- each scene is scheduled to perform at least twice

Sample Performance Schedule

	Wednesday	Thursday	Friday
Period Two	*Ord. People*	*Shoes*	*"Shakespeare"*
	S.N. Live	*Steel Mag.*	*John's Ring*
	Sorrows of St.	*(Nerd)*	*Odd Couple*
	(Anniversary)		*(Day Room)*
Period Four	*Imp. Embraces*	*Vinny/Ray*	*Anniversary*
	Nerd	*B'way Bound*	*Baby B'Water*
	John's Ring	*(And Stuff)*	*Streetcar*
	(Baby B'Water)		
Period Seven	*True West*	*Fables for Fr.*	*Ord. People*
	Odd Couple	*Lovers & Oth. S.*	*Day Room*
	Children L. G.	*Imp. Embraces*	*S.N. Live*
	Fables for Fr.	*(Shakespeare)*	*(Streetcar)*
Period Eight	*Shoes*	*Heidi*	*Vinny/Ray*
	Steel Mag.	*Children L. G.*	*Lovers & Oth. S.*
	And Stuff	*True West*	*Heidi*
	(B'Way Bound)	*(Sorrows of St.)*	

Parentheses indicate scene will perform if time permits.

Evaluating Scenes

With the tension quotient climbing for four straight weeks, the class needs a day now to take stock and unwind. They'll want to talk about how it all went—what exceeded their expectations, what surprised or disappointed them, audience reactions, near and real disasters, triumphs. This is the time to arrange the chairs in a circle, get comfortable, and hit the release valve. I'm not suggesting forty-five minutes of aimless banter. But the kind of formal evaluation I mistakenly launched one year (three pages of worksheets rating the actors from one to five on their ability to concentrate, pursue intentions, project their voices, and so on) makes even less sense because it keeps everyone straitjacketed, blocking out all the good, impromptu comments that don't quite fit the prescribed categories.

As everyone sits ready to swap impressions, they seem newly

poised and sophisticated. ("Oh, yeah, theatre scenes. Right . . . we've done those.") They've worked hard so I allow them a bit of this. Then I ask questions and offer opinions along with the actors, but I don't—as with the earlier feedback sessions—dominate the discussions with my take on the events. I'm one voice among many here.

In terms of format, we generally review the scenes one at a time, making sure to hit two main areas: the quality of the performances and the quality of the actor/audience relationship. This is one time I'm likely to call on specific kids, since the usually quiet students often surprise me with the most astute observations. I've listed below the range of topics we generally cover, some or all of which you may want to include. Obviously some questions are aimed at the performers in the scene under discussion, others for the class in general.

The Scenes

- In general, how do you feel it went?
- Were there things that occurred during the performances that you didn't anticipate in rehearsal? A character touch? A rhythm achieved? A flash of inspiration?
- Did the scene seem to take on a life of its own?
- Did you feel adversely affected by unwanted nervous energy?
- What were some moments that seemed particularly strong?
- In retrospect, were there some moments that could have been more successful if approached another way?

The Audiences

- Did the size of the audience affect the playing of the scene?
- Did you find yourself performing the scene in what felt like identical ways for two different audiences, yet drawing two totally dissimilar responses? How do you account for the disparity?
- Were there ways in which the audience signaled its attention or inattention? Its warmth? Hostility? Admiration?
- Did you feel the choice of material (as opposed to the performances) to be a key factor in the audience response?

- Did you find that differences in timing, stress, or intensity affected the audiences' reactions from performance to performance?

Throughout the discussions, I try to subordinate these individual questions to something more essential: What did you take from this experience? What did it teach you? I always hope the answer will include at least some mention of the ways in which the presence of the audience impacts the performance—separating it fundamentally from the world of TV and film acting.

I will abstain from offering you specific guidelines on what constitutes the difference between an A, B, or C scene. It's a decision you're forced to make, since pressure for objectivity in grading has never been more widespread than it is right now. But by the time the discussions have wound down, all students in the class will be more than aware of how well they've carried off this first major assignment.

Special Projects

*J*ust before we begin rehearsals for Theatre Scenes, I give the students a few days to complete the following written assignment for homework: "Describe in detail three or four original projects you'd like the class to attempt later in the semester." This request has produced some pretty original course content over the years; the kids have a way of coming through on any suggestion that promises a break from routine.

The day following the last evaluation sessions for the scenes, I seat everyone in a circle, return the papers, and ask the students to describe for the group the project from their list that they consider to be their richest inspiration. Then we select together the few we'd most like to pursue as a class, some slated for invited audiences, others not.

What follows are descriptions of the projects that came off especially well or resulted in interesting failures. A handful were later revised and recycled. Most enjoyed a brief place in the theatre curriculum and then faded. A few remained permanent staples. Pick and choose among them, or use these ideas to create ideas of your own. They can be introduced into the course whenever you find the right spot.

Scene Variations: Changes in Format

Some of the students' earliest suggestions were aimed at refreshing the Theatre Scenes format by organizing follow-up presentations some months later around specific themes.

Age Pieces

All material performed over a three-day period was chosen to show-case the actors' ability to portray convincingly an age other than their own. For instance, we offered within the same forty-five-minute session brief excerpts from Margulies' *Found a Peanut* (five- to fourteen-year-olds), Ives' *All in the Timing* (late twenties), Simon's *California Suite* (middle age), and Coburn's *The Gin Game* (old age). Or, similarly, from Hellman's *The Children's Hour* (eleven and twelve), Weller's *Moonchildren* (college age), Simon's *The Gingerbread Lady* (forties), and Pinter's *The Black and White* (old age). We made no attempt to alter the actors' appearances with makeup, and the costume choices were limited to whatever could be found in their own or their neighbors' closets, or in the theatre department storage rooms. That meant that the age transformation would have to be made through gesture, voice, walk, and especially attitude.

I'm usually cautious about asking beginners to play characters far outside their age range—a fourth grader lies within reach since the actor's memory of what it felt like to be nine years old is probably still fresh. To capture the essence of a person thirty years one's senior, however, is a tricky business. Obviously the job is made easier as the character approaches a stereotype (Aunt Harriet in Gurney's *The Dining Room*) and more difficult as she resembles a fully rounded human being (Lena in Hansberry's *A Raisin in the Sun*). But the assignment may be worth a try with the right group, especially if it's presented in the spirit of an experiment.

Kid Stuff

All scenes featured teenage characters as depicted in plays or films set between 1900 and 1999. We arranged the excerpts in chronological order, from earliest to most recent, so that during a typical period of the school day, the performance might begin with a piece from O'Neill's *Ah, Wilderness!* (1906), move on to Kingsley's *Dead End* (1935) and Ray's *A Rebel Without a Cause* (1955), and end with Crowe's *Fast Times at Ridgemont High* (1981).

Since one of the obvious aims of the project was to allow our audiences an amused look at teenage life a few generations removed, it became vital to caution the students against injecting the material with a cute or condescending tone. In a comic scene, the audience "laugh quotient" is guaranteed to increase in direct proportion to the seriousness with which the actors approach their characters. No mugging, no winking allowed.

The Amy/Virginia park bench scene from Hagan's *One Sunday Afternoon* (1930), which we performed a few years back, provides a perfect object lesson. The behavior of the teenage girls in this piece is hopelessly demure and precious by today's standards—not unlike an exchange between Judy Garland and Deanna Durbin from an early thirties MGM musical. Both actors were convinced that, unless they broadly parodied the situation, gestures, and voices, the scene would die an agonizing death. This direction, I assured them, while ideal for a skit from the old Carol Burnett show, would be a direct violation of the playwright's intent and an affront to the audience's intelligence to boot. They were adamant. We came to terms only after they agreed to test the opposing styles before two different audiences; their leers and sarcasm earned a few isolated snickers the first time through, lots of warm, appreciative laughter the second.

At the Movies

This round featured a selection of scenes from films only. The students were gung ho for this plan from the onset. They were drawn to it, I think, for two obvious reasons—excitement about trying well-tested material that had already impressed them onscreen and a hope that movie clips would draw instant recognition and thus larger audiences than scenes from "obscure" plays written for the theatre.

This is a false assumption, but the kids' true message still came through loud and clear: Among their friends, film is what's happening, and in presenting anonymous stage pieces, their best efforts might draw no more than yawns and a scattering of polite applause. We spoke in Chapter 4 about the special problems connected with the performance of film scenes (see page 117), and so long as the kids are careful to take these into account I have no objection to using them. There are, however, two further cautions to be observed. One is the matter of audience expectation. Especially among high school kids relatively unsophisticated in their theatregoing experiences, the student who sits down to watch your actors perform the opening sequence from, say, *Ferris Bueller's Day*

Off is going to expect nothing less than the full Paramount treatment. The actor playing Ferris had also better be prepared for the
inevitable comparisons to Matthew Broderick.

Making a movie scene stageworthy is the second necessity, but
this time the problem is easier to fix. Kids eager to perform their
favorite movie excerpts have usually overlooked a curious fact: that
single-location exchanges of dialogue onscreen rarely last more than
a minute or two at best (yes, there are exceptions). To win and then
sustain attention in a Theatre Scenes setting requires at least ten
minutes of running time. Put another way, when the lights come up
onstage, you've got to give the audience something to sink into
before the lights fade back down. The job usually consists of piecing
together several contiguous bits so that they emerge seamlessly in
performance. The exposition scene between the title characters in
When Harry Met Sally is an excellent case in point. On screen this
episode takes about ten minutes, encompassing four separate locations (car interior, parking lot, diner interior, and New York City
street corner) and several passages of time. The kids, on first reading
the screenplay, may feel stalemated. "Where do we go with this?"
But the whole sequence can work easily enough as an uninterrupted
theatre piece with only the simplest of adjustments: covering the
time lapses with brief interludes of mimed action plus music and
arranging a basic simultaneous set before the lights first come up
(two chairs RC for the car, empty space C for the parking lot, a table
and chairs DL for the diner, spot DC for the street corner). This kind
of stark simplicity is entirely defensible in a studio setting, where a
lively chemistry between the actors counts for everything, fancy
scenery and costumes next to nothing. (Of course there will still be
critics in the audience who, reviewing the scene in the hall with one
of your actors later in the day, won't be able to resist observing
smartly that in the movie "they had a whole diner and everything.")

Teacher/Student Scenes

The first time a student proposed the idea of organizing a medley
of teacher/student scenes, the class seemed skeptical of their teachers' acting abilities. "They're not exactly trained actors, right?" A
pregnant pause as everyone considered this question and then a
few, followed by more than a few, knowing smiles. "Yeah,
definitely. Let's do it!"

Good teachers *are* actors, of course. They're forced to be. Commanding the attention of some pretty demanding audiences for five performances a day makes that a virtual necessity. As soon as the kids had acknowledged this fact, they began shouting out names they considered perfect candidates. Each new suggestion drew a mixture of cheers and laughter. As the list grew, so did the crescendo of enthusiasm—along with everyone's awareness that we were on to something exciting, both in terms of personal reward and good old box office potential.

Just about every detail surrounding the completion of the project came down, thereafter, to a simple matter of logistics. Two weeks before our first planned rehearsal, I consulted the master schedule and posted on the board the name of every teacher in the building whose unassigned period corresponded to the time of day the class met. The kids were instructed to approach those they might especially like working with, or who they felt might show the right combination of flair and commitment. It was agreed that if some teachers politely declined the offer, no effort would be made to twist their arms. When two students expressed a preference for the same teacher, we held a simple coin toss.

The rest of the preparations went ahead exactly as for a standard round of all-student scenes. A few of the groups solicited my help in choosing material, while others knew exactly what they were after, in which case my job was to tell them candidly what I thought of the appropriateness of their choices. Everyone agreed that it would be time wasted to give the participating teachers a crash course in acting technique; their student partners would be present in rehearsal to fill any gaps and—in a pinch—so would one certified acting instructor.

The Scene Resource List in the Appendix (page 182) is rich in possibilities for this assignment, for example:

- the Terry/Charley car scene from Schulberg's *On the Waterfront*
- the Higgins/Eliza after-the-ball scene from *Pygmalion*
- the Bridget/Nancy confrontation scene from Sommer's *A Roomful of Roses*
- the Mark/Tim scene near the end of Act One of Davis's *Mass Appeal*

- the Norma/Joe meeting scene from Brackett and Wilder's *Sunset Boulevard*

- the Catherine/Beatrice scene from Act One of Miller's *A View from the Bridge*

Scene Variations: Changes in Location

Traveling Players: Cafeteria, Commons, Library, and Beyond

Watching a videotaped biography in class on the life of Molière some years back, a student was suddenly inspired by the example of the Illustre Theatre's twelve-year tour of the French provinces (1645–1657). "That's it! We've gotta go out on tour!" he insisted. "Hanging around the choral room every day is making us soft!" (This is the way kids once talked.)

His idea led to a class consensus that we could increase our visibility, and hence the size of our audiences, by bringing the entertainment to the crowd instead of vice versa. So the environs of the school became our "provinces." That meant taking actors, bare-bones sets, props, and costumes to some agreed-upon site and performing a set of two to three scenes (or whatever time allowed) for whoever happened to be present. Regardless of the spot, our one strategic need was for a reasonable playing space, which we sometimes configured as a small raised platform made of band risers, at others as a simple clearing or quasi-arena.

I can't say we enjoyed any memorable success with this venture, but we certainly learned a few things during the course of our travels. The first was that, in any of these "on location" settings, loud played better than soft, broad better than subtle, funny better than serious.

A few groups did give intensely emotional scenes a shot; these never really came off. The audience focus was often less than intense regardless of the quality of the performances. It becomes tougher with each passing year to win the unbroken attention of a group of high school students, and a lunchtime theatre class excerpt from *Antigone* set in front of the school cafeteria isn't exactly an ideal accompaniment to the consumption of pizza or burritos. Even a highly sensitive rendition of the Adrian/Rocky apartment scene, a rousing success in the choral room, didn't resonate fully here.

And therein lay our second discovery: Cafeterias remain best for eating, libraries for reading, commons areas for hanging out. This is not to say that we didn't profit from all these theatrical wanderings. Improv shows, especially, were often fabulously successful "on the road," ditto anything farcical or slapstick. And we did win that extra exposure we were after, most of it positive. In the end, though, we went back with renewed faith in the choral room as the ideal spot for theatre scenes. It was a setting just rough enough, just controlled enough, just comfortable enough. We had our lighting board, our bathrooms, our changing areas, and our prop tables conveniently at hand, and—all things considered—it just felt more like home.

Scenes to Order:
Social Studies, English, Science, You Name It

There was a single occasion when this wanderlust paid off handsomely. An acting student rehearsing a scene from *Inherit the Wind* mentioned to me that for the past two days his social studies class had been discussing the Scopes Trial in connection with a unit on landmark court cases of the twentieth century. He wanted to remind me to be sure to schedule at least one performance during a period available to them, since the curriculum tie-in would be irresistible (not to mention the chance to dazzle his classmates with the power of his portrayal of Henry Dummond). His classmates did attend, and about a week later the teacher sent a note expressing his students' gratitude at the chance for some lively follow-up discussion in class the next day.

Self-promotion aside, any course of study is enriched when the kids can witness a staged enactment of whatever topic they're working on. It helps make the abstract concrete and lends a human dimension to what would otherwise remain a sterile academic exercise. It's impractical to think that this can occur all or even most of the time, but when the demand is evident, the theatre classes are ideally suited to fill it.

And this was precisely "Drummond's" suggestion when it came time a few months later to submit his special projects assignment: The acting class would prepare a round of scenes to bring into subject classes as a curriculum enhancement, this time delivered directly to the customer's door. Every staff member in the school received a flyer from the theatre department six weeks in advance asking them to name plays or films that would benefit their program, suggestions for specific scenes we could perform in their classrooms, or—lacking that—for subjects or themes that would make for a meaningful connection. A good proportion responded favorably.

The setup was a snap since the necessarily small size of the playing area dictated that every choice favor a simple solution. We began by casing the room in advance, checking out its dimensions and the position of the electrical outlets for sound cues, figuring out how to adapt the blocking, entrances and exits, noting whether a bathroom was located nearby. We also timed the presentation in rehearsal to be sure to leave room for discussion on the day of the performance.

I wasn't sure early on whether we'd be able to line up enough suitable material for this project. "Let's see . . . *Inherit the Wind*, maybe *An Enemy of the People* . . . then what?" But the possibilities multiplied and fell neatly into place once we actually began compiling our list:

> French: *The Would-Be Gentleman* (Molière); *St. Joan* (Shaw)
>
> Social Studies: *Our American Cousin* (Taylor); *A Doll's House* (Ibsen)
>
> Spanish: *The House of Bernarda Alba* (Lorca); *Barcelona* (Stillman)
>
> Science: *Galileo* (Brecht); *Frankenstein* (Gialanella)
>
> English: *The Primary English Class* (Horovitz); *English Made Simple* (Ives)
>
> Music: *Amadeus* (Shaffer)
>
> Math: *The Lesson* (Ionesco)

It was the strange fate of this assignment to be tremendously well received and never once revived thereafter.

Inter-School Exchange Visits

This is the only entry that didn't originate with a student. It took shape during a phone chat I had with a friend and colleague from a neighboring high school. We discovered in the course of conversation that both of us happened to be rehearsing kids in Mark O'Donnell's *Marred Bliss* (from the first volume of *Ten-Minute Plays* from Actors Theatre of Louisville). As I remember, it was he who suggested that it would be fun to bring everyone together and play the scenes in succession, sharing comments and impressions, each learning through observation what the other group was—or wasn't—doing with the material.

We scheduled the meeting during after-school hours, so there was no friction over kids missing classes. And there were no complex preparations to be made, save the transportation arrangements.

We tried this once more with another scene and another school a couple of years later. This time we deliberately chose to work on the same piece. It all came off just as smoothly as the first time, and I think the kids enjoyed the swap and the follow-up discussions. But if you're at all acquainted with the convolutions of the teenage psyche, you've already anticipated the reason I never returned to the idea after the second try. Here's the comment I overheard in class the next day, just prior to the start of the lesson: "Oh, yeah, well *we* were a lot funnier during that part when they talk about the *ruses*, and Steve was soooo much better than the actor they had playing. . . ."

It may be that some stirrings of team rivalry are inevitable whenever kids from different high schools stand within hearing range of each other—that's natural enough when the activity is inherently competitive. But the notion of dueling Theatre Scenes strikes me as fundamentally suspect. It's the same sour aftertaste that can spoil the fun at competitive play festivals. You sit in the audience wanting to admire the talented work of another school's talented cast, and instead find yourself hoping desperately that the actors will forget lines and trip over the scenery. If you can work your way past these hurdles, I'd recommend giving the idea a try.

Dreamscape

This is just the thing for a group with above-average body temperature and a craving for the offbeat.

Two weeks before you're ready to get started with the assignment, ask all kids in the class to begin compiling a dream journal.

It should contain dated entries of the highlights of any dream remembered from the past night's sleep, set down in enough detail so that the narrative thread can be stitched together at a moment's notice. Kids who say they have difficulty recalling their dreams should be encouraged to get them on paper the instant they rise to consciousness in the morning. The chances of retaining "plot" developments are thus maximized.

Day One

Everyone sits in a circle and, in their own words, shares briefly with the class the dream from their journal with the strongest theatrical punch—the one they'd most like to see onstage. Students are asked to exercise good judgment: Anything inappropriate for public consumption is off-limits. To maintain the dignity of their own personal lives, students can generally be counted on to do the right thing.

Once everyone has contributed, the class decides on the handful of scenarios they'd like to green-light for production. Ideally, you should wind up with four or five mutually exclusive groups, each at the service of one "dreamer," who will cast and stage his own opus. Although questions do arise, such as How to agree on which scenes to pursue, which to chuck? How to make certain each cast has the actors it needs? How to ensure that every student is satisfied with his role?, I can only say that somehow the kids work it out so everything falls mysteriously into place.

Day Two

The groups meet separately in class. The dreamer runs the rehearsal, directing his actors in assembling an improv that effectively dramatizes the dream. Suggested playing time is a maximum of five minutes. Some pointers include the following:

1. Directors should not worry about literally recreating every detail of the dream. Frequent adjustments will be necessary to "make it play."
2. If a group has three assigned actors and requires, say, five or more characters, simply double up on the parts. Unless the tone is deadly serious, which is a rarity, males should be able to play females and vice versa.

3. The plot of a dream develops according its own strange logic. Characters may float on and off. Bizarre objects may appear and disappear without reason. Things may come together as strangely as on a Dali canvas. The directors should not impede the free-flowing of images. Encourage your students to let it happen. The audience will come along for the ride.

Day Three

A showing of the work-in-progress. Kids will moan and demand additional work time. A five-minute brush-up rehearsal is reasonable, but don't allow them a lot more than that. The immediate purpose is to discover where things stand at this point. Each run-through is followed by a brainstorming session in which classmates offer suggestions for changes and improvements.

Day Four

Polishing rehearsals: Props, music tapes, costume elements should all be brought in and incorporated into the scene. Keep the tech simple.

Day Five

Performances for the class: On occasion, when the results are especially satisfying, we've scheduled these for invited audiences. And once, on Halloween, we varied the format by offering an "all-nightmare" program.

Lyric Pieces

This idea was a favorite in the acting classes and remained in steady demand among Theatre Scenes audiences for almost a decade.

One week in advance, ask all kids in the class to search their memories for a song with particularly evocative lyrics. Not necessarily poetic, beautiful, or even memorable (although none of these qualities is of itself a liability) but rather well-suited to dramatic treatment—words that might spawn a good scene.

Then, a few days later, ask the students to present you with a legible printout of the lyrics, which can then be copied for the entire class. Of course, the good taste clause remains in full force and effect.

Day One

Arrange all chairs in a circle. Kids come to class with a CD containing their song of choice. The teacher brings in the collated packets of song lyrics (number the pages before you reproduce them!) and a CD player.

The students take turns introducing their songs, after which the class gets to hear a minute or so of each, following the lyric sheet as they listen. Ideally, you'd want to sample the pieces in their entirety, but time constraints will probably make that impractical.

Day Two

Set up shop exactly as you did for the dream scenario project: Select four or five choices (kids whose songs are chosen become the directors), assign actors, and allow the groups to meet separately. Their job for the remainder of the period is to brainstorm the possibilities for using the song lyrics as a creative springboard to a five-minute improvised scene. By the end of class, each group should have formulated their basic concept, talked through the scenarios, and completed their casting.

Day Three

Rehearsal day; directors should be guided by a single principle—to transform the material imaginatively and to use the words as a catalyst for stage action, *not* to slavishly match the lines of the song to the events of the scene. For example, one group of five actors working with Foghat's "Slow Ride" chose to set its sketch inside an SUV. Two noisy teenagers driving home from a local party decide to have fun picking up a series of oddball hitchhikers. The mood inside the van gets a little stranger and a little rowdier as the ride continues.

Note that the original lyrics are in no way at odds with this scenario, but nor—by the same token—do they parallel it.

Day Four

Run-throughs for the class of work-in-progress, followed by feed-back sessions and suggestions for improvements.

Day Five

We focused on polishing the scenes.

Day Six

Performances for the public were set up so that, on entering the choral room, each audience member was given a program containing the lyrics for the five songs being used in the show. The music department loaned us its high-performance stereo for the period. As the house lights went down before the start of the first scene, we faded in on the CD and pumped up the volume, allowing the audience to listen to the music in the dark for about ten seconds. Then we faded the music out as the stage lights came up on the actors already in position. The scene played out, after which the music was repeated. We followed this same format for the remaining songs.

Solo

This project was originally suggested as an enjoyable way to spend the three days prior to Christmas vacation. Students were offered a list of the five possible choices below, and a period of two and a half weeks to prepare at home.

1. a reading of their own poetry
2. a stand-up comedy routine (their own material!)
3. an original monologue (in their voice, as opposed to a character's)
4. a performance of an original song or dance
5. a published monologue provided by the teacher (only as a last resort, if they absolutely could not find inspiration in choices 1 through 4)

Time Limit: three to five minutes.

We agreed in advance that the emphasis would be on the personal, on presenting oneself *as* oneself, without benefit of a mask. That's why we omitted from consideration such popular talent show favorites as lip-synchs, magic acts, juggling acts, and the like. But a few variations did surface nonetheless. One student, for example, did some impromptu sketching with colored chalk to music. Another dedicated a giant Christmas card to the class with a personal message for every student. Naturally, a few kids asked if they might present something as a team, but that seemed a violation of the solo motif, so I returned a respectful "no."

Someone generously volunteered to handle the emcee post for the three days; however, his job in this instance was not to crack jokes or entertain, but to preserve the intimate character of the event and keep everything moving.

The class voted not to invite outside audiences to this one. The assignment was a miniature, and everyone agreed to keep it in the family.

Variety Show

A simple expansion of "Solo," the variety show was our solution to the need for a fund-raiser. I'm not a major admirer of theatre as vaudeville, but the student who suggested the idea made a persuasive case: "Look, we do lots of respected plays by respected playwrights. Why can't we serve the community some 'plain folks' entertainment once in awhile, just as a change of pace?" Fair enough.

Once again, we positioned the show before the start of a vacation, but scheduled it for public performance and charged a small admission fee. By contrast with "Solo," though, this time we laid on the show biz a bit: house band, comedy emcee, auditorium setting. The acts were a medley of the usual fare, with the addition of a handful of some recently successful Theatre Scenes (which, ironically, given the mood of the occasion, were the *least* successful segments!) No better or worse than the typical variety show in the typical suburban high school, it was a tradition that nevertheless held on through my last year on the job. What I liked most about it was that it always revealed a few students in a new light, unearthing talents I had no idea existed.

Comedy Cabaret

Just about every section of theatre I ever taught had its share of
class clowns; the idea for Comedy Cabaret was conceived one year
by a class virtually teeming with them. *Saturday Night Live, Kids in
the Hall*, and *In Living Color* were all going full blast at the time, and
the students had in mind a kind of local hybrid of those popular
shows. We resolved to make an evening of it, drawing together
pieces performed by actors in several different sections of theatre
class: published scenes ("Business as Usual" from Ted Tally's *Silver
Linings*, the "tennis match" from Stoppard's *Rosencrantz and
Guildenstern Are Dead*); classic *SNL* sketches ("Slumber Party," "The
Thing That Wouldn't Leave"); and a few original scripts lampoon-
ing life at school.

To make this into a special event, we decided to give our audience the full nightclub treatment: dinner at 7:00, entertainment at
8:00. The lineup would begin with a comedy monologue from the
emcee, followed by the individual acts and, as with the Variety
Show, two brief sets from a house rock band (as I said, very *Saturday
Night Live*). The only remaining chores were to find the right setting—the choral room was too small, the auditorium too large—and
a suitable caterer. We solved the second problem first by approaching the home economics chairperson. She usually avoided getting
sucked into these extra duty assignments, but in this one instance
said "Sure . . . why not?" The rest seemed to fall easily into place.

The home economics suite in our school happened to be sit-
uated next to an open set of staircases flanking an indoor court-
yard, called the C Wing Commons. It was just large enough to
accommodate twelve small tables at ground level (we found six in
the basement left over from *West Side Story* and built the remainder ourselves), an adequate playing area, and a spot for the band.
We were a stone's throw from the kitchen, which made the serving
of the meal a lot easier. Planning, shopping, and preparing dinner
for almost fifty guests kept the cooking classes well occupied for a
few weeks; meanwhile the actors got busy rehearsing the nearly
twenty comedy segments they'd gathered from the most eclectic
sources imaginable. Typical in these circumstances, the production
elements were limited to lightweight tables and chairs, simple
props, a few wigs, and a handful of costume items.

To install a formal production in the auditorium is a four- to six-week affair. The Comedy Cabaret was assembled in two quick shifts: a single 7:00 to 10:30 rehearsal the night before and a setup session between the end of school Friday and showtime six hours later. We'd done a decent job rehearsing the separate acts, but the frenzied throwing together of so much gear into what was essentially an exposed corridor of the school—the decorations, candles, table-cloths, dinnerware, band equipment, props, furniture, costumes, stereo system, piano—did too much damage to everyone's nerves.

The audience surprised us at the end with a warm ovation. But while the evening was a triumph in its sloppy fashion, my colleague in home economics delivered the final verdict before we'd even finished the cleanup: "It was a smash success," she said good-humoredly, "and I'll never do it again!" She didn't, and neither did we.

An afterthought here about the special rules for playing comedy. I've read some textbooks that cover the basics: "Never move on a punch line." "Accent the seriousness of the situation." "Don't let 'em catch you trying for laughs." "Play the exposition straight." They're all valid, and they all serve a useful purpose in rehearsal. But I've also found the formal giving of "how-to-make-it-funny" lessons a waste of students' time. For one thing, their entertainment diets have been so glutted by a steady bombardment of high-pitched comedy that most with a flair for humor have already got most of the right wiring installed in their nervous systems. Those who don't won't acquire it from studying a set of notes.

Children's Shows

We produced about three Children's Shows during my tenure at the high school. These were short plays rehearsed in class and performed for the district's elementary school children.

The first time one of the acting students suggested trying one, the bulk of the class was underwhelmed. But I pushed the project because I knew at least two positive things would come of it—the actors would fall into the spirit of a good "little kids' play" once they got their hands dirty in rehearsal, and they'd be warmed by the innocence and fullness of the children's reactions during performance. (Elementary school kids are dazzled when high school students do no more than occupy the same room.)

We never produced these grandly, but whenever we took costume or scenic elements along with us on the road, we made sure
they were colorful and big.

Big is the watchword here. There's no need to slip into that
phony singsong delivery that debases so much children's theatre.
But size—of gesture, voice, intention, energy, projection—is indispensable for keeping those young faces riveted to the stage.

We found several plays we liked for this assignment: Mamet's
Poet and the Rent, Denson's *Playground*, and our own abridgment of
Sills' *Story Theatre*, but there are scores of other good choices out
there as well. Check the Samuel French, Dramatic Publishing Company, and Baker's Plays catalogues for more possibilities than you'll
know what to do with.

Project Video

A few years ago, in between major assignments, I spent two periods
showing an advanced theatre class Michael Caine's *Acting for the
Camera*. When the kids handed in their Special Projects assignment
a few days later, one student proposed an idea inspired by the videotape: "We were discussing that these days the majority of available
acting jobs are in film and television, so how about using the TV studio to try out some of the techniques Caine demonstrated? Not sure
yet what scripts to use or how to set it up, but I think the experience
would be practical and a good change of pace." Everyone jumped at
this suggestion, so I promised I'd speak with the media teacher to see
whether we could devise a workable plan.

Not all high schools offer well-funded media programs, and
those that do can't always afford a fully appointed television studio—a sorry fact since media savvy is only a notch less vital to survival in the twenty-first century than computer knowledge. But
ours was not only well-equipped, it was staffed by a teacher who
loved setting himself new challenges and (so far as I knew) had no
aversion to working with actors.

Commercials

We came up with the idea of dividing the class into teams and giving each the responsibility for producing a half-minute ad for any

product of their choice, real or imagined. A thirty-second spot was a perfect entrée to life in the studio because anything more would have wound up consuming too much class time. Fortunately, a video production class was scheduled during the same period, which meant we were able to assign a cameraman, sound man, and editor to each group of actors. The process began with the writing of the script—I had just completed an "Acting for Commercials" course in Manhattan, so I had plenty of actual ad copy on hand to inspire the kids before they started work—and moved quickly through the casting of actors, choice of location, gathering of props and costumes, rehearsal on the set with camera and sound, shooting, and postproduction (editing and, if necessary, adding of music and sound effects). This all sounds very elaborate, but in fact we gave the students only five class periods, start to finish, to complete the job.

One group invented an ad for a deodorant spray to take the place of the dreaded gym shower ("Locker Fresh") and set it inside the boys' locker room during gym class. Another shot a Holly Farms chicken commercial after school in the local supermarket. And so on. Whatever their take on the assignment, though, we set a rule that no one was to produce a parody of an existing commercial. Ad takeoffs being, arguably, the cheapest form of satire, we wanted to see what they could do plugging an actual product, real or invented.

Scenes for the Camera

The commercials worked so well that the following year someone asked if we could work up a full round of theatre scenes and then perform them—not, as we usually did, for live audiences in the choral room—but in the TV studio, expressly for the camera. This would have meant a more ambitious collaboration of actors and tech artists, with every moment of every scene—camera angles, close-ups, long shots, transitions—systematically laid out, along with the actors' stage positions and movements.

It was a terrific idea, but we never fully realized it. A few beat-up chairs just won't cut it as a set for a video production; the camera demands a much higher degree of realism. Even if we'd been able to afford the materials, the thought of constructing a naturalistic set for five separate scenes and then incorporating the remaining tech elements for each seemed a little over the top.

We reached an equitable solution, though. Over the months and years, whenever an individual scene felt made for the camera, we'd produce it separately in the TV studio. "Vinny and Ray" from O'Donnell's *Fables for Friends* was a perfect choice because most of the action is set in the front seat of a car, making the camera and lighting setups relatively simple. We found just the right car seat in a nearby junkyard, mounted it on a platform in the studio, and were able to create wind, sound, and visual effects that would have been impossible to pull off in the choral room.

The students involved in these and other video projects really did learn something about the difference between acting for the stage and the camera, but only a small handful. To expand the possibilities, I experimented using video cameras in the acting classes, taping exercises and run-throughs of scenes so that all the kids could step back and observe what they were actually doing up there. The idea seemed promising at first; I'd hoped it would supply the picture worth a thousand words. But I didn't stay with it for long. Most of the kids absolutely dreaded watching the playbacks. Instead of allowing them a closer look at the fine points of their performance, in reality the tapes fanned their insecurities and self-consciousness—reviving all the tensions we'd worked so hard to erase. I remembered interviews I'd read of professional film actors categorically refusing to view rushes on the set and finally felt that I understood why.

Understand too that this technique, if you're tempted to try it, doesn't actually teach anything about acting for the camera. You're taping a *stage* performance and using the electronic eye as a kind of "recording secretary." There's no more art in this than in Uncle Al's camcorder taping of the spring musical.

That said, it's important to remember that the small percentage of your students seeking professional careers will need to learn how to feel at home in front of the camera—increasingly as the years pass. Somehow your program must find ways to expose them, at least to the basics.

Director's Workshop

I always assume that at some point my enjoyment of directing will rub off on the students, that in observing the process, they'll eventually grow curious to try it themselves, at least for the wicked pleasure of playing boss to their peers for a few weeks. In fact, they seldom show an interest, even when I sweeten the pot with reminders that line memorization will for once be somebody else's problem.

The few times students in the advanced classes chose to tackle a project in directing, they *did* take enormous pride in the work—but only in the home stretch, watching a run-through and discovering, as if for the first time, their imprint on the finished product. That became a defining moment for them, when they were finally able to see it as their "baby," to connect the dots and realize where their hand had made a difference in the results.

Student-Directed Scenes

We set up the project precisely as for ordinary theatre scenes: five or six casts rehearsing separately, but with each now assigned its own director. I'd begin by asking for volunteers, always praying to look up and find just the right number of raised hands. Then I'd go home and hammer out the choices for scripts and casts myself. We thought first of conducting a brief set of auditions, allowing the directors a full stake in the process from first step to last, but scrapped the idea as being too awkward and time-consuming. Whenever a director expressed a preference for a particular piece, I always said "yes," so long as I thought it lay more or less within the actors' grasp.

On the second and third work days, the actors were permitted to run lines while the directors, in a separate room, took part in a two-day workshop to define their role and responsibilities—a brief apprenticeship, to be sure, but we were not shooting for graduate-level results with this first assignment.

Below is the outline of the lesson I used to teach these classes, a copy of which was given to each participant.

Directors' Guidelines

CREDO: *If you're going to err as a director, let it be on the side of over, rather than under preparedness.* This means that the actors deserve a clear sense of your purpose in sitting down with them. They're already familiar with *their* job description: to learn lines, create character, master blocking and stage business, isolate intentions, meet deadlines. It's a tall order. So what exactly are your responsibilities? I don't ask this question ironically. A lot of people, even those with a dash of theatre experience, honestly don't know. So here's my distillation of five immutable laws:

1. *The buck stops here!* Rehearsals should be dominated by an atmosphere of discovery and invention. They should be exciting to attend, even when the tone of the scene is gravely serious. But just as parties and concerts make life out there worth living, so does the daily grind of homework, laundry, and grocery shopping make it a sometimes insufferable bore. So too with play production: There are always props to be dragged in, furniture to set up, lines to be memorized, responsibilities to be met. One of your key functions is to communicate to the actors that excuses won't cut it. The world is drowning in excuses. You want everyone to have a good experience in rehearsal and to take pride in the results. But that can't happen unless the cast can be trusted to meet deadlines. You are the deadline police. Offer them assurance that *you* plan to set an example of preparedness and then make sure to do just that.

If all this sounds corny or schoolmarmish, rephrase the thought however you please. You can humor, cajole, soft-pedal, or charm. But make sure, as a bottom line, that the cast is firm in its commitment. I know this is a tricky business; these are your peers. But setting the right tone on day one is a must. They need to feel that your focus is on making the scene—and hence *them*—look good, not on showing them who's boss.

So what happens the first time you set a line memorization deadline and two of the actors don't come through? You can't panic, scream, throw a tantrum, or start kicking people. But make sure they understand that they have one day's grace to turn things around. It's the team effort and their own self-respect that are ultimately at stake.

2. *Nail the intentions.* Your own preparedness begins with

a thorough study of the script. Know it *well*. Read it through several times. Then, once you have a handle on its tone and themes, get busy nailing the intentions. These must be notated in your script *for all characters* in advance of the first rehearsal. Start with super-intentions and then break each down into beat intentions. Remember that, again and again, you'll be asking yourself "What does she want here?" and then pinning down the different ways she goes about getting it. Don't forget to express each intention as a strong, actable verb: ("I want to. . . ."). For clarity, set up a notebook and place a blank sheet, divided into two vertical columns, opposite each page of text. Then use the left column to record character intentions ("I want to *belittle* him"), the right to indicate how these intentions might be physicalized ("rolls her eyes, plops into the chair, and begins flipping pages of a magazine"). Pros refer to this as *the prompt book*.

Once you assign your actors the job of writing out their characters' intentions, don't be thrown when their responses differ from yours. It's never about bickering over who's right or wrong. If the actors' choices are working, go with them. If not, you're there to resolve their doubts, not to engage in a battle of wills.

"What are you going for here?" "What are you trying to get her to do?" "What are you trying to make him do?" Those are the questions that will rescue you every time. Often the process of rehearsal is a matter of pooling your thoughts and theirs, sorting through the rough spots together.

3. *Set the blocking.* This is the heart of your work. You must help the actors find the most vivid ways of *physicalizing* their intentions. If you block the scene expertly, the positioning of the characters and their movements will communicate the play's meanings to the audience every bit as powerfully as the playwright's dialogue (which is probably what Hamlet meant when he said, a great deal more succinctly, "Suit the action to the word, the word to the action."). For a scene staged in utopia, the actors arrive at all the best choices themselves, and

you, in the aftermath of the performance, stand modestly aside and accept the rave reviews. Unfortunately, the pieces almost never fall so neatly into place. You will have to picture the scene in your mind's eye and record the blocking on paper for homework—preparing all the crosses, bits of stage business, character interactions, and then penciling them into the text (see Chapter 4, page 136 for a review of blocking basics).

You're confused now, so let's be clear about this. During rehearsal, do you actually say to the actor: "Okay, Anna, in these next four lines, your intention is 'to belittle him,' so after you say 'Brilliant deduction, Sherlock!' I want you to roll your eyes, plop into the chair, and begin flipping the pages of a magazine."? Occasionally, sure. All directors stoop to this kind of shorthand when they're low on time or patience. But only as a last resort. The best stuff always emerges through collaboration. The actors, remember, have been trained not only to pin down intentions but behaviors as well, so they're accustomed to having their say. Disagreements about where, when, and how they should move are bound to pop up. How to resolve them? You try a few possibilities and determine together what feels most effective and/or comfortable. Sometimes you'll want to make adjustments; sometimes they will. The moves should be subject to change. Nothing gets fixed in stone.

Until the final week, that is. If you keep altering the blocking after that point, the actors will resent your indecision and rise to mutiny.

If you're thinking: "Man, the boundaries here are pretty slippery," then you're right on the money. A scene is not *solved* like a math problem. If you spell out all the moves you become a dictator; if you lead each time by asking "Well, what would *you* like to do here?" "Well, what would *you* like to try there?" you become exasperating.

An important key to success is to study your notations thoroughly at home and then try whenever possible to keep your nose out of the script during rehearsal. Nothing is more frustrating for actors than a director who's forever fussing through pages of the prompt book instead of focusing on *them* (unless it's the director who has no idea what he's after in the scene). If you do that, you'll never allow the piece to breathe; you'll be too busy making sure the cast slavishly executes every last move recorded in your notes. The scene will remain stuck on the page, stillborn.

A final caution: Don't make the fatal mistake of walking into rehearsal with no written plan. It's one thing to do your homework meticulously and then set it aside, another to read through the scene once or twice and decide "Yeah, okay . . . right . . . I'll figure it out when I get there."

4. *Define the characters.* If staging the scene is primarily the director's job, it's the actor who's ultimately responsible for creating the character. Remind your cast early in the game that this is *their* obligation, that it's not your job to decide how their character will speak and walk. Keep literary analysis to a minimum. You want always to remain focused on pursuing wants; these will supply the germ for all believable emotion in the scene. When you and your actors are at odds over details of character interpretation, there are no instant solutions. Find evidence in the text, test different intentions, try several contrasting behaviors. That's precisely what rehearsal is about: rehearing.

When an actor is at a loss to define some aspect of a character, you're there to help. The same process of trial and error applies. Review the whole arsenal of techniques we studied as preparation for Theatre Scenes: props to suggest the character, costume elements, real-life people who might serve as models, and so on. (See Chapter 4, pages 126–128.)

5. *Schedule.* Set target dates and then follow through. No one will come across with the goods unless they know what you expect and when. "Come in Monday knowing the first three pages." "No more scripts as of this Wednesday." "Bring in all props by the end of the week." When I'm directing the kids, I deal constantly with their

alibis and tales of woe. Excuses have become a way of life in our culture. So be assured you will be receiving more than a few. One of the finest lines you tread is knowing when to turn a deaf ear and apply the pressure, when to lay back and give them a bit of rope.

6. *Timing and rhythm.* You can't do much to set the pace of a scene until the actors are off book, so make this your last concern, just prior to run-throughs. Some people think "fast" is the only desirable rhythm—that directors must clap their hands nosily to keep the cast forever moving at lightning speed. In fact there is only one absolute rule: that there be no dead spots, no pauses without purpose. If one character advances on another with a sharp, penetrating stare, the brief silence can be more compelling than a torrent of words.

Dialogue cues should be picked up instantly unless there's a reason for the hesitation (such as waiting for audience laughter or for a character's—not an actor's!—thoughts to gel). While it's true that comedies usually move at a faster clip than dramas, even this generalization defies any hard and fast formulas. If this directing thing grows more comfortable for you as the days pass, you will rely more and more on your instincts to tell the actors when to speed up and slow down.

This minicourse in the art of the director is usually just enough to wet the kids' feet. The two days of lecture/discussion, together with their copy of the six-step packet, will sustain them when you can't be around to answer questions. But the vast bulk of the learning will take place on the set, outside your presence, in the act of doing.

There will be problems: Some directors will engage the actors in nonstop power plays that have little to do with the script; others will be so self-effacing as to disappear from the playing field. Your most important job during this period will be to help the directors behind the scenes—bolstering the shy ones, restraining the egotists, dispensing sage teacherly advice. But do it privately! Never sit in on a rehearsal and begin tossing out unsolicited opinions. That usurps the director's leadership role; it makes her a "pretend director" whom no one need take seriously because, as the cast well knows, it's the teacher who's really calling the shots.

These rehearsals can be organized precisely as for plain old theatre scenes (see Chapter 4, pages 112–143). Only two differences apply: The teacher is at all times an observer, visiting with two casts per day, offering help as needed, and the dress rehearsals notes come first from the individual directors, who may then welcome additional comments from the audience and the teacher.

Style Turns: "Cold"

This was our one excursion into the realm of theatrical style, a sophisticated subject whose finer points are best left to more advanced levels of study. It began with a student suggestion that we take a short scene, choose up casts and directors, and—without changing *any* of the playwright's lines—render the scene in a variety of contrasting styles: murder mystery, farce, melodrama, soap opera, romantic comedy, action adventure, spy thriller, and so on. (How many scenes you do depends, obviously, on the size of the class.)

The instructions to the directors were as follows:

> You have four days to rehearse your scene in the style assigned to you. If your "company" includes four people, you will have to use two actors for the speaking roles, perhaps another as a silent character who advances the plot visually, another who takes care of the tech elements. You can employ whatever devices you wish to enhance the atmosphere of your scene: music to set the mood, props, a simple set, and sound effects. All performances will be given in class on the fifth day. Lines must be fully memorized. *Most important:* Everything we see and hear should be justified. For example, if you're directing a farce and decide to incorporate sight gags, they must grow believably out of the story and not be pasted on for mere effect.

We found the perfect vehicle in David Mamet's "Cold," an excerpt from his *The Blue Hour: City Sketches*. The script is a mere page and a half in length, and the language is teasingly ambiguous—"open" enough to accommodate just about any variations of theatrical style.

Cold

[A man, "A," waiting for a subway, another man, "B," comes down into the subway and looks up and down the track.]

A: Everybody always looks both ways. Although they always know which way the train is coming from. Did you ever notice that?

B: Yes. I did. [Pause.]

A: You going home?

B: Yes. [Pause.]

A: I'm going home, too. . . . Did you ever notice sometimes when it's cold you feel *wet*? [Pause.]

B: Yes. [Pause. "A" looks up.]

A: [Of grating overhead.] They make those things to let in *air*. [Pause.]

B: Uh huh.

A: From outside. Listen: Listen . . . [Pause.] Where are you going now?

B: Home.

A: Do you live near here?

B: No.

A: Where do you live? [Pause.]

B: Downtown.

A: Where?

B: Downtown.

A: Where though? [Pause.]

B: In Soho.

A: Is it nice there?

B: Yes.

A: [Pause.] Is it warm?

B: Yes. [Pause.] Sometimes it's not so warm.

A: When the wind gets in, right? When the wind gets in?

B: Right.

A: So what do you do then? [Pause.] What do you do then?

B: You . . . stop it up.

A: Uh huh. [Pause.]

B: *Or* . . . you can put covers on the windows.

A: Covers.

B: Yes. Storm covers. [Pause.]

A: Storm covers.

B: To keep out the draft.
A: And does that keep the draft out?
B: Yes.
A: Have you been waiting long?
B: No. [Pause.]
A: *How* long? [Pause.]
B: Several minutes. [Pause.]
A: Are you going home now?
B: Yes. [Looks at sound of subway in the distance.]
A: That's the other track. [They watch the train passing.] Do you live alone?
B: No. [Pause.]
A: You live with someone?
B: Yes.
A: Are you happy? [Pause.]
B: Yes.
A: Are they there now?
B: [Pause.] I think so. [Pause.]
A: What are they called?
B: Hey, look, what business is it of yours what they're called. [Pause.] You understand? [Pause.]

Naturally, the response following the first reading of the script was a chorus of outrage from the five directors. "You can't possibly play this thing as a soap opera!" ("farce" . . . "romantic comedy" . . . whatever). "Besides, that's not even close to what the playwright intended."

This last point may be well-taken (though I can't imagine Mamet getting all that indignant), the first is not. To pursue the farce example, the text doesn't exactly suggest pratfalls, does it? Banana peels? Disguises? Mistaken identities? But again, who's to say? It's all in how you look at things, right? My advice to the director: accept as a given that the writer meant these lines to be performed as slapstick. Once you surrender to that premise and spend ten minutes poring over the script, the ideas are guaranteed to hatch. (Note: The terms *farce* and *melodrama* are not necessarily familiar to your students, so make sure to define and illustrate them thoroughly before you begin.)

Student Originals

I argued in Chapter 2 that acting is a teachable skill. I'd be a lot slower to make the same case for playwriting. It was not for casual reasons, I'd imagine, that Walter Kerr titled his 1955 opus *How* Not *to Write a Play*. The affirmative position would have been a lot tougher to sustain.

That's why I hesitated the first time a group of kids asked if they could produce some original ten-minute scenes. I liked the idea but had no clue about how best to prepare them. The process is still a mystery to me (and apparently to English teachers in general who, you've probably noticed, almost *never* ask students to compose pieces in dramatic form, although they often assign short stories, poems, and personal narratives). A student of mine some years back—no academic superstar—completed a forty-minute one-act play for his class to perform as a year-end project. There were six main characters and substantial cameo appearances for each and every member of the class. It was a light sitcom, of no enduring literary value, but it was hysterically funny and consistently entertaining. It frustrated me to admit to myself that, with thirty years of classroom experience in theatre, I could never have written anything half as good. How could I ask the students to invent their own scenes when I had nothing solid to teach them?

What gave me incentive was a look at the instructions to candidates submitting scripts to the Young Playwrights Festival. Aside from a few limitations as to running time, number of characters, setting, and form of the manuscript, the directions essentially read: "Write a one-act play." Ten minutes suddenly felt reasonable.

The first time we tried this, that's pretty much how I worded the assignment: "Compose a scene of approximately ten minute's running time. Try to limit yourself to four characters and one setting. Due date—three weeks from today." After I'd looked through the scripts, we did cold readings of everyone's work in class, selected a handful to produce, named a director and actors for each (the playwrights were all assigned to other casts), and started rehearsing.

The results were well-received, so the following year, feeling guilty, I decided I owed the students at least three days of carefully organized lessons, the outline for which is given below.

The new scenes were again well-received, but I'd be hard-pressed to say whether there was a substantial difference in the quality of the scripts—either for good or ill. So, for what they're worth. . . .

Playwrights' Guidelines

1. *In searching for material, start with what you know.*
   The teenage social scene, family and school life, race relations, sports probably make more sense as a point of departure than government, big business, the military, or labor relations. If you have a keen or playful imagination, disregard the above.

2. *It's not enough to talk about it.*
   The best scenes are *action-driven* and *visual*. Things will bog down if your tone becomes narrative. In short stories and novels you often *tell* (narrate); in theatre you always *show* (dramatize). That's why the visual is so important. Beware of characters doing little more than sitting around and talking. (Yes, there most certainly are exceptions!)

3. *Most good scenes start in the middle.*
   Throw the audience right into the thick of the action. There's always time later on to fill in the background (exposition).

4. *Strong characters work best.*
   Just by their entrance, we should know who they are. Give them strong wants that originate not in the head but the gut, and obstacles to achieving them. These wants—and the characters' efforts to overcome the obstacles—will drive the plot forward, not artificial twists and turns in the road.

5. *Stay clear of cliches.*
   Give the geeky, slide rule–toting computer whiz, the ditzy blonde, the intrusive mother-in-law, the wisecracking waitress a break. Or, if you absolutely must use them, let it be with a true splash of originality.

6. *The hard part—separate yourself from your characters.*
   You must care about them, but you cannot step inside them or take sides for or against them. The master playwright is one who can allow the different characters their individual voices without judging them or moralizing. Great scripts are not

there to teach lessons in ethics. They often force us to think through serious moral questions, but they're not written to dictate "righteous" behavior.

7. *Maintain unity.*
   Don't include a single word of dialogue, a single stage direction, without a reason.

8. *Some possible situations to develop*
   (Only if you're totally stuck for an idea.)

   - Two recently single middle-aged people are fixed up on a blind date.

   - A psychiatrist can't resist sharing his problems with a patient.

   - An overprotected suburbanite encounters a street-smart city dweller.

   - Two friends meet after a long separation.

   - A younger sister advises an older brother on the subject of girls.

   - A stranger arrives in town and comes between two close friends.

   - An "oddball" moves into a straight-laced neighborhood.

Theatre Sports and Improv Shows

Theatre Sports enjoyed a huge vogue in the eighties. The concept was probably the brainchild of an actor who one day hit upon the brilliant idea of transferring the frenzy of the sports stadium to the theatre stage. A direct outgrowth of the work of Spolin, Ward, Heathcoate, Johnstone, and Sills, "The Games" are still going strong—especially among kids, who love the fast pace, high-wire tension, roaring crowds, and random bursts of lunacy. They consist of a medley of improvisation formats played in an atmosphere not unlike that of a Roman circus: teams, rules, shouted audience participation, austere judges, and competition for points—which almost no one, thankfully, takes too seriously.

Theatre Sports uses improv as a springboard for pure fun and invention. There's something exhilarating about the sight of young actors driven by adrenaline and "psych" to the limits of their creativity. I've never seen even a touch of mean-spiritedness invade these proceedings. The tone is mutually supportive, even among members of opposing teams, who will applaud a clever or spontaneous moment onstage whatever its source.

The first time a colleague invited me to see his kids perform a formal Theatre Sports competition, I watched with a mixture of awe and cynicism. "Amazing stuff, but those are plants out there, right? The actors know all the audience suggestions in advance and simply reenact scenarios they've worked through in rehearsal."

Not at all. Not even slightly. It's the structures—the game formats themselves—that keep the actors in focus and free up their best intuitions. That and the long hours of ensemble building. Like any skill worth acquiring, this takes time. But the payoff is rich.

So where exactly do you turn for a complete description of the program and advice on getting it off the ground? The answers are to be found in three books—*Improv Comedy* by Andy Goldberg, *Improvisation Through Theatre Sports* by Lynda Belt and Rebecca Stockley, and its sequel *Improv Game Book II* by Belt—which together spell out every relevant detail, from the simplest trust exercise to the organization of a full-scale match. How much time you spend will depend on the enthusiasm of the kids and the space available in your curriculum. There is raw material here for a month, a semester, even a full year, of high energy workshops.

Grand Finale: Theatre Showcase

During my first year as theatre director, a final exam was mandated for every course taught in the school. Since a written test on the distinctions between upstage and downstage struck everyone as more than a little stupid, the kids asked me to find a good vehicle for a student-directed one-act play, assign jobs to everyone in the class, and enter the resulting grades in the final exam box. I was pleased by the symmetry of it: a forty-week course beginning with simple exercises and culminating in the preparation of an all-student-produced one-act play! Even the principal was won over by our pitch and granted us special dispensation. That meant exactly four weeks of rehearsal time prior to the end of classes. We got busy immediately—before he had a chance to change his mind.

There were some minor wrinkles. I wanted to make sure that

whoever was named director would be someone in it for the right reasons: a true test of leadership and endurance, not a program credit or an escape from the drudgery of line memorization. More troubling was the impossibility of granting everyone in the class an equal share of responsibility. Some would have big parts, others a handful of lines. Some would be designing and constructing a set, others gathering a few props. But my concerns didn't phase the kids. They argued that the director would have to be chosen on trust, and that after working with a class for thirty-five weeks, I should pretty much know the territory. As to the uneven workload, they said, "So what. Next time the stakes will be reversed and it'll all even out. We'll just agree to work it so that each kid has some kind of acting role and, depending on the number of lines, some kind of tech responsibility."

The last and most serious hurdle was finding something with enough parts to accommodate the whole group. (In fact there *are* a few excellent one-acts with casts of over twenty, but at that stage of the game I had no idea what they were or where to locate them [see pages 187–188].) The solution we found was to halve the class, pick out *two* good shows, assign each its own director, and prepare them simultaneously in different rehearsal spaces, such as choral room and auditorium stage. This may sound like bedlam, but in fact two smaller casts ultimately helped reduce tensions and keep the ship afloat. We decided on "Clevinger's Trial," a dramatization of a chapter from Heller's *Catch 22* (six men), and The Manhattan Project's *Alice in Wonderland* (flexible casting).

That left only a few loose ends to be resolved before getting down to business.

1. *Who would be our audience?*
   The students felt they'd be more likely to produce quality work if we scheduled a night performance and charged a small admission. The principal had no objection so long as the auditorium dates were available but did want to know what we planned to do with the proceeds. Before I could respond he had a brainstorm. "Since you can't just let the kids pocket the cash, why don't you take them to the city in early July and attend a Broadway show? Splitting the gate will increase their motivation and stave off possible objections from the Board of Ed about unauthorized use of funds."

The class was more than amenable. We dubbed the evening *Theatre Showcase*. Each student agreed to be responsible for the sale of four tickets, guaranteeing us at least a decent attendance. We'd design the shows simply, mounting them in the auditorium and seating the audience in rows of chairs set right up there with the actors. That way the eighty customers, instead of being scattered throughout a darkened one-thousand-seat auditorium, would feel like a sellout crowd.

A field trip was scheduled for the Saturday following the end of the school year, which, because of final exams, was the first available date we could agree on. The kids were sure no one would show up. "No," I countered. "It's a no-lose proposition. If the turnout is large, we enjoy a big celebration in the city. If it's small, we each get to pocket a huge chunk of cash!"

2. *How would the directors prepare themselves?*
The same guidelines that applied to the Director's Workshop project would be in effect here. The only major differences: instead of preparing a ten-minute scene, the directors would be rehearsing a forty-minute play—tough but doable—and instead of receiving a ready-made cast, they would be auditioning for the major roles. We agreed, once the staging rehearsals began, that the teacher should spend half the period with each cast daily since the stakes for mounting a one-act play would be higher, requiring closer adult supervision.

3. *How would the director hold the company accountable?*
The most responsible, fair-minded, self-possessed of student directors is helpless against the chicanery of a classmate in a bad mood on a bad day—especially around final exam time. Here's the solution we came up with: the directors, if necessary with the teacher's help, would distribute a fixed rehearsal schedule at the first cast meeting. Anyone not needed for staging on a particular day would of course be required to attend class, but they'd be free to use the period to study for other finals. Legitimate absence from school could be tolerated up to a bare minimum, in which case anyone available in class that day could fill in and inform the absentee of blocking decisions on their return. But uncooperative behavior would not be tolerated. Everyone entered a pact to respect the autonomy of the directors. That meant that if serious

conflicts flared, the directors' word would prevail. Anyone refusing to defer to her authority in a pinch would be subject to grade penalties or the possibility of being dropped from the cast. It happened only once.

Advantages to ending the course with Theatre Showcase

- The promise of a paying audience can rally the kids and summon one final blast of energy before "the final curtain."

- Producing a one-act play is a perfect culminating experience, testing every skill taught over the course of the year.

- For almost a full month, the rehearsal schedule cancels the need for any and all teacher lesson plans (no small advantage in the last weeks of school).

- The project is a supreme test of the kids' ability to function independently of the teacher.

- Like casts of the more lavishly produced extra-curricular productions, the acting classes would now get to display their wares in public.

Disadvantages to ending the course with Theatre Showcase

- The pressure of putting together a show against the background of final exam preparation and end-of-year hysteria can be nothing less than cataclysmic—a single, but formidable disadvantage.

Appendix

Scene Resource List

What follows is a list of every play and film I've used over the years as a source for Theatre Scenes. You may not consider all the titles to be age-appropriate for your actors or content-appropriate for your audiences, but I've left the list unedited in the interest of completeness.

Male

Dumb Waiter
Rosencrantz and Guildenstern
 Are Dead
Zoo Story
Odd Couple
Midnight Cowboy
Carnal Knowledge
Dead End
Tea and Sympathy
Table Settings
True West
Mass Appeal
Mr. Roberts
Luv
American Buffalo
One Flew over the Cuckoo's
 Nest
Death Trap
Shivaree
Equus
Happy Birthday, Wanda June
The Last Picture Show
Brighton Beach Memoirs
The Producers
Superior Decision

Marty
On the Waterfront
The Great Santini
Biloxi Blues
Where's Sally?
Of Mice and Men
Orphans
Catch 22
Play It Again Sam
Plane, Trains, and Automobiles
Stand by Me
My Bodyguard
Easy Rider
Who's on First?
Three Men and a Baby
Summer of '42
Tootsie
Hatful of Rain
The Field
Death of a Salesman
The Hitter
Only Kidding
Inherit the Wind
Princess Bride
Split Second

Night Shift
Catcher in the Rye
Shoes
Ordinary People
The Bogeyman
Day Room
Talk Radio
Lost in Yonkers
The Forced Marriage
Pseudolus
Lunch Break
Julius Caesar
A Few Good Men
In the Line of Fire
Fast Times at Ridgemont High
Boys Next Door
Yorkshire Men
Lumberjack
Bachelor Party
The Line That Caught a
*   Thousand Babes*
Goodfellas
What About Bob?
Scent of a Woman
Dumb and Dumber
Dead Poets' Society
Pulp Fiction
Billy Madison
School Ties
Diner
Hello
Beverly Hills Waiting for Godot
Louis and Dave
Tape
Vinny/Ray
Barcelona
Broadway Bound
Clerks
Swing Shift
The Would-Be Gentleman

Galileo
Frankenstein
Dinner with Friends

Female

Vanities
Children's Hour
Bad Habits
Roomful of Roses
The Effect of Gamma Rays on
*   Man-in-the-Moon Marigolds*
Alice Doesn't Live Here Anymore
Alice in Wonderland
A View from the Bridge
Album
Bad Seed
Table Manners
Agnes of God
Crimes of the Heart
Faculty Lounge
University
'Night Mother
Killing of Sister George
The Miracle Worker
The Glass Menagerie
The Importance of Being Earnest
Madwoman of Chaillot
Macbeth
Table Settings
Gemini
Turning Point
Carrie
Between Friends
All About Eve
Terms of Endearment
Your Honor
Something Blue
Men!
Survival

Tartuffe
Mommie Dearest
Bernice Bobs Her Hair
A Young Lady of Property
Lunch Hour
Daughters
A Taste of Honey
Indulgences in a Louisiana
    Harem
The Crucible
Postcards
Hooters
Witches of Eastwick
Steel Magnolias
Beaches
Come Back to the Five and Dime,
    Jimmy Dean, Jimmy Dean
Mystic Pizza
Graceland
Casual Sex
And Now a Word
Babies Having Babies
Eastern Standard
Nine to Five
Pretty Woman
Sunday Afternoons
Odd Couple
Heidi Chronicles
Children
A Streetcar Named Desire
Lysistrata
Romeo and Juliet
The Miss Firecracker Contest
Annette and Gina
Lost in Yonkers
Heathers
Thelma and Louise
Single White Female
Shakespeare
Family Names

Catholic School Girls
John's Ring
Slumber Party
Five Women Wearing the Same
    Dress
The Gingerbread Lady
Isn't It Romantic?
Chapter Twelve: The Frog
The Black and White
The House of Bernarda Alba
Dinner with Friends

Mixed

Taming of the Shrew
Hatful of Rain
Bad Habits
Ordinary People
Prisoner of Second Avenue
Sunset Boulevard
The Graduate
Morning's at Seven
Five Easy Pieces
Lovers and Other Strangers
Harold and Maude
Rocky
Annie Hall
Saturday Night Fever
When You Comin' Back Red
    Ryder?
Oh Dad, Poor Dad, Momma's
    Hung You in the Closet and
    I'm Feeling So Sad
Come Back, Little Sheba
Saint Joan
Pygmalion
Barefoot in the Park
Table Settings
Gemini
Moonchildren

I Never Sang for My Father
Next
Tevye and His Daughters
Butterflies Are Free
Did You Ever Go to P.S. 43?
Luv
The Tiger
The Typists
Play It Again Sam
One Flew over the Cuckoo's Nest
The Glass Menagerie
A Taste of Honey
A Thousand Clowns
Inherit the Wind
Ah! Wilderness
Blue Denim
Flowers for Algernon
Mother/Son
Spam
Argument Clinic
Interview
The Lesson
Rebel Without a Cause
Balm in Gilead
Little Murders
Blithe Spirit
Brighton Beach Memoirs
Beyond Therapy
Bald Soprano
Big Time
And Stuff
Enter Laughing
'dentity Crisis
Gin Game
The Doctor in Spite of Himself
The Diary of Anne Frank
Present Tense
Tender Mercies
Waltz of the Toreadors
Sixteen Candles

Risky Business
American Graffiti
Psycho
Breakfast Club
Tootsie
University
Golden Boy
Network
Where's Poppa?
Found a Peanut
Swing Shift
Biloxi Blues
A Streetcar Named Desire
Fast Times at Ridgemont High
The Sure Thing
Nothing in Common
Boys Next Door
Less Than Zero
Split
The Nerd
Diner
Ferris Bueller's Day Off
A New Approach to Human
    Sacrifice
Fixed Up
Pizza Man
Personal Effects
"Sure Thing"
Ground Zero Club
Dirty Rotten Scoundrels
Heidi Chronicles
Heathers
Marred Bliss
When Harry Met Sally
Prelude to a Kiss
Coastal Disturbances
Women and Wallace
Happy Together
Seventy Scenes of Halloween
Rain Man

As the Stomach Turns

Transmogrification

Burn This

Naomi in the Living Room

Cover

Teeth

The Problem

Who's on First? (Rock version)

Anniversary

Sorrows of Stephen

Baby with the Bathwater

Cape Fear

Fun

Psycho Beach Party

Marvin's Room

Wonderful Party

Scapino

Last Day of Camp

Pickup Artist

Going Nowhere Apace

Interrogation

Eye to Eye

Vas Difference

After School Special

Extremities

My Cousin Vinny

The Honeymooners

Reckless

Pillow Talk

Supreme Beings Create the World

Kris and Jeff

Hank and Karen Sue

Little Footsteps

Intellectual Discussion

Goober's Descent

Business as Usual

Mental Reservation

Made for a Woman

The Philadelphia

Scruples

Ancient History

Father of the Bride

Oleanna

Pyramid

English Made Simple

Lost in Yonkers

Veins and Thumbtacks

Pulp Fiction

Slacker

Downtown

Cheek to Cheek

Strictly Personnel

Your Life as a Feature Film

Parenthood

The "M" Word

Your Mother's Butt

The Acting Olympics

Group

Procedure

Clara and the Gambler

Honey, I'm Home

Natural Born Killers

Women in Motion

Domestic Violence

The Art of Dating

Captain Neato Man

By the Sea

Splatter Flick

Scenes from the Ex-Pat Cafe

My Left Foot

Greater Tuna

Breaking the Chain

Dinner with Friends

Fools

Our American Cousin

A Doll's House

The Primary English Class

Amadeus

One-Act Play Resource List

Below are the titles of all one-act plays I presented as part of Theatre Showcase over the years. Plays labeled *flexible* generally offer enough roles to accommodate an entire class. Some, such as *Adaptation*—originally written for a small number of actors playing many parts—can be adapted for large groups. Others, like *Impassioned Embraces* and *The Dining Room*, are full-length plays that, being composed of many self-contained scenes, can be reduced to a single act without causing structural damage.

The Forced Marriage	Moliére	6M 5F
Manhattan Project's Alice in Wonderland*†	Carroll/Gregory	Flexible
Clevinger's Trial	Heller	6M
The Patient	Christie	5M 4F
Sorry, Wrong Number	Fletcher	3M 4F + extras
God	Allen	Flexible
Bald Soprano	Ionesco	3M 3F
Adaptation*	May	Flexible
Black Comedy	Shaffer	5M 3F
Death	Allen	Flexible
The Dining Room*†	Gurney	Flexible
Voices from the High School†	Dee	Flexible
And Stuff†	Dee	Flexible
University†	Jory	Flexible
Zoo Story	Albee	2M
Motoring†	Coleman	Flexible
Silver Linings*†	Tally	Flexible
Fables for Friends*†	O'Donnell	Flexible
Scenes from American Life*†	Gurney	Flexible
Senior Square	Williams	Flexible
Actor's Nightmare	Durang	2M 3F
New Approach to Human Sacrifice	Getty	4M 2F
Go Ask Alice	Shiras	5M 4F

This Is a Test	Gregg	Flexible
A Thurber Carnival*†	Thurber	Flexible
Present Tense	McNamara	3M 3F
Personal Effects	McNamara	3M 2F
Twelve Angry Men (abridged)	Rose	15M or mixed
Impassioned Embraces*†	Pielmeier	Flexible
Seven Menus	Ives	4M 4F
Crossin the Line	Bosakowski	5M 3F
Who?	Scanlan	2M 3F
Line	Horovitz	4M 1F
Snap Judgments†	Walden Theatre	Flexible
The Day I Tried to Live	Lauckhardt	Flexible
Bachelor Pad	Baumeister	Flexible
Road Test	Grosselfinger	Flexible
Out at Home	Canzoniero	Flexible
Monty Hall High	Squillante	Flexible
Competition Piece	Wells	Flexible
WASP	Martin	2M 2F
All in the Timing*†	Ives	Flexible
Your Life as a Feature Film	Minieri	3M 2F
A Tribe Called Man	Davis	Flexible
Choices†	Walden Theatre	Flexible
Parallel Lives: The Kathy & Mo Show	Gaffney, Najimy	Flexible
Greater Tuna*†	Williams, Sears, Howard	Flexible

---

* = Can be adapted for large group
† = Can be reduced to single-act play

Bibliography

Acting

Abbott, Leslie. 1987. *Active Acting*. Belmont, CA: Star.

Albright, Hardie, and Arnita Albright. 1980. *Acting: The Creative Process*. Belmont, CA: Wadsworth.

Barkworth, Peter. 1980. *About Acting*. London: Secker and Warburg.

Barton, John. 1984. *Playing Shakespeare*. London: Methuen.

Boleslavski, Richard. 1933. *Acting: The First Six Lessons*. New York: Theatre Arts.

Bruehl, Bill. 1996. *The Technique of Inner Action*. Portsmouth, NH: Heinemann.

Chekhov, Michael. 1953. *To the Actor*. New York: Harper & Row.

Cohen, Robert. 1984. *Acting One*. Mountain View, CA: Mayfield.

Dezseran, Louis John. 1975. *The Student Actor's Handbook*. Mountain View, CA: Mayfield.

Hagen, Uta. 1973. *Respect for Acting*. New York: Macmillan.

———. 1991. *A Challenge for the Actor*. New York: Macmillan.

Kahan, Stanley. 1985. *Introduction to Acting*. Needham Heights, MA: Allyn and Bacon.

Lewis, Robert. 1980. *Advice to the Players*. New York: Harper & Row.

McGaw, Charles. 1955. *Acting Is Believing*. Austin, TX: Holt, Rinehart and Winston.

Meisner, Sanford, and Dennis Longwell. 1987. *Sanford Meisner on Acting*. New York: Vintage.

Morris, Eric, and Joan Hatchkis. 1977. *No Acting Please*. Los Angeles: Whitehouse/Spelling.

Richardson, Don. 1988. *Acting Without Agony*. Needham Heights, MA: Allyn and Bacon.

Shurtleff, Michael. 1978. *Audition*. New York: Walker.

Silverberg, Larry. 1998. *The Sanford Meisner Approach: Workbooks 1–3*. Lyme, NH: Smith & Kraus.

Tanner, Averett. 1977. *Basic Drama Projects*. Topeka, KS: Clark.

Improvisation

Atkins, Greg. 1994. *Improv!* Portsmouth, NH: Heinemann.

Belt, Lynda. 1993. *Improv Game Book II.* Seattle, WA: Thespis Productions.

Belt, Lynda, and Rebecca Stockley. 1991. *Improvisation Through Theatre Sports.* Seattle, WA: Thespis Productions.

Bernardi, Philip. 1992. *Improvisation Starters.* Cincinnati, OH: Betterway Books.

Caruso, Sandra, and Paul Clemens. 1992. *The Actor's Book of Improvisation.* New York: Penguin.

Elkind, Samuel. 1975. *Improvisation Handbook.* Glenview, IL: Scott, Foresman.

Goldberg, Andy. 1991. *Improv Comedy.* New York: Samuel French.

Halpern, Charna, Del Close, and Kim "Howard" Johnson. 1994. *Truth in Comedy.* Colorado Springs, CO: Meriwether.

Hodgson, John, and Ernest Richards. 1993. *Improvisation.* London: Methuen.

Johnstone, Keith. 1979. *Impro.* New York: Theatre Arts Books.

Jones, Brie. 1993. *Improve with Improv!* Colorado Springs, CO: Meriwether.

Novelly, Maria C. 1985. *Theatre Games for Young Performers.* Colorado Springs, CO: Meriwether.

Polsky, Milton E. 1989. *Let's Improvise.* London: University Press of America.

Spolin, Viola. 1963a. *Improvisation for the Theatre.* Evanston, IL: Northwestern University Press.

———. 1963b. *Theatre Games for Rehearsal.* Evanston, IL: Northwestern University Press.

Directing

Ball, William. 1984. *A Sense of Direction.* New York: Drama Book Publishers.

Brook, Peter. 1968. *The Empty Space.* London: MacGibbon & Kee.

———. 1998. *Threads of Time.* Washington, DC: Counterpoint.

Clurman, Harold. 1972. *On Directing.* New York: Macmillan.

Grote, David. 1997. *Play Directing in the School.* Colorado Springs, CO: Meriwether.

Morrison, Hugh. 1973. *Directing in the Theatre*. London: Pitman.
Rossi, Alfred. 1977. *Astonish Us in the Morning: Tyrone Guthrie Remembered*. Detroit, MI: Hutchinson.

Monologues

Bogosian, Eric. 1983. *Fun House*. New York: Samuel French.
———. 1987. *Drinking in America*. New York: Samuel French.
———. 1991. *Sex, Drugs, Rock & Roll*. New York: Samuel French.
———. 1994. *Pounding Nails in the Floor with My Forehead*. New York: Samuel French.
Devlin, Joyce. 1989. *Women's Scenes and Monologues: An Annotated Bibliography*. Quincy, MA: Baker's Plays.
Earley, Michael, and Philippa Keil, eds. 1987. *Solo: The Best Monologues of the Eighties*. New York: Applause Theatre Book Publishers.
———. 1988. *Soliloquy: The Shakespeare Monologue*. New York: Applause Theatre Book Publishers.
———. 1993a. *The Modern Monologue: Men*. New York: Theatre Arts Books.
———. 1993b. *The Modern Monolgue: Women*. New York: Theatre Arts Books.
Emerson, Robert, and Jane Grumbach, eds. 1976, 1983. *Monologues: Men*. Vols. 1 and 2. New York: Drama Book Publishers.
———. 1976, 1983. *Monologues: Women*. Vols. 1 and 2. New York: Drama Book Publishers.
Hooks, Ed, ed. 1994. *The Ultimate Scene and Monologue Sourcebook*. New York: Back Stage Books.
Lane, Eric, and Nina Shengold, eds. 1992. *Moving Parts: Monologues from Contemporary Plays*. New York: Penguin.

Scenes

Dixon, Michael Bigelow, Amy Wegener, Michael Volansky, and Liz Engleman, eds. 1989–2000. *Ten-Minute Plays*. Vols. 1–5. Actors Theatre of Louisville. New York: Samuel French.
Handman, Wynn, ed. 1982. *Modern American Scenes for Student Actors*. New York: Bantam.

Karton, Joshua, ed. 1983. *Film Scenes for Actors*. New York: Bantam.
———. 1987. *Film Scenes for Actors, Volume II*. New York: Bantam.
Lane, Eric, and Nina Shengold, eds. 1988. *Actor's Book of Scenes from New Plays*. New York: Penguin.
Lane, Ruth, ed. 1973. *Scenebook for Student Actors*. Los Angeles: UCLA Press.
Nicholas, Angela, ed. 1999. *Ninety-Nine Film Scenes for Actors*. New York: Avon.
Olfson, Lewy, ed. 1984. *50 Great Scenes for Student Actors*. New York: Bantam.
Pike, Frank, and Thomas G. Dunn, eds. 1988. *Scenes and Monologues from the New American Theatre*. New York: Mentor.
Price, Jonathan, ed. 1979. *Classic Scenes*. New York: Mentor,.
Schulman, Michael, and Eva Meckler, eds. 1980. *Contemporary Scenes for Student Actors*. New York: Penguin.
———. 1984. *The Actor's Scenebook*. New York: Bantam.
———. 1987. *The Actor's Scenebook*. Vol. 2. New York: Bantam.

Catalogs

Applause Theatre Book Review and Catalog. Applause Theatre Books, 211 W. 71 St., New York, NY, 10023. (212) 496-7511.
Dramatic Publishing Catalog of Plays and Musicals. Dramatic Publishing, 311 Washington St., Woodstock, IL, 60098. (800) 448-7469.
Dramatists Play Service Catalog. Dramatists Play Service, 440 Park Avenue South, New York, NY, 10016. (212) 683-8960.
Samuel French Basic Catalog. Samuel French, 45 W. 25 St., New York, NY, 10010. (212) 206-8990.

General

Kerr, Walter. 1998. *How Not to Write a Play*. Woodstock, IL: Dramatic Publishing Company.
Merlin, Joanna. 2001. *Auditioning: An Actor-Friendly Guide*. New York: Vintage Press.
Rogoff, Gordon. 1987. *Theatre Is Not Safe*. Evanston, IL: Northwestern University Press.